Chapter One

London 1706

Edward, the Right Honourable Captain Howard, dressed in blue and white, which some of the officers in Queen Anne's navy favoured, strode into Mrs Radcliffe's spacious house near St James Park.

Perkins, his godmother's butler, took the captain's hat and cloak. "Madam wants you to join her immediately."

Instead of going upstairs to the rooms his godmother had provided for him during his spell on half pay—the result of a dispute with a senior officer—Edward entered the salon. He sighed. When would his sixty-one year old godmother accept that at the age of twenty-two, he was not yet ready to wed?

He made his way across the elegant, many-windowed room through a crowd of expensively garbed callers.

When Frances Radcliffe noticed him, she turned to the pretty young lady seated beside her. "Mistress Martyn, allow me to introduce you to my godson, Captain Howard."

Blushes stained Mistress Martyn's cheeks as she stood to make her curtsey.

Edward bowed, indifferent to yet another of his grandmother's protégées. Conversation ceased. All eyes focussed on the threshold.

"Lady Sinclair," someone murmured.

Edward turned. He gazed without blinking at the acclaimed beauty, whose sobriquet was "The Fatal Widow".

The countess remained in the doorway, her cool blue eyes speculative.

Edward whistled low. Could her shocking reputation be no more than tittle-tattle? His artist's eyes observed her. Rumour did not lie about her Saxon beauty.

Her ladyship was not a slave to fashion. She did not wear a wig, and her hair was not curled and stiffened with sugar water. Instead, her flaxen plaits were wound around the crown of her head to form a coronet. The style suited her. So did the latest Paris fashion, an outrageous wisp of a lace cap, which replaced the tall, fan-shaped fontage most ladies continued to wear perched on their heads.

Did the countess have the devil-may-care attitude gossips attributed to her? If she did, it explained why some respectable members of society shunned her. Indeed, if Lady Sinclair were not the granddaughter of his godmother's deceased friend, she might not be received in this house.

The lady's fair charms did not entirely explain what drew many gallants to her side. After all, there were several younger beauties present around whom the gentlemen did not flock so avidly.

He advanced toward the countess, conscious of the sound of his footsteps on the wooden floor, the muted noise of coaches and drays through the closed windows and, from the fireplace, the crackle of burning logs, which relieved the chill of early spring.

The buzz of conversation resumed. Her ladyship scrutinised him. Did she approve of his appearance? A smile curved her heart-shaped mouth. He repressed his amusement. Edward suspected the widow's rosy lips owed more to artifice than nature.

"How do you do, sir," she said when he stood before her. "I think we have not met previously." Her eyes assessed him dispassionately. "My name is Sinclair, Katherine Sinclair. I dislike formality. You may call me Kate."

"Captain Howard at your service, Countess." Shocked but amused by boldness more suited to a tavern wench than a great lady, Edward paid homage with a low bow before he spoke again. "Despite your permission, I am not presumptuous enough to call you Kate, yet I shall say that, had we already met, I *would* remember you."

"You are gallant, sir, but you are young to have achieved so high a rank in Her Majesty's navy."

"An unexpected promotion earned in battle, which the navy did not subsequently commute."

"You are to be congratulated on what I can only assume were acts of bravery."

"Thank you, Countess."

The depths of her ladyship's sapphire cross and earrings blazed, matching his sudden fierce desire.

Kate, some four inches shorter than Edward, looked up at him.

He leaned forward. The customary greeting of a kiss on her lips lingered longer than etiquette dictated. Her eyes widened before she permitted him to lead her across the room to the sofa on which his godmother sat with Mistress Martyn.

With a hint of amusement in her eyes, Kate regarded Mrs Radcliffe. "My apologies, madam, I suspect my visit is untimely."

Her melodious voice sent shivers up and down his spine; nevertheless, Edward laughed. Had the countess guessed his godmother, who enjoyed match-making, wanted him to marry Mistress Martyn? No, he was being too fanciful. How could she have guessed?

"You are most welcome, Lady Sinclair. Please take a seat and partake of a glass of cherry *ratafia*." Frances said.

"Perhaps, milady prefers red *viana*," Edward suggested.

"Captain, you read my mind. Sweet wine is not to my taste."

In response to the lady's provocative smile, heat seared his cheeks.

Kate smoothed the gleaming folds of her turquoise blue silk gown. The lady knew how to dress to make the utmost of her natural beauty. Her gown and petticoat, not to mention sleeves and under-sleeves, as well as her bodice and stays, relied for effect on simple design and fine fabrics. He approved of her ensemble, the elegance of which did not depend on either a riot of colours or a multitude of bows and other trimmings. Later, he would sketch her from memory.

Kate inclined her head to his godmother. "Will you not warn your godson I am unsound, wild, and a bad influence on the young?"

Edward gazed into Kate's eyes. Before his demise, had her husband banished her to a manor deep in the country? If it were true, why had he done so?

Kate's eyebrows slanted down at the inner corners. She stared back at him. He laughed, raised her hands to his lips, and kissed each in turn. "I look forward to furthering my acquaintance with you."

"High-handed." Kate gurgled with laughter. "Captain, please release me."

What did he care if she were some nine years his elder? He wanted to get to know her better. Edward bowed. "Your slightest wish is my command."

His godmother fluttered her fan. "Edward, Lady Sinclair, please be seated."

They sat side-by-side opposite Mrs Radcliffe on the sofa upholstered in crimson damask.

Although Kate smiled at him, the expression in her large blue eyes remained as cool as it had been when she first entered the salon. "Tomorrow, please join those who visit me daily at my morning levee."

"I fear my voice would be lost among many, thus casting me into obscurity," Edward replied, much amused.

"I don't take you for one to be ignored, sir. However, I respect your wishes. Besides those who seek my patronage, there are many gentlemen eager to wait on me. 'Tis more than my porter's life is worth to deny them entry." She looked at his godmother and raised a pencilled eyebrow. "Mrs Radcliffe, do you not agree it is pleasant to lie abed in the morning while indulging in conversation with one's admirers?"

Frances toyed with her fan. "Receiving one's admirers does help to pass the time."

"Come, come, madam, confess you value their advice," Kate teased.

"Sometimes." Frances looked at her most favoured admirer, Sir Newton.

Kate turned her attention to Edward. "I have no doubt you would become a cherished member of the group of those who seek my favour."

"Countess, life at sea teaches a man to be wary of enemies, not to compete with them. I am not a flirt who is given to haunting ladies' bedchambers."

"If I seclude myself with you tomorrow morning, may I have the pleasure of your company?"

"Alone with you in your bedchamber? How improper. Are you always so careless of your reputation?" he asked with a hint of laughter in his voice.

Her eyes widened. "I have no reputation to guard, Captain." She had spoken in a forward manner he was unaccustomed to in polite society.

"Have you not?" Edward needed a plunge in icy water.

A frozen glimpse of despair deep in her eyes unsettled Edward. Did he imagine it? He could not speak. Why should a lady like the countess despair?

He recovered his voice. "If it is your custom to take the air in The Mall, I shall be pleased to be your sole escort."

Kate fidgeted with one of the diamond buckles that fastened her satin-covered stays. "Are the battle lines drawn?"

"Don't confuse battle lines with a mere skirmish at sea." His voice hinted at the chuckle he restrained.

"There are those who would welcome an invitation to a *tête-à-tête* with me."

He preferred to take the lead in affairs of the heart. "Perhaps I am not one of them," he teased. "Maybe I would like to be your friend."

"My friend? Is that all you want of me?"

His eyes widened.

Kate laughed. "No, I thought not."

Chapter Two

Kate breakfasted in bed, drinking hot chocolate and eating two slices of thinly cut bread and butter. With pleasure, she breathed in the perfume of narcissi arranged in a pair of tall blue and white Delft flower vases, which stood on two small inlaid tables on either side of the marble fireplace.

Later, Kate washed her face and hands with the finest Smyrna soap. Before she returned to her bed, she first painted and powdered her face with particular care.

At eleven o'clock, the porter admitted the first of her guests to the house. Each time the door opened, she looked across the bedchamber with the expectation of seeing the captain. Unaccustomed to any gentleman declining her invitation, her annoyance and disappointment increased as the minutes passed. An hour dragged by. Still Captain Howard had not come. Wasted time, and what was more, it had been an equal waste of time to send her tirewoman, Jessie, to Lillie's for perfume. Kate put her scented handkerchief to her nose to inhale the fragrance of the distillation of roses and sandalwood. Delicious! Indeed Mister Lillie deserved his title, "The Prince of Perfumers". Soon, however, the levee would end.

She glanced at her most persistent admirers, Mister Tyrell, both dashing and bold, and Mister Stafford, conservative and somewhat hesitant. As usual, they had arrived before her other admirers. Now they sat at their ease on gilt-legged chairs near her canopied bed.

Kate decided she could delay no longer. She rose to make her toilette behind a tall screen, still conscious of the rose-pink night robe she had ruffled around her shoulders with great care before Tyrell and Stafford arrived.

With Jessie's help, after Kate removed her nightgown and night rail, she donned her under-linen, stays, and a bodice, cut lower than the current fashion and loosely laced in front to reveal gold buckles inset with pearls, which clasped her satin-covered stays so tightly that she could scarce draw breath. "Gentlemen, which petticoat shall I wear?" she asked, giggling deliberately and playing the part of an indecisive female. "Jessie, please show both of them to Mister Tyrell and Mister Stafford."

Over the edge of the lacquered screen, Jessie dangled the full petticoats to be worn displayed beneath skirts parted down the front.

Kate stood on tiptoe. She peeped over the top of the screen, decorated with a blue and white pot containing tulips, passion flowers, lilies, roses, and sprigs of rosemary.

"Gentlemen, the cream petticoat is made of Luckhourie, a newly fashionable silk from India. The lavender one is of the finest quality Pudsay."

"Stap me, they are uncommon plain," said Mister Tyrell.

Kate knew he admired feminine apparel trimmed with folderols such as gold or silver lace, ruched ribbons, bows, and rosettes. She suppressed a chuckle in order not to offend him.

11

"My mother approves of modest attire," Mister Stafford said.

Before she withdrew her head from their sight, Kate choked back her laughter. Stafford's contemptuous glance at his rival did not escape her notice.

She doubted Mrs Stafford found much about her to praise, but she cared naught for Stafford's mother, a creature with the languishing airs of a pseudo-invalid, who bound her son cruelly to her side. Indeed, the gentleman's determined courtship surprised Kate. It proved he was not, as the saying went, completely under his mother's thumb.

"Which one shall I wear?" Kate repeated. Although she had already decided to wear cream, she followed the custom of prolonging what amounted to "The Art of the Levee".

First, Jessie retrieved the petticoats. Next, she dressed Kate in the Luckhourie one, a gown, and lace-edged apron.

Stafford spoke first. "I have no doubt her ladyship will favour the cream petticoat, which will enhance the natural delicacy of her appearance."

Delicate? Heaven forbid. She did not want Captain Howard to consider her delicate. "'Pon my word, Stafford, I have no wish to give the impression of one who suffers from lung rot."

Mister Tyrell laughed. "I am sure you don't, Lady Sinclair. For my part, I beg you to wear the lavender. It will enhance the colour of your blue eyes."

"I shall surprise both of you." Kate ignored their petty war of words and wondered why she yearned to see Captain Howard.

Oh, the young gentleman was tall and broad of chest, and she supposed his face was handsome enough. In her mind's eye, she tried to reconstruct the captain's high cheekbones, broad forehead, and square jaw. Well, of one thing she could be certain; his was the complexion of a gentleman accustomed to being out in all weathers.

Restless, she smoothed her apron. There were many good-looking men in town, some of them far more handsome than the captain. Why did an insignificant naval officer occupy her thoughts? Kate shook her head, unable to build a complete mental picture of him and capture the fiery light of his eyes in her memory. Whatever his complexion, it did not matter because the very essence of him would remain the same.

She shrugged in an attempt to convince herself she was not piqued. Why should she care if Captain Howard chose not to visit her? Her lips tightened. She did care.

Jessie twitched the last fold of the lavender gown—worn over the cream petticoat—into place.

Kate left the shelter of the screen. "Behold, gentlemen, have I not pleased both of you?"

Mister Tyrell laughed. "May I say you are a minx, madam?"

She fluttered her eyelashes. "You may not, sir."

Kate sat at her dressing table to complete her toilette. She greeted yet more of her admirers, who praised her to the skies and offered their advice, while Jessie also admitted purveyors of fine wares, an artist, and a playwright who sought her patronage.

By the time Jessie pinned a wisp of point lace to Kate's hair, it lacked a quarter hour before one of the clock. Kate gave up all hope of the captain's arrival. *"Odds' bodikins!"* she exclaimed to vent her irritation. "Go," she said to the purveyors of fine goods and the playwright.

Mister Stafford sighed as he shook his head. "Lady Sinclair, I never expected to hear such an oath issue from your pretty lips."

"Upon my honour, Stafford," Mister Tyrell began, "your objection to such a pretty little oath smacks of the schoolmaster."

Someone knocked on the door. Hope bubbled through Kate. Perhaps the captain had changed his mind.

Her tirewoman answered the summons. "Flowers, my lady."

John and Simon, two of Kate's lackeys, entered the bedchamber, their arms overflowing with red roses which filled the room with fragrance more potent than that of the narcissi.

"How beautiful! Please hand me one of the flowers, Jessie." Kate looked at her lackeys. "Who sent them?"

Simon inclined his head. "Captain Howard brought them with his compliments."

"Is the captain still here?"

"No, my lady," John said.

She indicated the Delft vases on either side of the marble fireplace. "Have them refilled with the roses."

Mister Tyrell's eyes narrowed. "Such extravagance. I would not embarrass a lady thus."

Her face alive with curiosity, Gertrude Corby, Kate's plump, widowed mother, bustled into the room. "What beautiful roses. Pray tell me who sent them?"

Stafford and Tyrell bowed to her mother while Kate peered into her mirror, a treasure from the east, framed with carved rosewood. She scrutinised her face, grateful because her mask of powder and paint concealed her heightened colour.

Satisfied with her appearance, she shortened the stem of the rose with scissors, stripped it of its thorns, and tucked the fragrant blossom into the bosom of her gown.

"What a sweet boy," Kate mused. "Where did he find roses in May?"

"The weather is mild enough to advance the season," Gertrude remarked. "If they were picked in bud and brought indoors, I think they opened in the warmth."

Mister Tyrell clenched his fists. Stafford's tight pressed lips reminded Kate of a baited mousetrap. A clock chimed the hour of one. Both gallants made their farewells, bowed, and withdrew with the other visitors.

Gertrude sank onto a chair. "A boy, you said, Daughter, I hope you are not about to trifle with yet another green youth's affections."

"I don't trifle with any man's affections. 'Tis not my fault if I am admired."

"Be warned. One day, when you are old, no one will admire you."

Kate scowled. Heavens above, she would never allow anyone to treat her in the manner her odious husband had treated her, carping and criticising, as well as punishing her for minor misdemeanours. She shifted

15

on her chair, imagining she could still feel the sting of his cane. "What do I care, Mother? I live to amuse myself."

Gertrude's weak chin quivered. "You will care one day. You have never suffered. For now, you are too heartless to understand what it is like to be alone and unloved at my age."

Her parents had never dealt well together. Kate knew her mother frankly preferred widowhood, so the words did not touch her heart. "Oh, don't be so histrionic. You are not alone in this house full of people."

Kate's brow furrowed. Could anyone blame her for not loving a parent, who, when she was a small child, relinquished custody of her as though she had no more importance than an unwanted kitten? A mother, who had not even been concerned with her education.

She shrugged. Nothing could change her past, so why waste time blaming her impoverished parents, who handed her over to her father's elder brother and his barren wife in the expectation of him settling his fortune upon her. They could not have foreseen that Uncle Matthew would lose everything at the card tables. A young girl's voice, hurt and betrayed, whispered deep within her. *Mother should have done her utmost to dissuade Father from consenting to my uncle marrying me off to Sinclair. By law, Uncle was not my legal guardian so Father could have prevented the marriage but he did not want to.*

Gertrude tapped her foot on the floor. "Have you nothing to say?"

"I trust you don't think I have failed in my duty toward you, Mother," Kate replied, unable to bring herself to make a false declaration of daughterly love. "Please have the goodness to excuse me. I am going to shop at The Exchange."

* * *

Halfway to the famous shopping mart, Kate changed her mind and ordered the men carrying her sedan to proceed along the narrow streets to Mrs Radcliffe's house. She alighted from the sedan with the firm intention of obtaining Captain Howard's address. Near the doorstep, she attempted to justify her decision. After all, politeness required her to either thank the captain in person for the roses or to leave him a note of thanks. She fingered the fragrant blossom at her bosom while gazing down into its golden heart.

When she raised her head, she saw Captain Howard walking toward her with brisk footsteps. Upon catching sight of her, he increased his pace.

"Good day, Lady Sinclair. I trust you are well." His dark eyes gleamed. He indicated the rose. "I am flattered to see red and white nestled so charmingly together."

For a moment, she did not understand his comparison of the skin of her partially revealed bosom to a white rose. When she did, she pressed her hand to her breast. "Captain, you make me blush. I cannot imagine what prompted you to speak thus."

"Can you deny it is as though the red rose of Lancaster, and the white rose of York, battle within you?"

Kate stared over his shoulder. "It is nonsensical of you to allude to the 'Wars of the Roses', Captain." She

17

scrutinised his face. "Sir, I came to procure your direction from Mrs Radcliffe so that I could write a note of thanks for the roses. Our meeting spares me the task. Thank you for sending such beautiful flowers. Good day to you."

"I am honoured, milady, because you came in person instead of sending your foot page to make enquiries."

Kate bent her head, hoping he did not guess she had wanted to see him again.

"Milady, I am staying with Mrs Radcliffe. Will you not come inside and partake of refreshment?"

"No. Thank you. I must go."

"Good day, *milady*." The captain emphasised the word but did not seek to detain her. In silence, he tucked her hand into the crook of his arm, and then led her to the sedan emblazoned with the Sinclair coat of arms.

"The Exchange," Kate ordered her coachman.

Captain Howard's luminous eyes looked into hers for a moment before he broke the spell and handed her into the conveyance.

Chapter Three

Edward watched Kate's sedan until it turned the corner at the end of the street. Her pride, high spirits, her vivacious manner and unique style of dressing, intrigued him.

He turned to stare at Mrs Radcliffe's house. His godmother's superfine gallant of gallants, Clarence Newton, stood by the railings.

Edward's lips twitched. Older than Mrs Radcliffe, Sir Newton dressed like a youngster newly come into an estate; his slim body encased in finery like a sausage in a skin. Edward grinned. No doubt "stays" compressed his lordship.

"Good day, m'dear boy," Newton said.

"Good day, sir."

"Ah, can't help noticing you are looking at m'hat. A fashion entirely m'own." He stroked his hat as though it were a pet. "Why, I asked m'self, do gentlemen always wear black beaver hats? So, for a change, I chose cherry red felt." He patted the hat. "A bold venture is it not?"

"Yes," Edward said, on the verge of laughter. "You will cause a sensation both at the coffeehouse and your club."

"So say I. If the ladies, bless 'em, cover their heads with red mantles, why then, I said to Paine—he is my valet you know—Clarence Newton can wear a red hat."

Edward did know. Since boyhood, he had been acquainted with Newton's devoted, but long-suffering valet. He laughed to himself, imagining Paine's horrified expression when confronted with the reality of *that* hat.

Newton looked at his headgear with evident satisfaction. He perched it on top of his full-bottomed grey wig. "Enough of hats. Though your business is not my affair, I must say I don't care to see you keeping company with the Countess of Sinclair."

"You are right, Sir Newton, my business is *not* your affair."

"No need to take umbrage with me, m'boy. I recall the day when your nurse said, 'Pull up your skirts and piss like a man.' Now, will you come into your godmother's house with me?"

"Yes, sir," Edward said, chastened by the elderly gentleman's words.

After Sir Newton ascended the shallow flight of steps, he applied the brass knocker in the shape of a ferocious dragon's head.

Edward sighed, ashamed of his anger toward an old man with naught but his best interests at heart. "It is always a pleasure to see you, sir."

Newton turned around. His smile explained why his godmother liked Sir Newton so much. Despite the gentleman's vanity, he possessed a heart as warm as his smile. He did not gossip and had no known vices in this age of debauchery and excessive gambling.

Edward decided to make a peace offering. "Do you know the Countess of Sinclair well?"

Newton nodded. "Yes, she is a distant relative of mine. I must say I pity her. Old beliefs concerning men's rights over women die hard, but her husband's treatment of her was deplorable." The front door opened while Newton continued. "I am not one for tittle-tattle so I must not say more. Forgot m'self for a moment. Forgive an old man."

Edward's jaw tightened. Why had the late earl banished his countess? He kept pace with Newton while they followed the butler to the salon, with walls hung with wallpaper imitating white marble, a foil for many mirrors and oil paintings.

Seated on a sofa opposite the tall, narrow windows, his godmother held court among her afternoon callers. Several ladies, including Mrs Martyn and her daughter, and half a dozen or more fashionably attired men, filled the salon.

"My two favourite gentlemen," Frances said, a smile in her eyes when Edward approached with Newton.

Edward disengaged his arm before he kissed her cheek, his mind filled with thoughts of the bewitching countess.

Sir Newton lowered himself onto the sofa beside Frances Radcliffe and kissed each finger of her white, diamond-ringed hand while she cooed with appreciation.

All his thoughts still of Kate, Edward retreated to the opposite side of the salon. He stood between a pair of tall potted palms, recreating Kate's unique smile in his mind's eye.

The movement of a fan, wielded by a young lady seated on a sofa opposite him, attracted his attention. Upon recognising Mistress Martyn, his brow creased.

He choked back his amusement, well aware of Mrs Radcliffe's determination to alter his bachelor state.

Well versed in the language of fans, he understood what Mistress Martyn meant when she put her fan near her heart. *You have won my love,* the unspoken message stated. To whom was the silent message addressed? Bold of Mistress Martyn to risk such a declaration while seated by her mother, yet the sly puss had chosen her moment well. Mrs Martyn's head was turned away from her daughter while she conversed with another matron seated beside her.

Edward glanced around the room. Had Mistress Martyn signalled to the foppish youth neatly attired in puce and cream who stood to one side of the fireplace? He raised his eyebrows. Could the chit have been foolish enough to communicate with Cyril Fenton, a man of mature age, whom, at the very least, gentlemen considered a very strange card? Thoughtful, he gazed at Fenton, who stood on the other side of the fireplace.

Despite his dubious reputation, Mister Fenton—a man of good birth and heir to his rich uncle, a baron— knew how to charm the ladies, although his heart never seemed to be in his fulsome compliments. Edward shook his head. Rumour said the baron's days were numbered while he lay on his sickbed, and Fenton would soon inherit the title, together with a large fortune.

Edward watched the fellow advance toward Mistress Martyn. Fenton bowed. "Good day to you, sir," Mrs Martyn said. "Will you not join us? I am sure my daughter is delighted to see you."

Mistress Martyn's hand gripped her fan until her knuckles whitened. She bent her head, her cheeks suffused with a rush of colour.

Edward frowned. It seemed his godmother's protégée disliked the gentleman. So, why did Mrs Martyn encourage him? Had she set her heart on a title for her daughter? Surely the woman could find a better match for the girl. Was she fool enough to be blinded by Fenton's superficial charm?

Mrs Martyn and the other matron stood. Fenton sat next to Mistress Martyn. To Edward's disgust, Fenton not only greeted Mistress Martyn with a prolonged kiss on the mouth, but also grabbed her hand and kissed it. Like Kate, would Mistress Martyn be offered up on the altar of unhappy matrimony?

Edward made his way to his godmother's side. "I am surprised to see that reprobate, Fenton, in your salon," he said under his breath, although Mistress Martyn's fate was not his concern. "Does your young friend need to be rescued from him?"

"Bah, reprobate is a strong word for a delightful gentleman, Edward."

He decided not to disillusion his godmother by repeating the rumours about Fenton circulating at clubs and in coffeehouses.

Frances snapped her fan shut. "I daresay you have some reason for calling Fenton a reprobate. Please be good enough to ask Mistress Martyn to join me. Sir Newton, would you be kind enough to make room for her to sit next to me?"

With good grace, Newton stood.

Edward, determined not to do anything in regard to the young lady that might be misconstrued by either his

23

godmother or her mother, inclined his head to Newton. "My dear sir, please oblige me by conveying my godmother's request to Mistress Martyn?"

A quiet laugh escaped Sir Newton. He inclined his head. "Mrs Radcliffe, I told you the boy is not ready to tie the knot, but you ignored me."

Edward refused to allow his irritation at being called a boy to show. "Sir Newton is right."

"Indeed." Frances pursed her rouged lips.

"Godmother, to be blunt, I am not ready to be hand-fasted and request you to cease your endeavours on my behalf."

"But, Edward, dear Jane is so eligible. Look at her, she is pretty and her manners are pleasing."

"I think," Edward began, "that Mrs Martyn desires a title for her daughter. Besides, my taste does not run to chicks newly hatched from the schoolroom. What is more, my means are sufficient for my needs. I don't need to marry money. My brother is generous. Also, I have my inheritance and my prize money which are more than sufficient for my needs. Please don't inconvenience yourself by introducing me to any more eligible ladies."

To take the sting from his frank declaration, Edward kissed his godmother's cheek. He wished his conscience had not prompted him to draw her attention to Fenton and Mistress Martyn. The chit did not interest him. How *could* she, when no lady compared favourably to Kate?

* * *

24

Frances snapped her fan shut. *Provoking boy!* Earlier on, she had seen Edward *tête-à-tête* with Kate from her window. Obviously, his taste ran to more sophisticated ladies than dear Jane. She pressed her lips together, worldly-wise enough to know she was powerless to prevent a man from pursuing his inclinations, even if they would lead to disaster. No matter how much she wished to, it would be impertinent to speak of her misgivings to Kate.

"Mrs Radcliffe." Jane executed a perfect curtsey.

Sir Newton bowed. "Now I have brought Mistress Martyn to you, I hope you will be good enough to excuse me."

"And please excuse me, madam," Jane said. "I am faint and need some air. With your permission I will take a turn in your garden."

The young lady looked at her mother, who, with her back to them, sat deep in conversation. Mistress Martyn gathered her skirts in her small hands before hastening across the salon.

"What extraordinary conduct," Frances remarked. "But 'pon my word the chit must not sally forth alone. Edward, see no harm comes to her."

* * *

Edward noted the young fop to whom Mistress Martyn earlier signalled was following her. His lips twitched. "I doubt she is at risk in your garden." Perhaps the youngsters fancied themselves in the roles of those blighted lovers, Romeo and Juliet.

"Edward," Frances insisted.

"I am pleased to obey you, madam, provided Sir Newton will accompany me." Edward had spoken, aware that if by malign chance Mrs Martyn discovered him on his own in the garden with her daughter, it would be tantamount to his making an offer for the young lady's hand in marriage.

In the vestibule, Edward grinned at Newton. "I doubt Mistress Martyn wishes for our presence."

Fenton rushed out from the salon. "Where is Mistress Martyn?" he asked a lackey.

Edward exchanged a knowing glance with Newton.

Before the lackey could reply Newton stepped up to Fenton. "Good day, tell me what think you of m'hat," he said with the obvious intention of preventing Fenton from finding Mistress Martyn.

"Your hat, Sir Newton?" Fenton asked, with palpable surprise.

"Yes, m'hat."

"A monstrosity, sir."

"You are too unkind, but I feared you might say so," Newton murmured as he seized Fenton's arm. "M'dear sir, do me the honour of coming to m'club to discuss the merits of red hats."

Edward grinned. Few gentlemen would turn down an invitation from wealthy, influential Newton.

"Come," Newton urged Fenton with the manner of one interested in nothing more in the world than fashion.

At the precise moment at which the lackey closed the front door behind Newton and Fenton, Mistress Martyn entered the vestibule, the colour in her cheeks heightened.

"Captain Howard, I did not expect to see you here. The garden is beautiful, is it not? I must return to the salon. My mother might be looking for me."

He took pity on her incoherence. "I trust the fresh air benefited you."

After Mistress Martyn nodded, she hurried back to the salon. A minute or two later, the handsome, puce and cream clad youth followed her.

Edward sighed as he went up to his rooms. There was more to Mistress Martyn than either his godmother or her mother suspected. He dismissed the young lady from his mind. When would he see Kate again?

* * *

Edward smiled. Glorious to lounge, at ease, with money enough to suffice in this, the queen of cities, with its bustling River Thames, the skyline of Sir Christopher Wren's beautiful churches, and a peaceful rural landscape on its fringes. He linked his hands behind his head. In comparison to the cramped conditions on board ship, it was luxury to stretch out on a four-poster bed in his godmother's London house— although his body, toughened by conditions at sea, had always adjusted to austerity without difficulty. Yet, when ashore, he could not relinquish his passion for the sea, and he painted seascapes, as well as landscapes of foreign countries.

He looked up at the red velvet canopy, embroidered with threads of gold, and sighed with satisfaction. An excellent hostess, his godmother placed great importance on physical comfort and good food. However, he must remain vigilant to avoid gaining weight and letting his teeth rot from over-indulgence in sweet dishes.

Maybe Kate would enjoy a picnic in the country. Edward smiled. He sat up, imagining a tryst that would not compromise her reputation. He knew the very place to take her.

The countess aroused his curiosity. Yes, she was high-spirited, but he had seen fleeting sadness in her eyes. Was it due to her unhappy marriage or something else?

She was a lady without comparison, beautiful, mysterious, and vivacious. After he dined, he would take the air in Hyde Park in the hope of encountering her.

Chapter Four

Kate and her mother sat in the splendour of Kate's wainscoted dining room, at opposite ends of a table large enough to seat eighteen people.

Gertrude sniffed in appreciation of the delicate scent of mace and cinnamon flavouring the sweetened boiled cream. She piled some onto her plate to eat with her second helping of almond pudding.

Gertrude ate with single-minded enjoyment.

"Some cheese?" Gertrude suggested to Kate.

Kate cut a small portion of the imported, very expensive Dutch cheese with its bright red rind.

"Upon my word, Daughter, you are extremely quiet," Gertrude grumbled. "I would find livelier company in a graveyard."

"Would you?" Kate murmured, thinking of the letter she received in the morning.

Damn her late husband! She hoped he suffered in hell. He ruined her life. Three miscarriages before she gave birth to an heir. No, she would not torture herself. Instead of dwelling on the past, she must be grateful for her good health and generous widow's portion. It cushioned her from want, as well as providing the opportunity to increase her income through investment in foreign trade. She glanced at her corpulent mother, who suffered from frequent toothaches. Kate took care not to ruin her own teeth by partaking of too many puddings and sweetmeats. Her eyes half-closed, she considered Captain Howard. One of the first things she noticed about him was his strong white teeth; a rarity among men of any age.

Gertrude prattled on about her new apple-green taffety gown, her friends, and the convenience of living near St James's Park on the outskirts of London. She remained silent for a moment before continuing on. "In spite of all that, you don't understand how miserable I am because I am denied my grandson's company. Of course, I refer to the Earl of Sinclair, not my other grandsons."

Kate's hand tightened around the stem of her wineglass. She wanted to scream. Did her mother not understand the pain *she suffered* due to the unnatural separation from her son? And what would Mother say if she knew of the *girl's* existence?

Kate cursed the letter she received earlier in the day. A letter, in which yet another agent employed to find the child, informed her of failure. She sipped some wine and tried to swallow.

"Did you hear me?" Gertrude asked.

"Yes," Kate snapped. "I regret you cannot see my son, but you can enjoy your other grandsons' company. I suggest you visit either my brother or my sister."

Gertrude helped herself to more cheese. "I am not unkind enough to leave you to rattle about on your own in this mansion."

It would be better for both of them if Gertrude were honest and admitted she held her daughter-by-law and her grandchildren's undisciplined behaviour in aversion. As for her sister's husband, he had made his dislike of their mother-by-law plain. Kate's relationship with Mother might improve if the woman learned not to interfere in her children's business.

"Kate, if only my dearest Jeremy and poor little Elizabeth had survived their childhood, I am sure they would be a comfort to me in my old age." Without the least evidence of sorrow in her expression, Gertrude popped another piece of cheese into her mouth.

Oh no, as though she had not done everything she could to help Mother, yet again, her parent was about to extol the virtues of long dead Jeremy and Elizabeth. She stood. Although respect for Kate's elders had been drummed into her since childhood, Kate vented her anger by slamming her crystal glass on the table and then standing.

Gertrude looked up from the selection of different varieties of cheese on her plate. "I have not finished my meal."

"I know, Mother, but you must excuse me," Kate said, forcing herself to be polite. "Please don't disturb yourself on my account. Eat your fill."

She hurried up to her bedchamber. She would ride in St James's Park and give the tabby cats, clad in their finery, something new to gossip about.

After changing, she smoothed the jacket of her scarlet riding habit, trimmed with as much gold braid as Captain Howard's fine sea-faring clothes. She chuckled, imagining the cats extending their claws and meowing maliciously about her outfit.

Would Captain Howard be in the park? Kate spent some time deciding how she would greet him if he were there.

* * *

31

It was not done; it was simply not done to ride along The Mall while ladies and gentlemen promenaded in the late afternoon and early evening. It was even more shocking for a female to ride without a groom in St. James Park, at that hour, on a fine spring day with a pleasant breeze.

She guessed what the ladies whispered. "No female of good birth would draw attention to herself by riding a mare theatrically caparisoned in scarlet and gold that matches Lady Sinclair's habit," muttered the shocked matrons. "But what else can one expect of *her*?"

The tabbies shook their heads, while the boldest of their daughters eyed her enviously.

Kate suspected that sedate ladies taking the air on foot, on horseback, or in coaches, complained to their husbands, and although the gentlemen paid lip service to their wives' opinions, even the oldest and most devoted husband's blood stirred at the sight of her, seated straight-backed on the side-saddle of her grey mare, Scheherazade.

* * *

Edward had just begun his ride along The Mall when, resplendent in her scarlet habit, Kate rode toward him on her spirited horse, as though the whole world lay at her feet.

Glad of the pale spring sunshine, Edward settled himself more firmly in the saddle. "Walk on," he commanded.

Scheherazade minced down The Mall, advancing to the path by the canal, then stepping with her knees high to where the countess drew the mare to a halt.

Edward reined in beside Kate who sat confidently in the saddle looking down at a pedestrian dressed in sober, snuff-brown velvet and a long, cream-striped, fawn waistcoat.

As Edward doffed his hat, Kate turned her attention to him. "Captain Howard," she began, "it is my pleasure to introduce Mister Stafford. Mister Stafford, Captain Howard."

"Good day, sir." Mister Stafford bowed.

Edward returned the bow from the saddle.

Her ladyship's eyebrows drew together while her attention shifted back to Stafford. Stony-faced, she frowned at the unfortunate gentleman.

"My dear Lady Sinclair," Stafford said, "I shall speak out of concern for your reputation and safety. If Mother were here, she would also caution you. Indeed, I shall ask her to offer you advice, for you might pay more heed to one of your own fair sex than to a mere gentleman. Mother will explain why your habit is too-too gaudy."

Kate's mare snorted as though speaking for her mistress.

For a moment, Edward thought Kate might mimic her mount. Instead, she pressed her lips together in a mutinous line.

Edward smiled at her. "I admire you, milady. Too few members of the fair sex are bold enough to trust themselves to a side-saddle."

A smile formed at the corners of Kate's mouth.

Stafford held up his hands. "Captain, I implore you not to encourage her ladyship's folly."

Kate's hand gripped the reins. Her mare side-stepped. With the expertise of a skilled equestrienne, Kate controlled the horse.

Edward replaced his hat. "Milady, this is not the place to enjoy a canter. Will you ride with me in Hyde Park?"

She nodded, looking at Stafford, the expression in her eyes as cold as icicles. "Good day to you, sir."

"Take care," her admirer said.

"My poor friend," Kate commenced, "you need a tame bird in a glass cage. No, don't speak. Only believe me when I say, you would not know what to do with a wild bird." Her lips twitched. Merriment glinted in her eyes. "Ask your mother. She will tell you I am right."

Edward restrained a chuckle. Without doubt, an imp of devilment prompted Kate's last sentence.

In silence, the countess urged her horse to a trot.

Edward bowed again from the saddle, this time to take leave of the unfortunate Stafford. In his opinion, her ladyship would never stoop to heed the snuff-brown gentleman's unwelcome advice.

At Kate's side, Edward rode through Green Park—keeping a wary eye out for highwaymen—and entered the less fashionable Hyde Park, where Kate led him to a deserted ride.

"How do you tolerate him?" Edward asked.

"Who? Oh, Stafford! He is kind and he is one of my most persistent gallants. Who knows whether or not, in a moment of madness, I might agree to marry him?"

Edward could not imagine Kate agreeing to marry one of Stafford's ilk. He chuckled instead of replying.

"*Ventre a terre*," Kate cried out. Obviously careless of anything other than her enjoyment, she put the words into practice by urging her mare into a gallop instead of a canter.

Edward spurred his black mare forward. Ahead of him, her tail neatly braided with gold ribbon, Kate's grey forged on. Too fond of Dark Lady to apply the spur and risk goading her beyond her strength, he cantered forward until Kate, somewhat breathless, her cheeks showing pink, drew rein.

"Captain, confess a landlubber has beaten you."

"I admit you are right, milady, and needs must think of a suitable prize to give you."

Sparks burned deep in her eyes. "Though I played unfair?"

He laughed. "I am at fault for not hearing you challenge me to a race."

Shame-faced, she spoke. "You are too much the gentlemen. Yet despite what is said of me, I never cheat."

"I believe you. Let us dismount, so that we may indulge in pleasant conversation. Look, the sun smiles on us through the trees."

"Very well, if you promise not to try to flirt with me."

He sat still in the saddle. "Do you not want me to?"

Mischief curled around the edge of her mouth. "Do you *not* want to kiss me?"

He raised an eyebrow. "Yes, at a time of my choosing."

Her eyes widened before he dismounted. After he led Dark Lady off the bridle path, he fastened her reins to the branch of a tree. He then took Kate's reins from her. "You have not introduced me to this lovely lady. What is her name?"

"Scheherazade."

"Ah, I hope *you* will tell me a thousand and one tales, for it is my desire to know everything about you."

Before she disengaged her foot from the stirrup, something sparked in her eyes, but faded too fast for him to interpret its meaning. "I will not bore you with the commonplace story of my life."

"I promise nothing about you will ever bore me and that you could never be commonplace." He put a hand on each side of her slender waist, in order to lift her down from the saddle. For a second, Kate stiffened. Oh, the lady was less bold than she pretended. Her feet touched the ground. He released her.

Kate shrugged. "Is it possible for anyone to be truly interested in another person?"

He looked down at the top of her charming hat. "Are you really so cynical?"

"If I am?"

Fascinated by her quicksilver changes of mood, he tilted her chin with one finger while gazing deep into her eyes.

Kate jerked her chin away from him. With one hand she indicated the sunshine dappling the path. "I refuse to be serious on such a beautiful day."

"Lady Sinclair, I *am* at your service."

A frown creased her forehead.

He kissed her hand. When Kate snatched it away, he raised his eyebrows. Indeed, the lady was an enigma.

"Come, sir, the hour grows late. I must return home." She hurried back to Scheherazade, her skirts swaying with each step.

A squirrel chattered. Kate looked up. Her foot caught on an exposed tree root spread across the bridle path. Edward reached for her too late. She stumbled and fell, face down.

He hurried to kneel by her side. "Are you hurt?"

She rolled over, gazed up at him and smiled. "No, only winded."

"Allow me to help you."

"No thank you, I don't need assistance from any man."

He smiled down at her embarrassed face. "Do you not?"

Kate shook her head as she sat.

"With your permission." Edward drew Kate to her feet and removed a twig and several dry leaves from her hair before he picked up her hat.

* * *

After Kate parted from Captain Howard, she rode home alone, all the while nervously tapping her crop against her skirt and thinking about the captain.

She left Scheherazade at the stables, and then strode into her house, stripped off her gloves, removed her hat, and handed them to a lackey together with her riding crop. Deprived of the crop with which she could have swished the air to express her agitation, she hastened up the stairs to her bedchamber where Jessie waited.

"Help me out of my riding habit."

Jessie complied. Within a half hour or less, Kate, attired in a pretty nightgown, sat by the fireside in her

37

closet, where she kept money and jewellery in a strong box. Before settling down to work, she glanced around the small room crowded with chairs, a desk, sofa, bookshelves, and her sewing basket, the contents of which she occupied herself on rare occasions.

With impatient fingers, Kate sorted her correspondence: a sheaf of bills, invitations, begging letters, and other communications. After arranging them in four groups, she rose and placed them on her desk, a pretty piece of red-lacquered furniture from China inlaid with mother of pearl

She blinked away the tears forming in her eyes before returning to the fireside. Yet again, she had not received a letter from her son. She had written to him on innumerable occasions. But more likely than not, his letters had been confiscated by his uncle. Her son, Charles, would not know she had written to him.

Did Charles ever ask for her? Did his uncle and aunt ever speak of her to him? Had they poisoned his mind against her? She bowed her head. What did their opinions matter? Regardless of whatever they believed, they could not alter the truth. She remained an innocent victim of the terms of her late husband's will which gave the guardianship of her son to his uncle and denied her access.

Kate sank onto her favourite pink-upholstered chair and thought of the girl. In spite of her exhaustive inquiries since her husband's death, every trail led to a dead end. Should she give up the search? No, she would not. The child might have survived the perils of infancy.

* * *

On the following afternoon, Kate prepared to attend the theatre. Dressed like an ice queen in a white Cushlahs silk gown, trimmed with silver bullion lace and bedecked with diamonds, she regarded her reflection in the mirror with satisfaction.

Unbidden, thoughts of Captain Howard entered her mind. What would he think if he saw her dressed thus? She hurried to the desk to pen an invitation for him to join her in her box at The New Theatre. She smiled. The captain's presence at her side would make both Tyrell and Stafford jealous. After all, she did not want to give either of them false expectations of securing her hand in marriage.

Kate shrugged. She must not allow preoccupation with her son to sour her life. Only a girl when she married, the late earl had never allowed her to make merry. She suppressed an incipient laugh. She liked being a widow. Kate's tense body relaxed as she rested her head against the back of the wing chair. Captain Howard added a new dimension to London life. Confident that such a young man would never consider marrying her, she could flirt with him as much as she wanted.

Yet, the captain seemed older than his years. She closed her eyes. Did she still want to make him sorry for refusing her invitation to attend her morning levees? Perhaps not, although she would be interested in his opinion of poets, artists, musicians, and others who came to seek her patronage. She would also be interested in his estimation of those who sought to sell her valuable items, such as carpets and jewellery. With a swift, unladylike motion, she stretched out her legs.

Edward Howard, a strong name for a strong man, an unusual man.

What did the captain want of a woman nine years his senior? To be his mistress? His godmother was right. It would be more suitable for him to pay court to Jane Martyn or other young chits instead of a mature woman, a woman embittered by marriage to an insensitive, intolerant man who not only used her to breed but also mistrusted her.

Kate's hands clenched. Enough, she had not repined thus for three years or more. Her days were filled with activity, which was exhausting. Every day, when she went to bed long past midnight, she fell asleep without delay. Perhaps it would be unwise to allow the handsome captain to be part of her coterie.

She frowned. Unlike other young men in the past, it might be difficult to have the heart to dismiss Captain Howard. She laughed at the prospect. So be it.

Kate returned to the escritoire. She picked up the invitation for the captain to join her at the theatre before ringing a hand bell.

When Simon responded to her summons, Kate handed him the hand-written invitation while instructing him to have it delivered to Captain Howard at his godmother's address.

"A moment," she said. "How is your mother?"

The young man smiled. "Grateful to your ladyship for the cottage on your estate. Now she's away from London's foul air, she's recovering her health and blesses you."

"I am glad to hear she is much better. Away with you now. Send my foot page to deliver the invitation."

"Yes, Lady Sinclair. Thank you, my lady." Simon backed away as though she were royalty.

Kate inclined her head. She had learned compassion through her husband's neglect of those in his direct service and those working for him in various capacities. Unlike him, she never treated anyone with no more consideration than the straw beneath her feet.

By the time she sat down at the dining table with her mother, Captain Howard's acceptance of her invitation had arrived. He would call for her in his godmother's coach.

Kate laughed. What would Captain Howard think of Colley Cibber's play, *Love Makes a Man*? One day, would love make the captain?

"What amuses you, Kate?" Gertrude asked.

"Nothing of importance, Mother."

Kate ate some apricot pie. Whatever else she might say or think of Captain Howard, no one could accuse him of being a fop; although his gold buttons shone and his boots gleamed, and his blue coat and white breeches fitted perfectly. Yet they were not in the foppish mode employed by some officers in the army and navy. Her spoon clattered onto her plate. Heavens above, could she think of nothing other than Edward Howard?

Chapter Five

Seated in a box at the theatre between the Countess of Sinclair and her mother, Edward waited for the play to begin. "Are you looking forward to seeing the play, Mrs Corby?"

"Yes, Captain, I am also eager to attend the opera next week. That is always a treat."

"I hope you will enjoy it," he responded with his usual politeness, but most of his attention on Kate. Garbed in snowy white, her diamonds glittered like icicles. He imagined her reigning over snowbound landscapes like those he saw when his ship had blown off course to Iceland in mid-winter.

Last night, on the verge of sleep, images of fair Kate drifted through his mind, Kate, alternatively distant and mischievous. An inscrutable countess with cool, secretive eyes, which on the rare occasions they were off-guard, hinted at something he could not define.

What did he want of her? His heart answered the question. Her feminine allure challenged him to breach her barriers of satin, silk, and mystery. The thought of the intimate touch of their warm flesh aroused him.

The countess picked up the thread of his conversation with her mother. Her clear voice drew him from his thoughts. "Captain Howard, my mother indulges her taste for music whenever she can. Indeed, were she not a gentlewoman born, her soprano might grace the stage. Instead, my mother entertains close friends in the privacy of my music room where she spends much of her time. When the sound of her voice fills my house and floats out into the street, passers-by pause to listen."

Edward turned his head to look at Mrs Corby. "I congratulate you on your gift, madam, and hope to hear you sing."

The lady, a vision of purple silks, lilac satin, and silver lace, favoured him with a demure smile. "Thank you, Captain." With palpable delight, she leaned forward to look across him at her daughter. "I did not realise you take such pleasure in my voice."

Kate returned the smile before she surveyed the theatre. "Look, Captain, your godmother has just entered the box opposite us with Mrs Martyn, her daughter, and a gentleman whom I presume is Mister Martyn." She scanned the audience. "I see Mister Tyrell in His Grace, the Duke of Marlow's box, but I do not see Stafford anywhere. I daresay his mother has contrived to spoil his pleasure with either another sermon or her perpetual palpitations. She does not approve of the theatre. In Stafford's situation, I would either consign the woman to my country estate, or remove her from my house to her own establishment in town. The wretched creature does naught but mouth complaints and platitudes."

"How you rattle on," Edward joked.

Kate laughed. "Tut, tut, Captain, I am not in the habit of rattling on. Perhaps it is the result of your shocking effect on me."

He bent his head to whisper in her ear. "I want to have an even more shocking effect on you."

Kate fluttered her fan. "Whatever can you mean?" she asked, her voice almost drowned by the noise from the audience standing below.

"Can you not fathom my meaning?" He glanced at Mrs Corby to make sure she had not overheard him.

Kate pouted. "I am not skilled in the art of solving mysteries." She raised her fan and peered at him over the edge of it.

"Perchance I want you to fall in love with me."

Did he imagine alarm in the depths of her eyes? Maybe—despite her forward ways—the lady was not all she seemed.

Kate admonished him with a rap of her furled fan across his knuckles. "I would say pay attention to the play. Perhaps you will learn from it. Consider the title, *Love Makes a Man*." Her tone matched his playful one.

He tilted her chin with his thumb—his fingers spread over her mouth—and gazed into her eyes. "Consider your principal admirers. Stafford needs love to make a man of him. Foppish Tyrell lacks manly attributes."

Kate jerked her head away from the slight pressure of his gentle fingers. "What do *you* need, Captain?"

He hesitated for fear she would freeze before gliding away from him on invisible skates. "Need? I think you can guess."

The fan fell onto her lap. "You are, oh, I cannot decide what you are."

He raised her cold, be-ringed hand to his lips. "Precipitate," he suggested as he turned her hand over to kiss the flesh of her tender palm.

Kate gurgled with laughter. "You are too bold. Let go of my hand."

"All seafaring men are audacious, milady."

"Look, Daughter," Mrs Corby interrupted, "your brother-by-law and his wife have arrived. I wonder if they have brought my grandson to town. You cannot imagine how much I want to see him."

Kate clenched her hand around her closed fan.

Why was the countess so pale? "Wine," Edward said to a lackey, "a glass of wine for your mistress."

Throughout the graceful dance, followed by music and song, his ice queen sat like one frozen to her seat. She faced the candlelit stage as though she were blind. By the end of the performance, tears glistened in her eyes. But why? He wanted to comfort her. "How lovely you are," he murmured in her ear. "I want to capture you on canvas. May I paint you as you are now, wearing snow white and diamonds?"

Kate blinked her tears away. "Ah, you are a gentleman of unsuspected talents."

Why on earth did the eyes of the beautiful, rich countess drown in sorrow? He smiled as he handed her his handkerchief.

"Now I understand," Kate said.

"What do you understand?"

"You are an artist accustomed to acute observation." She dabbed her eyes. "You must not think there are tears in them. There is something in the right one."

He doubted Kate was telling the truth.

* * *

45

Annoyed, because she had not controlled her sensibilities at the theatre on the previous evening, Kate rose long before Jessie came to wake her. She parted the curtains at the window and folded back the shutters, thoughts of her son uppermost in her mind. Since yesterday, when she saw her brother and sister-by-law at the theatre, she had burned to find out whether or not her boy had come to town with them.

My son, she thought again with unwelcome tears in her eyes. By all accounts he is plucky, well-mannered, somewhat bookish, and a promising equestrian. He is nearly thirteen. In three years or more, he will make his bow at court. In five years, he will take his seat in The House of Lords. After he does so, no one shall stand between us. I shall introduce myself to him. Although many precious years have been lost, somehow or other I will forge an indestructible steel bond between us.

Kate nibbled her forefinger. If the Sinclairs had brought him to town she must see him, albeit from a distance.

She stared through the drizzle at a milkmaid guiding two brown cows to her house.

A simple life in the country where fat cattle grazed on green pastures would suit her current mood. How her head ached. In an hour or more, Stafford, Tyrell, and other gentlemen would wait on her while she made her toilette. She sighed again. After yesterday evening spent in Captain Howard's pleasant company, she did not look forward to seeing them.

The milkmaid knocked on the door. Simon answered the summons and handed the young woman two churns. Shoulders hunched against the persistent drizzle, the milkmaid removed her milking stool from her back and balanced it on the cobblestones.

Kate rang the hand bell. Two or three minutes passed before her tirewoman came.

Smoothing her apron, Jessie bustled into the bedchamber. "My lady, up already? You'll take a chill." She fetched a fur-lined nightgown for Kate to wear over her thin linen night rail. "Put this on."

"Never mind about me, Jessie, the milkmaid has arrived."

"What of it?"

"She is cold and wet. Give her one of the black cloaks with a hood which I wore while in mourning for the Earl."

"Too good for the likes of her," Jessie said with the familiarity of a much-valued servant.

"Why do you object to giving the woman a woollen cloak thick enough to keep the rain from her back?"

"I don't want every Tom, Jack, and Dick to come knocking on your door trying to take advantage of you, my lady."

"Give her the cloak!"

"As you please." Jessie sniffed.

Kate stood at the window until she saw her tirewoman hand over the cloak.

To the tune of her sigh, Kate sank onto the window seat. She visualised a girl with hair as fair as her own and hoped someone was taking good care of her.

* * *

With Jessie in attendance and, in accordance with her custom, Kate readied for her levee. Somewhat less interested in her appearance than usual, she powdered her cheeks but applied no paint.

When Stafford and Tyrell arrived, they annoyed her by not commenting on her pallor. Did they have no genuine concern for her well-being?

"Would you be kind enough to read snippets from the broadsheets, Mister Stafford?" she asked.

Stafford smirked at Tyrell. Their rivalry bored her. More gentlemen arrived, filling the bedchamber with chatter. Stafford put down the broadsheet. He began a discussion about the iniquitous window tax. Kate shrugged. Well, what did she care if they did not ask her to express her opinion? What else could she expect of men with such shallow natures whose visits had become no more than routine?

Until today, they had amused her. She now realised she did not need suitors who courted her only for her face and fortune. At this moment, she wanted nothing more than to be rid of them.

A poet read some lines in the hope of gaining her patronage. Time seemed to pass even more slowly than when she had still hoped Captain Howard would wait on her at one of her levees.

* * *

Alone at last, Kate proceeded along the hall to her closet where a letter from her bailiff awaited. She would open it later.

In need of fresh air, she decided to exercise high-spirited Scheherazade. She returned to her bedchamber to change into her riding habit.

On the ground floor, a lackey responded to an impatient rat-a-tat-tat on the door. Captain Howard's voice echoed around the hall below and up the stairs to the second floor.

Kate hesitated. Was the captain too late for her levee? No, he had made plain his intention not to call on her early in the day while she chatted, discussed politics, gossiped, allowed artists and writers to speak with her, and merchants to display their valuable wares.

She hurried back to her bedchamber to scrutinise herself in her dressing table mirror. Too pale? With expert hands, she quickly painted her cheeks and tinted her eyebrows. A great improvement!

Someone rapped on her door.

"Come," she called.

John entered. "Captain Howard asks if you will receive him, my lady. He awaits you in the green salon."

Her palm tingled. She remembered the exquisite sensation of his kiss on it at the theatre. Never before had she experienced such a surge of desire for any man. Breathless passion set her heart afire, then left her yearning for more.

With pleasurable anticipation at the thought of seeing her new beau, Kate stepped along the corridor and into the salon with its many mirrors and row of tall sash windows which filled the room with light, regardless of the window tax.

She advanced across the room. How handsome the captain appeared in his blue coat, white waistcoat embroidered with gold, white breeches, and stockings. The flutter of her heart surprised her. It was something she had very rarely experienced and had not known since the days before her marriage. Instead of looking at him full in the face, she eyed his gold-buckled shoes to hide her agitation. "Good day to you, Captain Howard."

Edward, whom she thought of by his given name, bowed. He took a few hasty steps forward. Facing her, his large dark eyes alert in his tanned face, he inclined his head and then kissed her lightly on the mouth in accordance with the prevalent custom when greeting a lady. The brief touch of his lips warmed hers. Heat coursed through her. She clung to sufficient presence of mind to indicate a wing chair upholstered in sage-green damask. "Please be seated, sir. A glass of wine? I have some fine Annadea. Would you care to taste it?"

Edward sat quite still, his posture that of a man very much at his ease. One strong hand, with a ruby ring on the little finger, rested on the smooth arm of the chair. "I shall be guided by you." The manner in which he drew out his vowels made the mundane acceptance of her offer of a glass of Portuguese wine seem intimate.

Kate sank onto the chair opposite him. He did not look like the type of gentleman to be guided by anyone. With a wave of her hand, she gestured to the lackey on duty to serve them. While waiting for the man to do so, Kate sought for something to say to the young officer whose self-assured manner made him seem much older than his years.

Edward accepted a glass, sipped, and rolled the wine around his mouth before he swallowed it. "Excellent, but I did not expect less of you."

She recovered her wits and chuckled. "Sooner or later you will discover my feet of clay."

His eyes laughed at her. "I am sure you wrong yourself." He stared at the tips of her slippers resting decorously side by side on a footstool. His eyes gleamed. "Truth to tell, I would like to paint you with your skirts drawn up a little to reveal your ankles."

Kate willed herself not to cover her feet with her quilted petticoat. "Impertinent jackanapes," she reprimanded him, conscious of a rush of hot colour into her cheeks.

"Not as impertinent as you might imagine, for I am come to request you to join me on a picnic in the country and to allow me the privilege of sketching you."

Accustomed to artists who clamoured to paint her, she shook her head.

"Come, come, my lady, do not be bashful." A "toast of the town" shy?

"No, you may not paint or sketch me. At my husband's command, I sat for my portrait. Never have I suffered such ennui. I never wish to experience it again."

"Shameful of the artist to bore you. If I promise to regale you with entertaining conversation, will you allow me to draw you?"

She toyed with her fan. "No, I detest picnics because it either rains when one is planned, or the sun is too hot to eat and drink in comfort."

"What will you wager that neither rain nor sun nor cold shall spoil our picnic?"

"I never gamble."

Edward laughed as though he did not believe her. "Never?"

"No, to do so would be to risk becoming one of those women who wager their last coin on the turn of a card, on a horse, or some other foolish thing. I shall not chance poverty."

"May I remark how uncommon you are? I scarce know a gentleman or lady who does *not* play cards."

The corners of her mouth turned down. "Then you know not that my uncle, who adopted me, lost his fortune at the gaming tables and sold—" she broke off in confusion.

The captain's forehead creased. "I am sorry to hear that. What did he sell?"

Kate shook her head in disbelief. She had almost confided in this young officer whom she liked better than most men of her acquaintance. In her right mind, nothing would have induced her to even hint that her uncle sold her in marriage to the Earl of Sinclair. The captain really did have an astonishing effect on her. "No need to be sorry, for it is past history."

His lips parted in a charismatic smile. "I shall suggest a gamble of a different nature."

"You shock me, Captain Howard. Yet if I accept, what do you wager?"

"Would you agree to a lover?"

Kate did not want one. She shook her head, this time with annoyance. "I am too old for foolish games."

"Rejection, how sad." He took his kerchief out of his pocket, pretending to dry his eyes.

Her lips twitched. "You make yourself ridiculous."

"I hoped to melt your frosty heart."

Burdened with her late husband's betrothal and wedding rings, her hand trembled, a reaction to Edward's teasing. She clutched the arm of her chair. Although this youngster amused her, it would take much more to melt her heart.

Edward stood. He bent forward to put his hand over hers. "Yesterday, when I saw you dressed in white, I compared you to an Ice Queen. How presumptuous I am to think I can shatter the frozen wastes of your heart with a kiss. Please forgive me." He sat again. "What shall I wager? Ah, I know the very thing to appeal to a lady, particularly one as deliciously fragrant as you are. Shall we agree on a flask of perfume blended for you by Lillie?"

"Agreed. Shall we shake hands on it, Captain?" She stared at him. How had he persuaded her to go on a picnic with him?

Edward stood. "Though you venture naught, I guarantee I shall win." He took her cool hand in his warm one.

At his touch, her body tingled in the most peculiar way. Wide-eyed, she gazed at him but managed to retain her spirited manner. "Bah, you are insufferable. Do you think you are God?"

"No, but sea-faring men lay careful plans."

She did not rise to his challenge. "Whether or not you win, do your sketches do their subjects justice?"

"Some people say they do."

"Ah, you are now modest."

Edward shrugged. "You cannot expect me to be judge of my talent or lack of it."

Kate unfurled her fan. "Are you in the habit of sketching ladies?"

"To be sure I am. I have portrayed them in every port I have visited."

At the thought of the beauties he must have known, she experienced a sharp pang in her chest. She snapped the fan shut. "I do not know why you want to add me to your collection."

"You, my lady, are a diamond of the highest calibre. Jewels are always worthwhile adding to a collection."

"You are premature, Captain. You have not won your wager."

"But I shall." Edward tilted his head back and laughed.

His youthful laughter reinforced her awareness of the difference in their ages. Stafford and Tyrell, who were one or two years older than she, always restrained their mirth no matter how amused they might be. Come to think of it, Stafford laughed little. When he did, he tittered to indicate his amusement.

Edward smiled. "Name the day for our jaunt, my lady."

She peered out of the window at the dull April sky. "A week from today. The weather might be warmer by then. But even so, I warn you that you will lose your wager."

Chapter Six

At Horse Ferry, Kate shivered. She drew her sable-lined cloak closer around her throat. Her hands snuggled into her matching fur muff. She looked at Edward, who sat opposite her in Mrs Radcliffe's coach.

"You are mad, Captain Howard, quite mad to plan a picnic when the rain pours down in sheets," she teased, while the coach rumbled onto the ferry that would carry them across the Thames. She removed one hand from her muff and pulled her hood lower over her forehead. "Moreover I must be equally mad to have agreed to accompany you."

Edward chuckled. "Perhaps I am not in my right mind. However, I cannot vouch for the state of yours."

"Wretch, for speaking to a lady thus. Come, come, sir, admit you will lose your wager, and take me home."

"The day is not yet over."

Why did the self-assured officer seem so confident he would win? "If you think the rain will cease, the clouds roll away, and the sun shine on your venture, I fear you are doomed to disappointment."

"My only thought was to please you. May I remind you, nothing is more injurious than the heat of the sun? It is known to overheat the blood and turn the human brain rabid. Indeed, our summer parlours are situated to avoid the dangers of both the sun and the south wind."

"So, we are to partake of our picnic *al fresco* soaked to the skin?" She pressed her hand to her heart with genuine apprehension. "Oh, please tell me we are not going to eat our meal in the fields amongst the cowpats where the milkmaids disport themselves on May Day."

The corners of Edward's mouth twitched. "Trust me to have made provision for your comfort."

"You cannot sketch me in a downpour, so I shall win your wager of a flask of perfume blended especially for me by Lillie." Waspish over her failure to discover his plans, she rested her head against the down-filled squab attached to the back of her seat.

Kate pretended to doze. Instead, she turned her face toward the window and peeped out once or twice before the coach disembarked. Afterward, it moved on at a good pace. When it drew to a halt, she rubbed her eyes as though she had slept.

Edward inclined his head to her. "I trust you have awakened refreshed?"

To her annoyance, it seemed as though he guessed she had feigned sleep because he refused to satisfy her curiosity about the picnic. Moreover, she would not be surprised to learn he now laughed quietly and rolled his eyes, knowing her inability to draw information from him had piqued her interest. Kate pretended indifference to his reaction and made a show of pushing a tendril of hair back into place beneath the hood of her cloak. "Where are we?' she asked, although she suspected they were in Chelsea, for where else did the road through broad fields lead?

"Chelsea." His eyes alight with mirth, he doffed his hat and flourished it elegantly.

How dare he be amused at her expense? Her other gallants were more respectful. This young captain needed a sharp set down. "Oh," she began, "the village in which there is naught more interesting than the Physick Garden, the barracks for old soldiers, and boarding schools for young ladies. Captain Howard, I cannot imagine why you should wish to picnic in such an unfashionable place."

The coach halted. A groom opened the door. Parasols in hand, two menservants advanced along a weathered brick path from a house built in the Tudor style. Captain Howard sprang down from the coach. "Come, milady."

She rose, rested her gloved hand on his arm, and stepped out. "Where are we?" she asked with genuine confusion.

"Come, I don't want you to be drenched." Edward cupped her elbow with his hand. He hurried her along the path and through an arched side gate.

"Where are we?" she repeated.

"At my house which I inherited from my great-aunt."

Edward guided her into a walled garden some thirty square yards in size, laid out in neat beds edged with low, green-painted rails. Daffodils made a bright display, although their heads drooped in the onslaught of rain that showed no sign of cessation.

"As you see, I am a man of property," the captain said with an air of quiet satisfaction, no trace of envy of her fortune in his voice or demeanour. "The ornamental garden is small, yet it is a treasure Great Aunt tended lovingly with the help of her gardeners and several lads." Edward indicated a door in the wall. "Through there is the fruit and vegetable garden she took great interest in, and beyond it, a knot garden in which she cultivated herbs." He led her through an arch cut in a yew hedge. "We shall picnic in the summerhouse."

She paused for a second to admire the octagonal building, its exterior painted with *trompe l'oeil* that deceived the eye into believing the garden extended farther than it did. "I believe you have cheated me, sir."

"I have not. The summerhouse is part of the garden. We shall enjoy our picnic protected from inclement weather." He opened the door. "I trust everything is to your satisfaction. My sole aim is to please you."

With a theatrical swirl of her scarlet cloak, Kate brushed past him. She looked around. A ceiling with a painted blue sky and frescoes of the four seasons delighted her eyes. "How beautiful. Words almost fail me."

"Thank you for praising my attempt to portray paradise gained, not in a faraway land, but in a miniscule portion of 'this sceptre'd isle'."

"'This other Eden, demi-paradise','" she quoted.

"Ah, you read Shakespeare and are familiar with his play, *Richard II*. On board ship, I whiled away many a long hour with him." The laughter quit his eyes. "How many times did I yearn for England when shivering with cold in the desolate wastes of the north, or perspiring profusely in the searing heat of the tropics? When surrounded either by grey seas beneath a sullen sky or oceans shimmering brighter than bluebells beneath the torrid sun I read:

'This fortress built by nature for herself
Against infection and the hand of war,
This happy breed of men, this little world,
This precious stone set in the silver sea.'

"I leave it to you to imagine how much I hoped I would live to see England again."

Kate sank onto one of the chairs grouped together around a brazier set in a hearth. Captain Howard surprised her. When he requested permission to paint her, she assumed it was a ploy by a gentleman of no particular artistic ability. She had been mistaken. Not only did evidence of his talent surround her, but his voice, with its rich timbres, had thrilled her.

The captain doffed his hat. He bowed. "Have I bored you, milady?"

She shook her head. Far from it, few men captured her interest and commanded her full attention as he did.

"A glass of wine?"

"Yes, thank you." She pushed back her hood and looked at the rain streaming down the sash windows. "How far from home you have travelled. I have often wished I could board one of the merchant ships I have shares in."

His face grave, he handed her a glass of wine. "I trust you are not serious. For one thing, most sailors believe a woman aboard is bad luck."

"Do *you*?"

"No, but sea-faring is dangerous. Sailors are ever at risk from privateers, pirates, and disease."

"That I know. *The Seagull,* with a cargo of molasses and sugar from the West Indies, is overdue. I and the other shareholders are anxious about her fate."

She sipped her wine while Edward spoke to a servant. Not for a moment did she regret purchasing a country estate with the profits made by investing the income from her dower lands in foreign trade. Besides, both the West Indies' trade, and spices and silk from the Levant, brought her rich rewards. Kate hummed as she considered whether or not to fling her net wider across equally lucrative seas. Of course, no female dealt in person at the Royal Exchange, but she could inform her agent she wanted to invest in trade with India and China.

Edward pointed at a round mahogany table covered with a fine linen cloth laid with silver cutlery and blue and white Delftware. "Shall we dine before I sketch you?"

"Yes," she replied, still distracted by her thoughts of business.

"Ah, I have won."

How clever he was. In an absent-minded moment, she had agreed he won the wager.

"What was that tune you hummed?" Edward asked, while servants carried trays of food to the table.

"'Under The Greenwood Tree'."

"Ah. Let us hope we will picnic outdoors when the weather is more favourable. With your permission, I shall sketch you beneath the boughs of a spreading oak tree."

The servants withdrew. Edward offered her his hand. She placed the tips of her fingers on it, then crossed the floor to the table with him. "Please be seated, milady." He drew her chair back.

Intrigued by the scene on the opposite wall of woodlands carpeted with bluebells, she noticed rabbits partially concealed in the lush growth, a badger peering out from his set, and a fox peeping from behind a gnarled oak tree. "Were you not an officer in Her Majesty's navy—and if you had the need to do so—you could command a living as an artist."

Edward ladled soup into a bowl. "Do you think so?"

She nodded.

"I trust you have no objection to serving ourselves. I dismissed the servants to give us an opportunity to become better acquainted."

Kate appreciated his honesty. "Yet you refused to attend my levee. You even refused my offer to permit you to be the only attendee."

"So I did, milady, because I am accustomed to taking command."

"Should I be ashamed?"

He shrugged. "Do you think you should? Now, shall we eat?"

Kate bowed her head before she said Grace. After she said "Amen," the captain regarded her with what, surprise, because she invoked the Lord's blessing as she had done since childhood? Shy for the first time in years, she bent her head, and spread butter on a slice of crusty bread.

"I hope you will enjoy your meal." He indicated the symmetrical arrangement of roast meats, sallet, a dish of pureed carrots, condiments and sauces.

"I am sure I will. It seems you have been at pains to please me."

"My late great aunt's elderly cook was delighted by my request for her to prepare a meal for a guest. The other servants were equally pleased by your impending visit. They have been at pains to air and cleanse the house, which I hope you will agree to visit later. It is small but charming. My great aunt whiled away many happy years in it."

"Since you don't occupy the house, why have you not dismissed her servants?"

"How could I?" He shifted on his seat. "They grew old in service in this place, the only home they have known for more years than I can count. To pension them off would break their hearts as it would the gardener's." He cleared his throat. "I daresay you think I am a sentimental fool."

"On the contrary, your consideration for them does you honour."

Silence reigned until Kate spoke again. "Do you weary of being a land lubber, Captain?"

"Not at the moment, but I shall if we go to war with France."

War, something very much at the back of her mind. She again tried to decide whether or not to buy her own ship and trade with the Orient, or if it would be wiser to remain content with investments in joint ventures.

She put her soup spoon down. "Do you think war will break out?"

"I think the question of who will succeed to the Spanish throne, and thus rule its vast territorial holdings in the Old and New World, makes war inevitable. England and her allies will never allow a French claimant to become king of the vast Spanish Empire."

"I agree." How would the war affect her investments? Kate's appetite faded away. She made pretence of eating a small portion of roast mutton with some pureed carrots. War put ships at risk. The insurance never covered the full cost of losing them at sea. She decided against purchasing a merchant ship. Instead, she would continue to spread her cautious investments amongst several consortiums.

"What is your ladyship's pleasure?"

She eyed the ham, game, fowl, fish, and sweet dishes. He had gone to so much effort to provide an excellent picnic, if one could really term it thus, so she must eat more.

"You seem troubled, milady."

"Somewhat. I fear the future. Suppose the second King James's papist son becomes king after Queen Anne?"

"Let us suppose he does not and put aside wearisome matters. Some marzipan bacon or some stewed venison?"

She should guard her teeth from all things sweet but the bacon looked so delicious in its marzipan coating that her appetite returned. "A small portion of bacon please. Lord, your cook has prepared enough to feed an army. What will she do with the remainder?"

"After the servants eat their fill, the rest will be distributed to the poor of the parish. Some more wine, milady?"

"No, thank you."

"Do you not like it?"

"It is excellent but I despise drunkenness. I never over-indulge." She relished her last forkful of succulent bacon and marzipan.

"A piece of apple pie? Great Aunt once told me her cook has a very light hand with pastry."

"No thank you, I can eat no more."

Edward rang the hand bell to summon the servants to clear the table. After they did so with quiet efficiency, Kate refused his offer of sweetmeats and then allowed him to lead her toward a chair that faced the window.

He fetched her cloak and spread it over the chair, inside out, to reveal the sable lining. "Please be seated, Countess, while I arrange my easel."

Kate admired his deft movements as he arranged his paraphernalia.

When he requested her to raise her skirts to reveal her ankles she hesitated.

"Afraid to reveal them?"

Afraid? No, she was not. After the treatment she endured from her husband, she would never again allow herself to be in a situation in which she needed to fear any man. With her right hand, she fingered the small, but deadly dagger strapped to her arm in its sheath beneath her left sleeve.

"Why should I be frightened, Captain?"

He laughed. "Ladies have strange fancies. Perhaps you think your ankles are too thick."

Although her nostrils flared, she did not fall into his trap. Instead, she pulled her petticoat up to reveal her feet shod in high-heeled Morocco leather shoes and her ankles sheathed in green silk stockings. To her annoyance, her cheeks warmed while the captain scrutinised her.

"Hmm, with your permission." He rumpled the folds of her apple-green gown then arranged the hem of her cream petticoat.

Her cheeks grew even warmer.

"No need to look so startled because I rearranged your skirts. Artists are a strange breed. Now, rest your head against the back of the chair and arch your neck a little. As for your hands, clasp them on your lap. No that is too demure. Rest one hand on your knee. Toying with a curl with your other hand would be very effective."

Without so much as a polite "by your leave" he removed her lace cap. Before she could protest he unpinned the plait wound around her head, released it from the ribbon, then drew a ringlet forward over her shoulder. "How I have longed to do that. Ah, what beautiful hair you have. It is as soft as silk to the touch and fair as silver gilt in this light."

The scent of his spicy pomade filled her nostrils. A thrill gathered in the pit of her stomach. "Outrageous of you to take the liberty of loosening my hair," she protested, confused by the novel sensation and not knowing whether to be shocked or amused by his presumptuous behaviour.

Edward inclined his head and set to work. Every time she opened her mouth to speak, he motioned her to silence. Whenever she moved to stretch her stiff limbs he protested that she spoilt her pose.

"I am done," he said at long last. "You have been very good. Although you explained you are careful not to over imbibe, you deserve a glass of wine." His eyes brightened as though he returned from a far place. "Forgive me for breaking my promise that you would not be bored."

"I shall not reproach you because I understand you were absorbed in drawing me." Kate plaited her hair, pinned it up, and replaced her lace cap.

"Well," she asked, regaining her customary pretence of high spirits, "are my ankles too thick?"

Edward gazed at his work. "What? Oh, if they were I would have altered them in my sketch."

Taken aback, she said not a word. She stared at him, annoyed, because she knew other gentlemen would have flattered her after being granted such a privilege. Kate swallowed, unable to think of a dignified retort. "May I see the sketch?" she asked after she stood and shook out her skirts.

"Sketches," he corrected her. "No, they are mere outlines for an oil painting." He covered his easel with a cloth. An inner voice told her an undignified struggle would ensue if she tried to remove it.

He glanced at the embers of the fire. "A million apologies, milady, are you cold?"

"A little."

"I am sorry. Shall we go to the house to sit by the hearth while we partake of sweetmeats and wine?"

By now the rain had lessened but a chill breeze tugged at their clothes as they made their way to a side door leading into a narrow hall with a slightly uneven red brick floor.

Edward smiled at her. "Come, shall we enjoy our refreshments before I conduct you around the house?"

* * *

Hours later, while she dressed to attend a rout, Kate thought about the small but delightful house. Every room was furnished not only with charm, but with an eye for convenience, yet it was too feminine for the new owner. Redolent of the faint fragrance of pressed roses and dried lavender, its daintiness did not suit Captain Howard.

Her lips parted in a smile. Bold, the captain was too bold and greedy. He also wanted to paint her as an

Ice Queen. She must remain on guard. Already, when he asked if she liked his property, she had replied, "Yes," and said it reminded her of Missendene Manor. But she had not told him she purchased the estate with *the girl* in mind. Kate trembled, despite her anguish, never could she think of the missing child as other than 'the girl' for she had never seen her face. She only knew she must find her.

Chapter Seven

To please Mrs Radcliffe, Edward agreed to accompany her to St James Church. He realised a less fashionable place of worship would not do for his godmother and concealed his amusement in order not to hurt her feelings. He knew that in her opinion, only her chosen church, situated between fashionable Piccadilly and Jermyn Street, merited her attendance.

Like Mrs Radcliffe, he admired St James. He considered it one of the finest of Sir Christopher Wren's churches, although many people considered the exterior too plain. They wanted it to be plastered with a mixture of lime and stone, but he liked the unpretentious appearance of the two-storied building with tall, domed windows.

The coach drew up outside the red brick building dressed with Portland stone, and Edward had only a moment to admire the tall steeple topped by a weathervane before he handed his godmother out of the coach on the south side.

When Mrs Radcliffe's feet touched the ground, she smoothed her burgundy coloured satin petticoat and adjusted the skirts of her damask gown. Amused, Edward smiled. Like many other fine ladies and gentlemen, Mrs Radcliffe came to worship, not out of piety, but to be seen in her finery. On weekdays, she often came here on the pretence of saying her prayers, but in fact did so to observe others and to gossip outside the church.

"Come, Toby," Godmother said to her small black page. "Don't drop my prayer book. Straighten your turban, child." Her eyes alight with curiosity, she turned her head to survey those entering the church. "'Pon my word, Countess Sinclair. I did not look to see her here." She sniffed. "The lady is wearing blue again. Does she wear it so often because it matches her eyes? If so, it is a pretty conceit, is it not?"

Edward patted her gloved hand. "As ever, the countess looks well, very well indeed."

"Look there at Tyrell and Stafford, hurrying after her like a pair of devoted servants." Mrs Radcliffe laughed. "They are racing her other admirers to her side."

Indoors, the pure white walls dazzled Edward's eyes. Soon they adjusted to the glare so he looked appreciatively at the barrel-vaulted ceiling supported by Corinthian columns.

His godmother poked his arm with her fan. "Come, Edward."

They passed Kate, who was already seated in her pew. When she noticed him, she inclined her head. This place of worship, with a congregation of bejewelled lords and ladies, suited Kate. It would be a brave cleric who delivered a sermon on the subject of ostentation to a proud congregation famed for its lack of docility and humility. Edward doffed his hat and bowed to Kate, conscious of his godmother's tightened grip on his arm.

"Come, Edward."

He followed her, waiting patiently each time she paused to greet acquaintances on her way to her pew.

When seated, he could not see the countess. Later, when he and his godmother emerged from the church, Kate approached him. "Captain Howard, once again allow me to thank you for a delightful picnic."

Godmother fluttered her fan. "A picnic! How extraordinary! We have not enjoyed one mild day for an age."

"Indeed, sir, you are careless of her ladyship's health, thus deserving any reprimand her friends care to issue on her behalf," protested Stafford who stood close to Lady Sinclair.

"Do you number yourself amongst the countess's friends?" Edward asked.

"I think the lady will agree that I am one of her oldest, most devoted friends."

Out of the corner of his eyes, Edward noticed Kate's amused smile, which she hid quickly behind her painted fan. Were Stafford a cockerel, he would have crowed. "You are to be congratulated, sir."

From his position opposite Kate, Tyrell bowed. "If you wished to picnic, you had only to ask me, my lady, for as you know, your every wish is my command."

Stafford and Tyrell glared at each other as stiff as a pair of tomcats commencing hostilities.

Kate gurgled with naughty laughter. "Thank you, Tyrell, but your offer comes too late. Captain Howard anticipated my every desire, and truth to tell, I hope to picnic with him again."

Tyrell looked down his nose at Edward.

Unperturbed by the gentleman's hostility, Edward raised an eyebrow. The countess deserved to be called a minx.

Her ladyship favoured him with a smile before she inclined her head to his godmother. "Before I bid good day to you, madam, please allow me to ask if you enjoyed your recent visit to my brother-by-law and his wife?"

"Sir Newton," Godmother called out as though she had not heard Kate's question. She waved at the gentleman with his treasured red hat perched on his grey wig.

"Are all of the Sinclair family in good health, Mrs Radcliffe?" Kate asked a little louder than before.

Edward pursed his lips. Why had the countess clenched her fists until the knuckles shone white?

His godmother beamed at her favourite gallant. "Good day to you, Sir Newton, I declare the sun shines in your honour for the first time in a week."

Sir Newton executed a perfect bow and kissed her briefly on the lips.

"You are remiss, Godmother, the countess asked you how the Sinclairs are," Edward said, although Kate had opened her mouth to speak.

"They were in good health when I returned to town," his godmother replied.

The countess no longer appeared to notice any gallants who hovered around her. "I trust the children did not inconvenience you, madam. I hear they are over-indulged," Kate said, her expression enigmatic.

"Countess, it is public knowledge that you have no love for your late husband's relations, so why waste time inquiring about them when there are so many more agreeable things to speak of?" Tyrell asked. "Allow me to escort you to your carriage."

Kate shook her head and laughed.

The sound seemed forced to Edward.

"Off with you gentlemen," she ordered. "I wish to converse with Mrs Radcliffe."

Edward remained while her other admirers protested. Nevertheless, they bowed and went their separate ways.

Kate faced his godmother. "Are the Sinclair children over-indulged?" she persisted.

Godmother tapped him on the arm. "Lud, look at Lady Davencourt. I vow she can scarce walk for the weight of her diamonds."

Edward observed Kate, inquisitive about her determination to have an answer to her question. She glanced at him. Without doubt his curiosity must have been blatant for her eyelashes fluttered and she looked away as though reluctant to be observed. Even more inquisitive than before, he turned his head toward his godmother. "Lady Sinclair asked you a question."

Godmother watched the crowd. "What? Oh yes, the countess asked me about the children at Sinclair Place."

Kate nodded. "Yes, I did." Heightened colour deepened the shade of her tinted cheeks.

"Countess, I am not fortunate enough to be blessed with children. I know little about them, but neither your son, whose tutor ensures his manners are pleasing, nor any of his cousins, inconvenienced me. Truth to tell, I enjoyed their company."

Kate's hands relaxed. A sigh parted her lips. "I am glad to hear it. Good day to you." She nodded at Mrs Radcliffe. "Sir Newton, Captain Howard, good day to both of you."

"Lady Sinclair, please allow me to escort you," Edward said. "I am sure Sir Newton will be only too pleased to escort my godmother to her home."

"No, Mrs Radcliffe must permit you to accompany her so that she has yet another opportunity to warn you about me." Having fired her broadside from a metaphorical cannon, Kate's lips curved into her famous, languorous smile.

"Godmother knows better than to do any such thing, for she understands I make my own judgments."

"Yes, I believe you do. Your chin confirms you are a gentleman with definite opinions of your own."

"Come, Edward," Godmother said, "I am both famished and dismayed."

"Dismayed?" he echoed.

His godmother nodded so vehemently that the ribbons which secured her starched headdress wobbled. "Yes, dismayed! The sermon put me out of patience. What business is it of the vicar if his congregation chooses to honour The Lord by dressing '*finer than Solomon in all his glory*?' As for his suggestion that each of us should contribute one of the jewels we wear this day to the poor, never before did I hear such a thing and hope I will never hear it again."

"I approved of the suggestion, so I donated a ring," Kate said.

"Did you indeed?" His godmother turned to face her page. "As for you, Toby, I hope you realise how fortunate you are to be owned by a mistress who has the means to see to your comfort and educate you as a good Christian."

"Yes, Mistress, I do."

Edward smiled at the child and wondered what his future would be. Of course, it was the way of the world to own slaves, and some ladies were fond of their little black pages. However, he had no desire to own another person body and soul. His godmother's voice interrupted his thoughts.

"Do you have such a black jewel of a page, my lady?" Godmother asked Kate.

"I have a page, but he is from Ireland not Africa."

"You must buy one. Negro pages are all the fashion."

An ominous gleam appeared in Kate's eyes. "Yes, I know they are as fashionable as pet birds in glass cages. No thank you, I am not ruled by fashion."

It seemed something in Kate's expression deterred his godmother from arguing about the advantages of owning a slave boy.

Godmother looked at Toby kindly. "Must I forever be telling you to straighten your turban?"

The child rolled his eyes, tucked the prayer book under his arm, and adjusted it.

"Do you disapprove of slavery?" Edward asked Kate in an undertone.

She shrugged with what was most likely practiced daintiness. "I neither have a slave nor trade in slaves."

"You have not answered my question."

"You will receive no other from me."

He bowed, not from the waist but from the shoulders. "May I escort you home?"

"You *must* give Mrs Radcliffe another opportunity to warn you about me," Kate said once more. After this shot across turbulent waters, Kate's lips again curved in her renowned smile.

"I hope to have the pleasure of accompanying you on another occasion." He bowed, this time more deeply.

Followed by a maid and two lackeys, Kate departed with a swirl of her skirts. Her fragrance lingered in the still air, reminding him of a summer flower garden underlain with a hint of some spicy herb.

The soft expression in his godmother's eyes revealed her devotion to her elderly swain. "May I take you home, Sir Newton?"

Newton shook his head and then gestured to his sedan chair.

"Ah, there is my coach," Godmother said. "I hope to see you later today, Sir Newton. Come, Edward." She put her hand on his arm and allowed him to lead her to the coach. Godmother patted his hand. "My dear boy, when are you leaving for Hertfordshire to visit your brother and his family?"

He raised his voice to be heard over the clatter of wheels from vehicles arriving to collect their owners. "There is no hurry. For the moment, I will remain in London."

Her laugh mocked him. "Before you met Lady Sinclair, you told me you were looking forward to visiting your relatives without delay. In your shoes, I would avoid danger by doing so."

"You are not in my shoes. Moreover, I have never feared danger. But what of you? Did you enjoy your recent stay at Sinclair Place?"

Godmother fingered one of her emerald earrings. "Oh, I confess that after the innumerable cold draughts at the charming young Earl of Sinclair's country seat, I was glad to return to the comfort of my own bed in my warm house."

He handed her into the coach before sitting opposite her.

His godmother tilted her head to one side. "So, you picnicked with the countess."

"Yes, she is magnificent is she not? I am at her feet."

"Then you are in an unfortunate position." His godmother sank back in her seat while the coach gathered speed. "Society condemns her ladyship. She provokes censure with behaviour not suited to a widowed mother. However, even though her ladyship is a flirt, in my opinion she is to be pitied."

"Pitied? Why should anyone pity a lady with beauty, intelligence, and wealth?"

"In spite of all that, I am sorry for her. By the time she reached the age of sixteen, Kate's uncle, who adopted her, had gambled away his entire fortune. To recoup it, he married the poor girl off to the Earl of Sinclair, as unpleasant a man of sixty or more years whom I had ever seen. Whenever I think of it, I boil with anger. His lordship made no concession to Kate's youth and he did not appreciate her natural high spirits. After he fathered an heir, he banished her. Later, under the terms of his will, his brother, George Sinclair, became the child's guardian. Mister Sinclair does not permit Kate to see her son," she grabbed the strap when the coach took a steep bend, then continued, "not that Kate seems to care—if one is to judge by her enjoyment of fashionable pursuits. She is to be seen everywhere, riding in The Mall, at the theatre, at routs and balls, in addition to every other fashionable diversion one can think of." Her sharp eyes stared at him. "Most likely it is true she cannot abide any of the Sinclairs, her son included. After all, why should she care for a child she has never seen?"

A frown furrowed his forehead. "Why did her husband banish her?"

Godmother shrugged and sniffed her nosegay of fragrant herbs. "No one knows. He remained at Sinclair Place with his infant son and housed Kate in seclusion elsewhere."

His hands tightened within his leather gloves. "A monster!"

"I agree."

"It is common enough for an old man to marry a young girl but my blood boils at the thought of Kate married to one."

"My dear Edward, however much you sympathise with Lady Sinclair, put aside all thought of her. Such marriages are common enough. I dare to say her fortune consoles her for any suffering she might have experienced. Besides, though sinned against, she is now a merciless coquette."

Edward raised an eyebrow.

Mrs Radcliffe sighed. "When you look at me thus you remind me of the engaging child you used to be. Yet for all your charm, you were ever a stubborn boy as unwilling to heed good advice then as you are now. And even then, you seemed older than your years." She rapped his arm with her fan. "Come to think of it, you still don't want to accept good counsel, but please believe me when I say a lady such as my young protégée, Mistress Martyn, would be a better wife than any heartless widow."

"The subject of marriage yet again. Godmother, please be done with it. The thought of the parson's trap terrifies me." He yawned, one deliberately languid hand over his mouth.

Though his godmother laughed, she seemed abstracted. She frowned. "Maybe I am mistaken." She shook her head as if for once she was unsure of her thoughts.

"Concerning what?"

"To accost me at church of all places, perchance Kate is desperate for news of her son. If it is so, maybe she *has* a heart."

Edward frowned, his mind racing. "Now there's a thought to meditate on instead of the sermon on the subject of charity."

"My dear boy, why should we think of the lady instead of the good dinner awaiting us?"

Easier said than done, Edward thought, his mind occupied by Kate, who intrigued him more each time he saw her. Every time they parted, he burned to see her again. By his faith, his blood was more at risk from overheating in her presence than when the sun beat down on him in foreign climes.

* * *

During the days which followed, Edward sought Kate's company. The more he participated in her world of fashion, frivolity, and people jostling for her attention, the more she interested him.

With mingled curiosity and pleasure, he accepted the countess's invitation to attend a private performance of Cibber's play *Love's Last Shift*. Curiosity, because the subject of play seemed an odd choice for a lady with her past history. Pleasure, because he would enjoy mingling in her milieu, that of an influential, wealthy peeress. Upon his arrival at Kate's mansion, he handed his card to the butler, then proceeded to a salon in which coal burned in a pair of marble fireplaces, one at each end of the room. It seemed her ladyship did not fear the chimney tax.

A low whistle escaped him. No expense had been spared on the spotless black and white marble floor and the carved white marble swags which framed matching mirrors above the fireplaces.

Edward joined the queue of those waiting to pay their respects to their hostess, who sat on a padded, high-backed wooden chair placed at the far end of the vast salon with its many mirrors and windows. While Edward waited, he watched Kate. No trace of the flirt today. Seated beneath a green brocade canopy with gold fringes, she received her guests with dignity and graceful gestures of her hands. The queue moved forward until at long last he made his bow.

Kate looked deep into his eyes. "Captain Howard, I *am* pleased to see you again. Please be at ease and partake of some wine. We will soon adjourn to the music room to attend the play. I trust you will enjoy it. I regret Lady Marlborough is unable to be here because she is in attendance on Her Majesty. Had she come, I would have introduced you. I presume you are acquainted with her brother-by-law."

Was Kate testing him, trying to find out if, like the admiral, George Churchill, he was a Tory? What of Kate? Was she a Whig or a Tory? "No, I have not experienced the pleasure of meeting him," he replied belatedly.

"Something for you to remedy, Captain. I hope to converse with you later about the admiral and other matters which may be of interest to you." A wave of her hand dismissed him. He made way for someone else.

Was she going to try to advance his naval career?

The queue shortened. The master of ceremonies announced, "My lords, ladies, and gentlemen, the play."

* * *

Seated at the back of the music room, Edward faced the crimson velvet curtains hiding the stage, wondering if he had overestimated Kate's interest in him. This evening, she was very much on her dignity, very much the great lady whose actions and clothes the press reported daily, a noblewoman at ease at court and elsewhere, although some private doors were closed to her because of her reputation, which he suspected was greatly exaggerated.

He wished he could see Kate's reaction to the tale of the virtuous heroine's attempts to reform her rake of a husband with appeals to his better nature. The play had as great an effect on this small audience as it did when performed recently at The New Theatre. When he glanced around, he noticed a gentleman who rubbed his eyes with the back of his hand, and then blew his nose loudly to hide his emotion. The ladies sniffed and dabbed away their tears with dainty, lace-edged handkerchiefs. When the curtain dropped after the finale, silence reigned in tribute to both the play and the actors, before the audience rose to its feet and applauded.

Only the countess remained seated until the enthusiastic cheers and clapping faded.

Kate stood, then led the way to a room in which a supper of both savoury and fruit tarts, as well as wafer-thin slices of cold meats, cold fowls, cheese, bread rolls, jellies, syllabubs, and other culinary delights were set out on tables from which the guests could help themselves.

* * *

Kate stood next to Edward and the actor who had played the part of the libertine husband.

"I'faith, milady," began the actor, "begging your ladyship's pardon, you look much like a very young actress I saw playing a small part at The New Theatre some two or three months ago. Indeed, so greatly does she resemble you that you could be related to her."

Could he know *the girl*? Kate trembled with excitement—at the prospect of finding her—and shock over his casual words. She sank onto a chair and stared at him, speechless.

"A glass of wine for her ladyship," Edward said to a lackey. He stooped over her. "Shall I send for smelling salts, milady?"

Kate glanced at him, grateful for his concern. She shook her head. In control of her emotions, she stared up at the player. "How fascinating, pray tell me more about the girl you mentioned."

"I know not who she is, so there is little to tell other than I judge her to be between eleven and thirteen years old. Her hair and eyes are the same shade as yours, her face is shaped like your ladyship's, and her form is graceful. Milady, I trust you are not offended by the comparison. If you are, please accept my apologies for mentioning the child."

Kate straightened her shoulders and shook her head slowly. She needed to find out more. "I am not offended."

She must be careful not to arouse suspicion. If she found the lost girl, she wanted no stigma to attach itself to her. And heaven alone knew a former actress—no matter how young—would be looked on with grave suspicion in polite society. At all costs, to protect the child, she must proceed with caution.

Kate forced a carefree laugh. "I would like to observe this girl who so closely resembles me. It would satisfy my curiosity. Have you seen her at any other theatres?"

"No, my lady."

"Well, I hope to watch you perform again in the near future. For the moment, please partake of some refreshment. You must be tired after your excellent performance."

"Thank you, Lady Sinclair." The actor bowed and made his way across the room.

Kate looked up at the captain. "Captain Howard, don't allow me to detain you by my side, please go and eat your fill."

"To be detained by you would be a pleasure."

"May I congratulate you on the success of the performance," a sprightly young lady said to Kate. "'Tis so congenial to watch a play without rude interruptions from the gallery and the pit. I enjoyed it and swear the poor wife brought tears to my eyes. My handkerchief is soaked."

"I am glad you approve of the venture, Lady Pickering," Kate replied as though she had not a care in the world.

* * *

Thoughtful, Edward stroked his chin with his forefinger. Did the young actress the actor spoke of have any connection to the unknown child Kate had mentioned? If so, who could she be? He approached the man. Surely there must be more clues regarding her whereabouts.

Chapter Eight

Two days after they attended the play, Edward called on Kate. A lackey led him to the long gallery where Kate often walked up and down when the weather was too bad for outdoor exercise.

He made his bow to the countess who remained seated on a sofa opposite a tall window.

"I did not expect you to call today."

"I trust my visit is a pleasant surprise."

She laughed. "Fishing for compliments, Captain Howard?"

"I never fish off the anchor, though I would be sorely cast down should you not welcome my visit."

She tilted her head to one side. "Why should I not welcome it?"

He chuckled. "You alone can answer that question."

"*Touché.*"

Edward turned to take his portfolio from a lackey.

Perhaps Captain Howard had brought the sketches—which he drew at Chelsea—for her inspection. "Please be seated. Some wine?' she asked. He nodded. "Red or white viana, Canary wine or a glass of Madeira?"

"Oh, I share your tastes and hope you share mine," he said, a roguish gleam in his eyes. "Red, if you please."

Shared her tastes? Whatever did he mean? Oh, yes, now she remembered. When they first met at his godmother's house, he suggested she would prefer dry viana to sweet wine, or did he mean something else? She glanced at the lackey on duty. "Simon, you may also pour a glass for me."

She raised her eyebrows. All too many gentlemen presented her with gifts and then sought her favours, both pecuniary and sexual. What did the captain expect in return?

Edward put the portfolio on the low marble-topped table in front of their chairs.

Simon served the wine while Edward scanned the gallery. "You have some fine paintings, Countess."

"My late husband was a connoisseur, and I have added to the collection. Some of them are those I commissioned of my country house, Missendene Manor."

After Simon withdrew, Edward put aside his crystal glass. He opened the portfolio and handed her two sketches. Astonished, she gazed at him.

"My lady, I overheard the actor speak of a very young actress he once saw playing a small part at The New Theatre. He remarked on her likeness to you. One of the sketches is of you, as I imagine you when you were a young woman. The other is of the unknown girl."

Yes, the captain had captured her very face when she was young. As for the other sketch, could it be both her own and the girl's image at the age of twelve? Kate wanted to kiss it. She glanced over at Edward.

His expression serious, and perhaps questioning, Captain Howard looked deep into her eyes. "Without fear of judgment, you may confide in me if it pleases you."

Judgment? What had those tabby cats, the gossips, said about her? Did the captain think she might be weighed and found lacking?

"You are impertinent, sir." She looked away. "I have naught to fear from either your verdict or that of any other man."

"Forgive me, I did not mean to offend."

She rallied without the least desire for a confidant. "It is not uncommon for a person unrelated by blood to bear a close resemblance to someone else." Kate crossed her fingers behind her back, conscious of the lie she was about to tell. "Without doubt, such a likeness is no more than coincidence. I dare say this is true of the young person the actor referred to."

Annoyed by her childish gesture, Kate uncrossed her fingers and picked up the captain's drawing of herself as a young woman. Her eyes, what had the captain seen in them? Detachment? Melancholy? Longing? There was something she could not define.

Kate pursed her lips. Although the captain was too percipient, she liked him, liked him very much indeed.

"I hope my gifts please you."

"Yes, thank you. They are charming. I shall have them framed and hung in the gallery. Or perhaps they would look well in the green salon. Come, sir, you shall give me your advice."

In the spacious salon hung with sea-green wallpaper, she addressed the captain. "What do you think? Should I hang them here?"

"Yes, someone else might recognise the likeness and tell you where to find the actress."

She took a deep breath before forcing a laugh. "By my faith, sir, it might be amusing to see my double. Now, you must take your leave. I am going to ride in St James Park."

"Allow me the privilege of accompanying you."

"Oh, you would not care to cool your heels while I change into my riding habit."

Captain Howard's laugh rang out. "To the contrary, a sailor's needs must be patient while he awaits a favourable wind. I am only too pleased to wait for you."

"Your horse?"

"Is tied to the post outside your house. So, what say you?"

"I will ask Simon to bring the broadsheets for you to peruse while you wait for me."

Kate swept from the room to hide her impatience. Bother the man. Why could he not have taken her hint that she wished to be alone. Yet, she never found Captain Howard's company unwelcome. She smiled.

* * *

"My lady," Jessie said, "you're fidgeting so much that I can't tie your cravat."

Kate stood deep in thought while Jessie arranged the muslin folds. Had Captain Howard guessed her secret? Did he know why she wanted to find the girl? She restrained an impulse to nibble the end of her forefinger. Instead, she picked up a ruby-headed pin and thrust it through the cravat to anchor it to her lawn shirt.

Plumed hat on head, hands in perfumed leather gloves, Kate swished the riding crop against her scarlet wool skirt. By now Captain Howard's patience must be sorely tried for she had not hurried to get ready. On a whim, she prolonged it by wearing a powdered wig with several curls falling to her breast. After a quick glance in the mirror, she joined her gallant in the green salon.

The captain stood looking as though nothing in the world pleased him more than his long wait. He offered his arm. "How elegant you are, milady, and how delicious your perfume."

"Though you are a flatterer, I thank you for the compliments."

Kate rested the tips of her fingers on his wrist then proceeded out of the house.

The captain helped her up into the saddle and mounted his horse.

* * *

Appreciative of the mild April air, Kate rode into St James Park at the captain's side, as ever indifferent to any disapproval of her dashing riding habit. Her spirits raised by the blue skies and birdsong, she drew rein at frequent intervals to greet acquaintances, and once, upon sighting the Sinclairs' coach emblazoned with her son's coat of arms, reined in Scheherazade, and stared after the vehicle.

"Milady, what is your pleasure?" Captain Howard murmured.

"What? Oh, I beg your pardon. Shall we ride by the canal?" Without waiting for an answer, she guided her mare forward. A child darted across the road. Kate brought Scheherazade to a halt, but not before the little girl fell over almost under the dancing hooves.

The countess slid somewhat awkwardly to the ground and helped the child to stand. "Are you hurt? Don't cry. Please speak to me."

"I am not crying," said a small but indignant voice.

A woman hurried toward them. "Mary Anne, what were you about, running away from me in so disgraceful a fashion?'

Kate raised her eyebrows. "You are?"

The woman curtseyed. "This wretched child's unfortunate nursemaid," she muttered, straightened, and then grabbed Mary Anne's arm.

The child cried out, her face contorted with pain.

"Come along," the nurse said, "it will be bread and water for your supper tonight."

Conscious of the captain, who had dismounted and now stood at her side—and indignant on Mary Anne's behalf—Kate eyed the nurse from top to toe.

"*Oddsfish*," Edward said, "were I in your charge I think *I* would run away."

The narrow-faced woman blushed scarlet.

Mary Anne seemed terrified of her. No child should appear thus, with huge frightened eyes and cheeks devoid of colour. "Who is your mistress?" Kate asked.

"Begging your pardon, madam, it's none of your business."

"I choose to make it mine." Kate looked down her nose before turning her attention to the child. "Who are your parents?"

"Mother's name is Mrs Bellamy."

"Where do you live, Mary Anne?" Edward asked.

"On King Street."

A good address, thought Kate. Coupled with the child's expensive clothes, it indicated a wealthy family. *Bellamy.... Could Mary Anne be old Lady Bellamy's granddaughter?* Kate put her hand on the small girl's shoulder. "How old are you?"

"Eight."

"Why did you run away?"

Mary Anne's large blue eyes filled with tears. A shudder passed through her petite frame.

"Don't be frightened, I shall try to set all to rights if you tell me why you ran away."

"Nurse said my father died because I am so bad that he did not love me."

"I am sure it is untrue," Kate said in an even tone. Furious on Mary Anne's behalf, she glared at the nurse. "How dare you claim such an awful thing?"

The woman's chin jutted forward. "Indeed, I didn't."

"You did," Mary Anne protested.

The nurse ignored the child. "What's more, little Miss here is a shocking liar, always making up stories." The woman stared into the distance as though she could not look Kate in the eye.

"I am not lying," Mary Anne shouted, although she trembled. "I am not," she almost sobbed.

Kate believed her. She doubted a child would make up such a horrible story, and so she decided to use her rank to overcome any objections to taking matters into her own hands.

Immune to murmurs from spectators who had gathered around, she indicated the captain with a wave

90

of her hand. "Mary Anne, would you like to ride home on this gentleman's horse?"

"She shan't," the nurse all but shouted, her eyes dark with palpable anger.

Mary Anne glanced uncertainly from her nurse to Kate before she nodded. "Yes, please, I used to ride with my father, and sometimes Mother came with us." Her mouth quivered. "Now my mother says she has no appetite for living. She does not want to ride and will not allow me to go riding without her." The little girl sighed. "Although my grandmother scolds her for it, Mother lies in bed all day long."

Kate faced the captain. "If you will be good enough to mount your horse, I shall hand the child up to you."

"As you please, milady," he replied.

Within moments, pink-cheeked, Mary Anne was settled in front of him.

Kate smiled at a stripling who, unasked, held the reins of her horse. "Thank you for your help."

He coloured up to the roots of his hair. "Glad to be of service," he muttered. "An' it's an 'onour to be close to such a fine piece of 'orseflesh."

"Would you be kind enough to help me up into the saddle, sir?"

The man cupped his hands to assist.

"Do you think this is wise?" Captain Howard asked when she had gathered the reins.

Kate ignored the nurse's outraged squawks. "Would you prefer me to *walk* home instead of riding?"

Though the captain shook his head reprovingly, she noted the same roguish gleam in his eyes that he had displayed earlier.

"You know full well *riding* is not what I refer to. You could be accused of kidnap, milady, so I again ask you if you think this is wise."

She frowned down at him. "Wise? Are you not presumptuous to question my decision?"

"I doubt my gall will harm you." His laughter bubbled over. "No, I implore you not to scowl at me. You see me shaking in my boots."

Unable to resist his funning, she laughed.

"To be serious, milady, should you not reconsider what you are about to do?"

"No." Past suffering came to Kate's mind. Too many children endured cruelty for the lack of someone to confide in. "I shall take Mary Anne home and acquaint her relatives with this evil woman's wickedness. For what could be more sinful than telling the child the reason that her father died was because she behaved badly, and therefore, he did not love her? However, I shall not blame you if you withdraw from this sorry affair."

"Retreat? No such thing, milady, I am no craven. I shall act the part of a heroic merman and rescue you from monsters."

"Ones like her?" she asked while rudely pointing a finger at the nurse. "You iniquitous woman, may God forgive you for what you have wrought in this poor child's mind."

"You can't take Mary Anne," the nurse shrieked. "I'll call the watch. They'll arrest you. See if they don't."

"Arrest the Countess of Sinclair? I doubt it," said one of the spectators.

Aghast, the nurse wept. "Gawd, what's going to happen to me?"

"You should have considered that before you poured poisonous words into this child's ears," Kate said.

* * *

Edward held Mary Anne steady within the crook of his arm while Kate rode alongside. The rumble of traffic, the cries of street sellers, and the ringing of church bells prevented conversation. Ever conscious of the little girl's safety, Edward considered the countess. When he first met her, he admired her beauty and simultaneously experienced physical desire so strong that it literally took his breath away. She had shocked him by inviting him to call her Kate, as though she were a tavern wench making free with her name. He still fought his fierce sexual desire, but soon after they met, something in her eyes indicated she was not the flirtatious, pleasure-loving woman—without a serious thought in her head—that she seemed. He doubted many people realised this and attributed his own suspicion to his habit of seeking the true nature of anyone he painted or drew, even from memory.

Well, one thing about the countess was certain; her marriage had been disastrous, so ill-starred that her husband rid himself of her company by excluding her from his society. Edward pressed his lips together. Poor lady, even after his death, she suffered the consequences of the marriage when his will precluded her from seeing her own son. Edward wanted to know what she thought of that. Did she long to see her boy, or did she care naught for him? He shook his head. And what of her son? Did *he* wonder why he was separated from his mother?

Edward did not doubt the countess's intelligence. Since the late earl's death, her ladyship had increased her inheritance through trade, but she was more than a shrewd business lady. He was convinced she harboured some secret sorrow. Could it be connected with the young actress? He fancied it was.

His brow creased. Kate intrigued him. When she sat next to him at the New Theatre she had resembled an Ice Queen in both her dress and conduct. At other times, she revealed outstanding compassion. After all, she had referred to his godmother's Negro pageboy as a bird in a glass cage. Now she had responded to a little girl's desperation with decisive action. Despite the nurse's wicked words about Mary Anne's father dying because her behaviour had caused him not to love her, few would have the courage to take action.

Useless to attempt to define her ladyship, to him she remained just Kate, no more and no less. Not even her wig—instead of her familiar blonde plaits wound around her head—set her at a distance from him.

He looked at Kate, her back straight as a mounted knight of old, preparing to do battle on behalf of the innocent.

Other than sharing her bed, what did he want of her? To be her knight errant? The words popped into his mind. Yes, he wanted to be both her champion and a trusted friend who would never fail her. What, he asked himself, could he do to help her? He laughed. How presumptuous. What deed of daring could he perform for her? As for becoming his mistress, he doubted she would ever agree.

* * *

Kate guided her mare around a dray and manoeuvred between a coach and a horseman. What must Captain Howard think? He must consider it strange of her to champion Mary Anne. Yet how could she resist the sweet appeal of the frightened little girl when she had knelt to put her arms around the child? For a split second, Mary Anne satisfied Kate's hunger to cradle a small girl's plump, warm body. The child's mother did not deserve her. With her blue eyes, chestnut brown curls, and courage—which did not allow her to sob her distress—Mary Anne was a treasure to be appreciated. She should not be an unimportant daughter ignored by a selfish parent.

Mary Anne pointed when they turned into King Street. "There is my house."

"Where?" the captain asked.

"Opposite the sign of The Queen's Head."

"Whoa," he instructed his horse.

Captain Howard dismounted, then reached up, lifted Mary Anne out of the saddle, and set her on her feet.

The captain tied his horse to a hitching post before helping Kate to dismount. He looked around then beckoned to an urchin. "Two pence for keeping an eye on the horses."

The ragamuffin spat on the ground. "Done."

Kate rapped on the door. A maidservant opened it. "Yes?" She noticed Mary Anne. "Lord have mercy, where is your nurse?"

Mary Anne shrank back against Kate's full skirts. Kate put a reassuring hand on the child's shoulder.

"Tell Mrs Bellamy, the Countess of Sinclair and Captain Howard wish to have an urgent word with her," Edward said.

"I regret to say my mistress doesn't receive visitors." The woman transferred her attention to Mary Anne. "Where's your nurse? Come inside. Goodness knows what the mistress will say when she sees you. What have you been doing? Your hair's untidy and your apron and gown are dirty."

"Does it not occur to you that the child might be hurt? Have you no concern for her? No, don't answer. I am too angry to heed any reply of yours." Kate put a foot over the threshold. "I shall wait here until Mrs Bellamy can receive me."

Mary Anne darted inside. "I am sure my mother will want to see you. I shall tell her you are here." Her eyes grew larger. "Are you really a countess?"

Kate nodded.

"You must be very important," said Mary Anne.

"Some people might think I am, but it is not true. I am merely your friend."

"Oh, Mother's hand bell is ringing."

Mary Anne ran up the stairs.

Edward looked at the maidservant. "Announce us," he insisted.

* * *

No more than half an hour elapsed before Mary Anne's shocked mama thanked Kate for drawing her attention to the nurse's cruelty. During their conversation, she rose from the couch, where she had passed most of her days since her husband's death, and promised to ride with Mary Anne in the park on the following day.

Kate inclined her head. "I shall look forward to seeing both of you there. Good day to you."

"I hope to accompany you tomorrow," Edward said to Kate when they stepped out into the street.

"As you please. From now on, I think all will be well with the child."

"Thanks to you." After giving the ragged urchin the promised pennies, Edward saluted Kate before helping her into the saddle.

Edward looked up with a smile.

"What?"

"May I tell you how much I admire you?"

"No, too many men say so."

"My admiration is genuine. Few ladies would have spared the time from their pursuit of pleasure to help Mary Anne."

Kate blushed, the colour easily seen beneath her *maquillage*. "I am sure you are mistaken." She rode forward before he had time to mount.

She was too modest to accept genuine appreciation. Indeed, the lady was a jewel with many facets, all of which he hoped to discover.

Chapter Nine

"Captain Howard has arrived," Simon announced. "He is in the green salon, my lady."

"Thank you, Simon."

Before Kate reached the room, someone beat an impatient tattoo on the front door.

"Where is the countess?" a high-pitched voice demanded. "I will not be denied."

Kate did not know who had spoken. She paused, puzzled. Impatient steps thundered up the wooden stairs. She turned to rebuff the intruder, with the intention of sending him away, for she had been about to invite the captain to accompany her on a visit to Mary Anne and her mother, to see if all was well with them.

However, she could *not* send the visitor away, since before her stood a figure she had not dared hope to see so soon. At first, she thought her eyes deceived her, yet there was no mistaking her twelve-year-old son's fair hair, cool blue eyes, and arched eyebrows, replicas of her own. She gasped. Sudden fear assailed her. What did he think of her? Had his relatives filled his head with lies?

A miracle to observe him so close after many anxious years waiting for this moment. How handsome he was: broad shouldered, both muscular and tall for his age, and scarcely a head shorter than she.

"*You* are the Countess of Sinclair?"

Her heartbeat increased and she feared she would faint for the first time in her life. Speechless, she nodded.

He glared. "I want to know the truth," he said, grinding his words through his clenched jaw.

She feared he would blurt out something scurrilous. "Not here. Come. You may say whatever you wish in private."

This was the moment when, if she could make her son believe her, she had one chance to convince him of her innocence. If she failed, would her heart break? *Could* her heart break? No, it could not. She was fashioned of strong stuff. Kate jerked up her chin before leading Charles to the book room adjacent to the salon where Captain Howard awaited.

She faced the young man, trying her utmost to appear in control of her emotions. What did he know of her? Well, for him to be so white of face, whatever he knew must be to her detriment. With obvious reluctance, a lackey, his eyes alive with interest, closed the door leading into the hall. *Odds bodikins*, doubtless the servants would gossip about the boy's unexpected visit.

Fearful, Kate sat down behind her desk. "Please sit, Charles."

He refused, staring at her with eyes like her own, not only in colour but also in shape. Hands clasped tight, she regarded him in return. Charles bent forward, his fists on the desk, his face only inches from hers. "Countess," he began and then broke off.

He had not called her Mother. Curse etiquette; she did not want the formality of his addressing her by her title. Yearning to hold him in her arms, she hungered to create an indissoluble link between them. But whatever Charles said, however shocking, she must control herself with as tight a rein as she controlled Scheherazade.

Her son straightened his back. "Did you birth another babe when I was born?"

What had her brother-by-law told him? To avoid answering the question while she gathered her wits, Kate indicated a chair opposite the desk. "Please sit, Charles," she repeated, for the lack of anything better to say.

This time Charles sat, but fidgeted. "Will you not answer my question?"

Kate took a deep breath. "Yes, you are a twin."

"So, my lady, it *is* true that you slept with two men," he blurted out, his cheeks scarlet.

She could not bear the anguish in her son's eyes. Her hand crept across the desk toward his fist, clenched so hard that the knuckles shone white as a skeleton's. "It is not true. I have only slept with one man, your father."

Charles's unhappy young face did not look away for a second.

To collect her thoughts, she stood, poured a measure of apricot cordial, diluted it with spring water, and then handed him the crystal glass.

"My uncle says you slept with two men, Countess."

"Your uncle lies," she replied, her voice wrenched from the depths of her being. "I gave birth to you some five minutes before your twin sister. Your father recognised you as his legitimate heir and disowned our daughter." She looked into Charles's eyes. "I did not cuckold him. Both of you are legitimate."

"Why did he accept me and reject my sister?"

"Your father was too arrogant to admit I gave birth to twins, so he acknowledged you, cast out your sister, and condemned me to live in solitude in the country."

"Uncle George says Father banished you because you lay with another man."

She sat in a wing chair opposite his, her back, poker straight. "He says so because in the last century 'twas believed if a woman bore twins, they were conceived by different men. Today, most educated people don't believe twins result from adultery. Before you judge me, seek out young men of science and medicine to ask for their opinion."

For the first time since he entered the book room, her son looked away. "My uncle would not allow me to, but I *shall* when I come of age." Charles sighed. "Every minute of my day must be accounted for." He fingered a tear in his sky blue, velvet coat. "I climbed out of the window to come here. My uncle will punish me severely for leaving the house without permission, but I had to see you." He rubbed his moist eyes with his knuckles before he put his hands on the desk as though regretting the childish action.

"Why?"

Colour rose in Charles's face, still innocent of a razor's sharp edge. "My lady, Mister Milton overheard my uncle speak very ill of you to me. Later, Mister Milton told me you have been greatly wronged and maligned."

Kate remembered the gentleman of the cloth's compassion. When she married, Milton—who was at that time her husband's chaplain—had been very kind to her, not only kind, but also courageous. After the twins' birth, his was the only voice to speak in her defence.

Oh, how she had detested the thrice-married earl whose first two wives were barren. Kate pressed her lips into a thin line. When, after two miscarriages, she told his lordship it seemed she would carry a child to full term, he had looked at her approvingly for the first time. Her pregnancy became public knowledge amongst their peers in town and countryside. Out of pride, he accepted Charles as his son and rejected the daughter.

"Churchmen don't lie, do they?" Charles asked breaking into her thoughts.

"Not one of Mister Milton's good character."

"What of my sister?"

Kate breathed deeply. "Your father took both of you away at birth," she replied, trying utmost to steady her voice. "Since that terrible moment, I have been unable to discover her whereabouts."

Though Charles squared his shoulders like a man, a shuddering boy's sigh escaped him. "I dreamt of meeting you. Now I have confronted you, I believe you did not cuckold my father. When I come into my own, I will search for my twin sister." He squared his shoulders. "My lady, we will find her."

Blood surged through Kate. Could it be that Charles did not accept his uncle's accusations? Or did he want to believe what she had said for no other reason than she was his mother?

"We shall find her," Charles repeated.

"Don't build your hopes too high. Your sister might be dead."

"If she perished, we will find her grave and bring her bones home to Sinclair Place to rest."

Kate shuddered at the thought of so macabre an event but, thank God, it seemed her son believed in her innocence.

Charles gulped his cordial. "I pray the Lord in His mercy has spared her, for I always sensed—" he broke off, bowing his head as though something embarrassed him too much to face her.

"What? What did you sense?" She spoke in a deliberately gentle tone of voice.

Charles ran a hand over his neatly tied-back hair. "I am incomplete. In my dreams, a fair-haired girl sometimes touches my heart. In all but her sex, she is my mirror image. Oh—" He glanced at his mother. Again he hesitated before speaking. "I believe my twin lives. If she died, I would know." His fists clenched. "I cannot believe I have confided in you. Never before have I spoken of this to anyone, although, when I was a small boy, I whispered all my secrets in my dog's ear before my uncle banished her to the stables."

Kate lost her battle not to cry. In her eyes he was still a small boy. She dabbed the tears away with a handkerchief, pained by the thought of her son's lonely childhood.

"Are you crying?"

Too choked to speak, Kate shook her head. She rose to replenish his glass and try to gain control over her emotions, but after serving him, she could not resist the temptation to rest her hand on his shoulder. To her joy, he reached up and covered her fingers with his own—warm fingers strengthened by riding, shooting, and other manly pursuits.

"Your aunt and uncle, are they kind to you?"

"Mister Milton is kinder than either of them. He is much nicer than my tutor."

"Does your tutor whip you?"

Her boy's head drooped. She longed to console Charles and wrap her arms around him but feared he was not ready for such intimacy. "I am your mother, Charles. I swear to God there has not been a day since you and your sister were born when I have not thought of both of you. If you cannot be honest with me, with whom *can* you be honest?"

His hand clasped hers more firmly. "With Mister Milton."

She must do all in her power to help him. "He is the best person to give you spiritual guidance, but if you want me to, I shall speak with your uncle to yet again try to persuade him to allow us to see each other regularly."

Charles sprang to his feet, turning to face her. "Truly?"

"Yes, I will try my uttermost to make him agree, but in the past he has not listened to my pleas to see you."

"Perhaps he will consent this time." He pouted like a younger child. "By the way, nothing will make me marry my pudding-faced cousin."

Kate stared at him, simultaneously shocked to the core of her being by the Sinclairs' plan, and amused by his boyish way of broaching the subject. "Your aunt and uncle expect you to marry their daughter?"

"Yes."

Someone closed the book room door.

Charles ran across the room and reopened it. "Who is there?"

Captain Howard, smart in his customary blue and white, stepped into the salon. "Forgive me. The door to the book room was ajar." He looked at Kate. "You may trust my discretion."

Dear God in Heaven, Edward now knew the possible identity of the young actress. Could she trust him to keep her well-guarded secret?

Charles scrutinised the captain. "Who is this man, Mother?"

Her boy had called her, Mother, for the first time. Delighted, she sank onto a chair. "My Lord," she addressed Charles, when she was able to draw breath without difficulty, "may I present Captain Howard? Captain Howard, my son, the Earl of Sinclair."

Charles bowed with the grace instilled in young gentlemen by their tutors and dancing masters. She had a son to be proud of.

The captain bowed with equal style. She frowned. "'Twas ill-done of you, Captain, to listen to a private conversation. You should have made your presence known to us."

Her son stood motionless beside her chair, head high, hands clasped behind his back. "Indeed," he said, "Mister Milton says eavesdropping ill-befits a gentleman."

"I agree, but please picture the scene." The captain pointed at the book room door. "While I waited for you, my lady, I sat with my eyes half-closed, lost in a pleasurable dream of what the future might hold for us."

Charles's chin jerked up. He looked from her to Captain Howard. She wished the captain had chosen his words more carefully. Heaven alone knew what had been said about her to her son. She frowned. Did Captain Howard truly believe she would play a significant role in his future?

Before either she or Charles could protest, Captain Howard continued. "Milady, had I not eavesdropped, I would neither understand you better, nor be able to help you and Lord Sinclair."

Kate straightened her back. "I seek no man's sympathy. Besides, why should you help us?"

He bent over the chair to raise her chin with the tips of his fingers. "I shall not make a conceited claim to chivalry. To say I desire to serve you will suffice for now." He smiled at the earl. "In the navy, although corporal punishment is necessary, excessive brutality earned my deepest disapproval. I am on half pay because I prevented a sailor being flogged to death. Fortunately for me, my uncle is Admiral Rooke. He assures me I shall be spared a court martial and that I should soon be able to return to sea." A wry smile twisted his lips. "Is influence in high quarters not wondrous?"

How self-absorbed she must seem to him. Why had she never questioned the captain about the circumstances leading to his being on half pay?

Captain Howard smiled at her son. "I trust you don't bear scars from the rod, on your person."

The rush of colour to Charles's face revealed the truth. Kate clasped her hands together. "My poor boy, I disapprove of beating children and other ill-judged punishments."

"Truly, Mother?"

"I never lie, no matter how unpalatable the truth might be." She stood and drew Charles to his feet. For the first time, she held him in her arms, scarcely able to contain tears of happiness. When he rested his head against her breast, her joy reached such proportions that she feared she would faint.

Loud knocks reverberated on the front door. Startled, Kate inhaled sharply. "Charles, Captain Howard, please excuse me." She hastened into the corridor where she could hear George Sinclair's voice rising from the ground floor. "I insist on seeing your mistress. My business is urgent."

Hurrying to the landing, Kate peered over the banisters. Mister Milton—neat and trim as she remembered him—her corpulent brother-by-law, and Alice, his tall, waspish wife, stood in the centre of the hall confronting her lackey. Kate's stomach somersaulted. Her nails dug painfully into her clenched hands. Every nerve in her body protested at the thought of Charles returning to George and Alice's custody.

Simon addressed George. "Your name, sir?"

"Mister Sinclair." Her brother-by-law glared at Simon. "Make haste, I have no time to waste."

Simon opened the door to an anteroom and then bowed low. "Please wait in here."

"No, I will not," George snapped.

Kate clenched her jaw. Her brother-by-law was every bit as arrogant as her late husband.

"Has a young fair-haired boy, who resembles your mistress, come here?" Alice asked in a tone loud enough to penetrate every corner of the hall and corridors.

"I can't say, madam."

"Cannot or will not?" George demanded.

"I'll notify my mistress of your arrival," the lackey replied, signifying contempt by neglecting to address George as 'Sir'. "I'll ask my mistress if she will receive you." He turned and put his foot on the first stair of the flight leading up to the next floor. Instead of waiting to be announced, her unwanted visitors trooped past him.

Before the Sinclairs reached the half landing, Kate slipped back into the green salon. She gestured to Charles and the captain to be seated and then settled herself in the chair with a canopy over it, which she used on formal occasions.

The door opened. Simon announced the chaplain and Kate's relatives-by-law.

She dismissed the lackey, and eyes wide, feigned surprise. "Alice, George, a pleasant surprise. Mister Milton, it is good to see you again."

"Charles," George shouted, "how dare you come here without my permission!"

The muscles around Kate's mouth twitched. Her brother-by-law's cheeks were more florid than on the last occasion on which they met. "George, I fear your manners have not improved since I last saw you."

"How dare you address me as George," he sputtered, squirming as though his purple velvet coat were too tight.

For Charles's sake, she must be careful. "Please accept my apology and don't scold his lordship. After all, it is not unnatural for him to wish to meet me. Now that I have satisfied his curiosity, I doubt he will wish to further our acquaintance." Despite the perspiration seeping its way through the smock worn beneath her corset, she forced herself to speak as though she had no interest in her son.

Alice pointed a bony finger at her. "You are an unnatural mother. I could no more part with an arm or a leg than any of my dear children."

"Then it is fortunate that you have not been forced to part with them." Kate trembled with rage. "Unnatural, yes, it seems I am, but may I remind you my child was taken from me without my consent. Fortunately, I have no need to concern myself with his lordship. After all, he is happily situated in your family." Heaven forgive her for telling lies, but she would not admit to the odious couple that grief over the separation from her son, occupied much of her time. "And," Kate continued, "I doubt not, that, after his lordship's coming of age, he will provide for you and your children. When will that be? Ah yes, at eighteen he may take his seat in the House of Lords." She tapped her long fingernails on the arms of the chair. "'Tis possible he may take it when he is sixteen, or must he wait until he is twenty-one? It is his right, is it not?"

Her sister-by-law coloured up. *Good.* Her words had hit one of their targets. Rage seethed within as she regarded Alice. She did not doubt the income from her son's estate paid for the woman's Italian silk gown, flowered with green and gold, her gold satin petticoat, and the emeralds at her throat, in her hair, and on her fingers.

Alice glanced at George who remained lost in thought. "Of course, I am devoted to your son, my lady."

Kate stilled her hands and then clasped them on her lap. "My dear Mrs Sinclair, may I say how glad, how very glad I am, to know that in you, Charles has found a mother's tender care. Should I compliment you and his tutor on his excellent manners?" Unable to force more insincere words from her mouth, she smiled at the chaplain. "Mister Milton, I have no doubt you are the very man to guide my son in all things."

"Taking his seat in the House of Lords, you say," George mumbled.

Kate observed Charles, who sat straight-backed, with his eyes lowered. "Yes," she confirmed. "Moreover at eighteen, under the terms of my husband's will, his lordship comes into his inheritance, does he not? Unusual to come into it so young but maybe your brother did not have full faith in you." She forced herself to speak in an even tone. "I do not doubt Charles will continue to depend on you for wise counsel."

George frowned. "I hope you understand that sometimes one must not spare the rod for fear of spoiling the child."

Kate stared at him, inwardly furious. "I understand perfectly." She emphasised each syllable. "My lord, you are nearly thirteen are you not?"

"Yes, Mother." Charles looked at her with an obvious gleam of intelligent appreciation in his eyes. As she hoped, her acting did not fool him. He understood she was attempting to improve his situation.

"Let me think, how long is it until you gain control of your estates?" She counted the years on her fingers. "Ah, you have little more than five years to wait before you decide who may occupy your houses. However, I am sure you will not wish to evict your aunt, uncle, and cousins from your properties and from your life. After all, Mister and Mrs Sinclair are as parents to you, so I daresay your sentiments regarding them are too tender for you to act so cold-heartedly." With a deliberately impassive face, she watched George exchange an uneasy glance with his wife. "Charles, at your age, perchance it is time for your tutor to be replaced. He might not have the knowledge to advance your education with due consideration for your future position in life."

The Sinclairs glanced at each other, their discomposure obvious, while Mister Milton, a picture of propriety in clerical black, observed an oil painting of the biblical characters, Ruth and Naomi.

Alice broke a brief silence. "Madam, your son has lacked nothing required to foster his education, yet we might be too complacent. Perhaps the time has come to give it further consideration. What do you think, Mister Sinclair?"

George's hands shook. He nodded slowly. Satisfied there would be changes for the better in Charles's life, Kate turned her head aside to conceal a satisfied smile.

Mister Milton avoided her glance by transferring the subject of his regard to a painting of Christ overturning the tables in the temple.

Kate stood. She dipped a curtsey in Charles's direction. "My lord, Mister Sinclair, Mrs Sinclair, Mister Milton, I am engaged to ride in the park with Captain Howard. Your visit has delayed me. Good day to you."

"Do you not want to see Lord Sinclair again? Have you no concern for him?" Alice asked, obviously shocked by Kate's seeming indifference toward Charles.

Kate pretended to ponder the question. "Do I not want to see him?" She forced herself to appear indifferent to Charles's fate. If the Sinclairs guessed how much she yearned to see Charles as often as possible, they would further enjoy exercising their power over him. "Concerned for him? Why should I be? He is extremely well-cared for, is he not? When all is said and done, I have only the slightest acquaintance with Charles." She stood. "If you have no further business here, I wish all of you good day."

"Come, my lord." George hustled his wife and nephew out of the salon.

Kate beckoned to Mister Milton. "I lied to the Sinclairs. There is naught which concerns my son's welfare which I am not interested in. Please reassure Charles. Be good enough to tell him I want nothing more than to see him frequently."

"I shall be pleased to do so," he responded, his tone gentle.

* * *

Kate peered out of the window at the street. After the Sinclairs and Mister Milton entered their coach with Charles, she uncorked a bottle of Caravel, her favourite Portuguese wine.

"Will you share some, Captain?" she asked.

"Yes, please."

Kate poured the wine.

"Thank you."

She hesitated, although, as a rule, she never overindulged. At the moment, she needed a small measure to settle her queasy stomach. Without further vacillation, she poured a quarter of the small bottle into a crystal glass and drank it, albeit a little too fast. She eyed the remainder but refrained from partaking of any more.

How dare the Sinclairs allow the tutor to treat her boy so badly? Perhaps she should kidnap him and send him to Europe to complete his education. She squared her shoulders. No, he might be trapped if war broke out with France.

At the thought of George manipulating a marriage between his daughter and Charles, Kate's indignation rose to dangerous heights. Careless of creasing her skirts, she plopped down onto a chair.

"Kate." The captain knelt and took her cold hands in his.

"How dare they mistreat Charles? As for that conniving pair marrying him off to their daughter, I will not tolerate it."

Captain Howard rubbed warmth back into her hands. "How may I be of service to you?"

She took a deep breath before speaking. "With your discretion."

The captain stood. "My lady, words cannot express how shocked I am by your situation, the torment your husband caused you, and his vile accusation."

His kindness brought a lump to her throat. She snatched her hands away for fear she would lose control of her emotions. "Please say no more."

"It is my sincere wish to help you."

"But how can you?"

"Through being your devoted friend."

Kate inhaled deeply. Oh, without previously realising it, she had become so close to this man, with his decisive manner and air of command which made him seem older than his years. Even so, a bitter laugh escaped her. "It will be a new experience for me. Never before have I had a true friend."

He stood looking down at her, his eyes serious. "I suggest you employ Mister Hinchcliffe to make discreet enquiries about your daughter's fate."

"Who is *he*?" She struggled to maintain rigid self-control—something God alone knew she was well-practiced in.

"Hinchcliffe acts on behalf of those who seek information, lost property, runaways, missing relatives, and much more." He cleared his throat. "He once acted on a matter of great delicacy for a brother officer."

What did she have to lose? She pondered for a moment before reaching a decision. "Very well, if you are sure he is discreet."

"You may have complete trust in him. His livelihood depends on confidentiality."

How kind of the captain. She nodded her agreement. He really seemed to care about her and want to help. Yet, she must not be gulled into depending on him. In her experience, no one could be fully trusted.

Captain Howard smiled. "I shall contact Hinchcliffe and bring him to you as soon as possible."

* * *

Twilight lent mysterious charm to London's streets when Captain Howard and Mister Hinchcliffe arrived at Kate's red brick house, ablaze with candlelight, seen through unshuttered windows.

Simon opened one of the doors in the hall. "Please wait in the anteroom while I ask her ladyship if she will receive you."

Kate looked up when Simon told her of Captain Howard and Hinchcliffe's arrival, then hesitated while she looked around her favourite parlour, a sanctuary decorated in pale rose and cream, and furnished, not with modern box-like furniture, but with dainty pieces made by French Huguenot master carpenters. Should she instruct Simon to take the gentlemen to the green salon? No, she would receive them here, where it seemed more fitting to speak of her lost daughter.

Could it be? Could the agent really trace her child? Almost breathless with hope she stared at the panelled door. When it opened, the captain, followed by a middle-aged gentleman of medium stature, entered the room. A quick assessment of the agent assured her his unremarkable features, medium height, and plain attire would enable him to pass unnoticed in most situations.

She waved her hand at a chair opposite her own on the other side of the marble fireplace. "Please sit yourself down, Captain Howard."

Before the captain acquiesced, he captured her hand and pressed a kiss on the back of it. His lips all but scorched her flesh. She drew her hand away. Why did he have such a profound effect on her? Whatever the reason, she did not appreciate it. Her experience of marriage would suffice for a lifetime. Never again did she intend to risk being at the mercy of any man. But, there was no time to think of that now. Indeed, why was she thinking of marriage? She doubted the captain would ever ask for her hand. Why should he when he could wed a much younger lady?

"Mister Hinchcliffe." Captain Howard indicated the man with a gesture of his hand.

The agent cleared his throat. Drawn from her thoughts, she acknowledged him with a nod. "Do sit on the sofa."

"With your permission, Lady Sinclair, I shall sit at the desk and make some notes of our conversation."

"Very well," Kate said, confident they would not be overheard by servants. "You may go," she told Simon.

The door closed quietly behind the lackey.

Hinchcliffe sat, dipped a sharpened goose feather quill into a silver inkpot, and then drew a piece of paper toward him. "Please tell me what you require of me, my lady."

"I scarce know how to start."

Captain Howard would not have recommended Hinchcliffe if he did not believe they could depend on the man to keep his own counsel. Something about the agent reassured her.

"I suggest you start at the moment when your problem began," Hinchcliffe suggested.

Regardless of the embarrassment of disclosing such private matters, Kate explained her predicament. Although her hands trembled once or twice, she spoke in an even tone.

Hinchcliffe put down the quill. "My lady, I shall try to find out where your daughter is."

Kate's chest tightened. "You will explore every possibility?"

"Yes, my lady, and should you come into possession of any additional information, please let me know."

Hinchcliffe stood, bowed, and then left the parlour accompanied by the captain.

Air, Kate thought, I must have some fresh air. Perhaps I will retire to Missendene and enjoy the benefits of country life. For now, I shall stroll in the garden and seek composure.

* * *

Refreshed, and scarcely able to hope the agent could trace her girl, Kate entered her bedchamber to the sound of her mother's demands.

"Jessie, I insist on knowing where Lady Sinclair is."

Kate hesitated and watched her stout tirewoman take a step forward, her hands on her hips. "Haven't I told you I don't know?" Jessie's voice rose toward the end of the sentence.

"What an obstinate creature you are, Jessie," Gertrude snapped. "I know Lady Sinclair always tells you where she is going."

"Here I am, Mother."

Gertrude swung around. "Where have you been? What have you been doing? The hems of your gown and petticoat are filthy."

"Don't exaggerate, Mother, I daresay they are only a little muddy."

"Where were you?"

"I went for a walk in the garden."

"In the dark?" Mother pressed a small flask of *sal volatile* to her nose. "'Pon my word, Kate, you become more eccentric with each passing day. You pout, you frown, you ride at breakneck speed and you flirt—

besides conducting yourself in a manner ill-fitting for one of your rank."

"Enough! You are not my keeper, madam. You relinquished your rights when you agreed to my adoption."

Although Kate saw no trace of a remorseful tear, her mother dabbed her eyes with a handkerchief. "Kate, Mister Stafford awaits us below."

"Please keep him company while I change." She looked at Jessie. "I shall wear my cherry-coloured silk-plush gown, matching stays, cream bodice, and cream Pudsay silk petticoat."

Gertrude gestured to Kate with her handkerchief. "Heartless creature, you care naught for my sensibilities!"

"Yes, Mother, I am heartless enough to maintain you in luxury."

She must control herself. Although she would prefer to remain at home, it would be rude not to attend Lady North's amateur concert this evening with her mother and Mister Stafford.

A cold shudder ran though her. She would know no peace until Hinchcliffe returned with news of the girl.

Chapter Ten

Kate took a deep breath before entering the music room in Lady North's house. She forced herself to smile hoping her ladyship's guests would not notice the tremor of her hands. Head high, she stepped onto the black and white chequered floor and then glanced up at the high ceiling painted with cherubim and seraphim playing harps, lyres, and other instruments.

Perched straight-backed on a chair, Kate studied busts of famous musicians set on pedestals while a young lady butchered the high notes of a ballad to the accompaniment of an orchestra hired for the occasion. She endured an indifferent duet and a performance on the harp. At last, her mother stepped onto the dais with a waft of patchouli, her favourite perfume.

A ripple of admiration echoed around the room while Gertrude arranged her peach-coloured gown and matching petticoat, both trimmed with silver thread and pearls. After she sang "The Nightingale" in a glorious soprano, applause thundered. No doubt the performance came as a relief after the previous ones.

Too restless to listen to more music, Kate quit the room. She sought sanctuary in a large salon decorated in blue and gold set aside for those who preferred to play cards. She greeted Lord Carruthers, one of her admirers, and nodded to another acquaintance, but before she had time to participate in a game of ombre, the butler announced, "My lords, ladies, and gentlemen, refreshments are served in the yellow withdrawing room."

Kate made her way into a lofty chamber—redolent with the scent of beeswax candles—hung with a half dozen or more portraits, and furbished with many small tables, chairs, and sofas upholstered with velvet, the colour of old gold. She settled on a chair. To her amusement, Tyrell and Stafford positioned themselves on either side of her before anyone else could seize the opportunity. Other gentlemen, who hovered within her orbit, competed to fetch wine and delicacies with which to tempt her appetite: thin slices of ham, succulent lobster patties, as well as various sweetmeats.

Although Kate forced herself to display a semblance of careless enjoyment, she could not compel herself to eat. Charles's image remained with her constantly. She wanted nothing more than to keep him at her side. Her stomach churned. Captain Howard came to her mind. The memory of his gentle, yet purposeful manner, and his air of quiet command soothed her queasiness.

Kate sipped some Caracavella, a popular Portuguese wine. She toyed with a minuscule pie, filled with fish in a creamy mushroom sauce, while engaging in conversation, until Lady North's butler announced, "My lords, ladies, and gentlemen please return to the music chamber. The second part of this evening's entertainment will soon commence."

"Excuse me," Mister Tyrell said and hurried away, most probably in need of the water closet. Reluctant to join the crowd, Kate waited until it thinned before she eased herself out of her chair. To her amazement,

Mister Stafford gripped her elbow too tight for her to release herself without drawing unwanted attention.

"Let go of me," she said in an undertone, sickened by his spicy perfume, which did not mask the stale odour of perspiration that clung to his clothes.

Stafford ignored her protest. To her fury, he guided her into a small, somewhat musty withdrawing room lit by firelight and a pair of flickering candles which stood on the mantelpiece.

"How dare you insult me thus, sir."

Her unwanted cavalier locked the door, slipped the key into his pocket, and turned to face her. "I have something particular to say to you."

Shocked and upset by her suitor's outrageous behaviour, she forced herself to appear calm. "There is nothing you can say that I wish to hear in private, Mister Stafford," she said in a frigid tone.

"Don't be coy. Surely you understand I don't want Tyrell or any other person to interrupt us."

Kate frowned. Jealousy of his amiable rival must have prompted this insufferable behaviour. Stafford did not understand her flirtations were no more than an amusing means to idle away the hours. She never intended to break hearts, not even the outwardly meek Stafford's. Until now, she had believed he enjoyed his courtship of her because she was a toast of the town, and also because his pursuit of her added interest to his sedate life.

She did not believe Stafford's heart was engaged. Moreover, she had never believed his intentions were in earnest. For one thing, his widowed mother disapproved of her. She caught her lower lip between her teeth. Until now she took none of his declarations of eternal devotion seriously. So, in spite of his outrageous conduct, she looked at him kindly, reluctant to cause him pain.

Stafford puffed out his narrow chest. "Please sit, my turtledove. This evening's exertions must have exhausted you."

Her eyes widened with amusement. Stafford misread her. She had more in common with a fierce falcon than a cooing turtledove. Lord, how Captain Howard would laugh to hear her referred to thus.

"I have no intention of sitting. I must protect my reputation."

Would Captain Howard think the worst of her if he heard she had been secluded with the hitherto prosaic gentleman during an evening supposed to be devoted to music? Her nostrils flared. Why did Captain Howard's opinion of her matter more than any other man's?

Stafford's narrow forehead perspired. His cheeks coloured up. "My mother…." he broke off and shuffled his feet.

"What has she to do with your monstrous behaviour?" Kate snapped.

"Mother pities you for having married the late earl. She thinks you need a sensible, sober husband with the common sense to guide your footsteps in the right direction, a man to change you into a modest wife who busies herself only with domesticity and the care of her children."

No matter how much she wanted to house her children under her roof, his mother must be insane to visualise her in such a role. She sank onto a chair by the fireside, falling victim to gales of laughter.

Undeterred, Stafford knelt. He grasped her hand. "My dear Lady Sinclair, your mirth dismays me. I assure you I would be a kind and generous husband."

"Liberal with my wealth? Never." No longer did she care whether or not she wounded his sensibilities. As though a wasp had stung her, she snatched her hand away from him and stood. "Enough, I say. I have never given you any reason to believe I will marry you." She snorted. "As for your mother, she disapproves of me. I suspect my fortune is the only reason she has encouraged you to propose marriage. End this farce. Open the door."

With strength surprising in one so slight of build, Stafford pulled her against the length of his thin body and kissed her neck.

"How dare you!" she cried out, sickened by his moist lips against her skin, and shocked by his tight hold moulding her to his velvet-clad body, the stench of mingled perfume and sweat nauseating her even more at such close quarters. "Have you taken leave of your senses? What will your mother say when I tell her you forced your attentions on me?"

Mister Stafford's grasp slackened for a moment.

Long country walks and daily rides had strengthened her muscles. Kate seized her opportunity. She twisted out of his arms. He tried to grab her. She dodged. With all the force she could muster she punched him between the legs.

Her would-be-husband's face contorted in agony. He moaned and doubled up.

Kate glared at him. "From today, my porter will no longer admit you to my house."

Stafford crouched lower and groaned.

Kate removed the key from his coat pocket, opened the door, and slipped into the corridor.

To her annoyance, a nearby lackey glanced at her when she emerged. She held herself straight as a curtain pole. More than likely the man would spread gossip about her being sequestered with Stafford. After all, most servants were notorious gossips. Heavens above, she needed a glass of wine to restore her. Oh, to be a man and challenge Stafford to a duel. Kate laughed, albeit somewhat hysterically. If she were of the opposite sex, the situation would not have arisen. She would thwart Stafford regardless of whether or not the servants tittered.

Kate went to the water closet and dabbed her neck with cool water from a china basin. Ugh, Stafford's kisses repulsed her as much as her husband's had. How dare the wretch presume to think she would agree to marry him!

She squared her shoulders and returned to the card room, smiling as though naught troubled her in spite of her unsteady legs and queasy stomach.

Mister Tyrell approached her, handsome in his jade-green velvet suit.

She took deep breaths to calm herself.

The gentleman bowed. "A game of ombre, Lady Sinclair?"

"By all means."

A smug expression on his face, Tyrell handed her into a chair. "Where is your hound dog, Stafford?"

Had he observed her enter the withdrawing room with Stafford? Kate raised her eyebrows. "My hound dog?"

"An apt description of Stafford, is it not?"

"Come, come, sir, I hope you understand I am a cold-hearted widow who enjoys her liberty. There are no rivals for my affection because I have none to give."

"Not even to the handsome captain who hovers around you?"

She shrugged. "He is little more than a boy. What has he to offer me?"

Tyrell narrowed his eyes. "You would not be the first lady to be enamoured of a handsome face and a dashing air."

"You are ridiculous, sir." She put her hand over her mouth and pretended to yawn. "Forgive me. I have changed my mind about a game of ombre. I forget my duty. I must attend to my mother."

"By all means, please allow me to escort you to the music room."

* * *

Kate carried out her decision to ban Mister Stafford from her house. Despite his written apology, she did not allow him to attend her levee. After all her visitors left, Kate perused the broadsheets in her closet.

An advertisement caught her attention. Heaven above. Mister Martyn, father of the heiress whom Mrs Radcliffe wanted Captain Howard to marry, offered a reward for information leading to his daughter's whereabouts. She turned the page and read with close attention.

The conduct of Mister S----d toward Lady S---r at Lady N---h's private concert deserves censure. Lady S---r emerged in haste from a small Withdrawing Room leaving Mister S--- doubled over after receiving a forcible Rebuke from her Ladyship. This Broadsheet does not doubt Mister S---d conducted himself in a manner ill-befitted a Gentleman.

She shuddered at the memory of Stafford's revolting odour and the slimy touch of his lips.

With disgust, she crumpled The Gazette before tossing it into the fireplace. Soon, The Female Tattler joined The Gazette.

By now, she should be accustomed to public interest in her appearance and activities. Nevertheless, reports of her ensembles and of trivia such as a description of her new town coach irritated her.

A lackey brought a letter from Mister Robinson, the Sinclair family's man of business, a well-respected bencher, who had read law at Lincoln's Inn. To the accompaniment of several irritated sighs, she sharpened her quill again, prior to writing a reply to Mister Robinson about a share in a merchant ship she had decided to purchase. Her hand hovered over the writing paper. With her children never far from her mind, she could not concentrate on business. Would her brother-by-law treat Charles better? Would he allow her to see Charles? She forced herself to think of something other than her children. Why had Captain Howard not attended Lady North's musical evening?

The crow feather quill slipped from her grasp. Many men admired her. Some were charismatic. Others resembled the handsome hero of a novel or play, the stuff of a silly maiden's dream. Innocent fools! Hero or husband, the result would be the same—degradation and shame in the connubial bed.

Kate stiffened her spine.

Despite the delightful dimples at the corner of the captain's mouth, not to think of his eloquent, heavy lidded eyes beneath a pair of arched eyebrows, she decided never to soften toward him

To be honest, she valued the officer's courteous manners, and his cheerful countenance, but she would no longer accept his advances. Indeed, did she wish to encourage those of any man? Recently, flirtations wearied her. Reluctant to admit she found the captain exceptionally attractive, Kate again considered retiring to Missendene Manor. After all, she need not remain in London to continue her search for her daughter.

Kate bent her head over the blank paper. She composed the necessary reply to Mister Robinson and signed it with her usual flourish before sealing it.

Physical inactivity irked her. Kate tapped her slipper on the wooden floorboards. She would ride in the park.

An hour later, garbed in her scarlet riding habit—reminiscent of a military uniform—and a hat sporting a jaunty cockade, Kate descended the stairs, gauntlets and riding crop in hand. Perhaps Captain Howard would be in the park. She shook her head. What was she thinking? Had she not decided to rebuff him? Yet did she really want to do so? It was unlike her to be confused. Kate shook her head. London wearied her. She would retire to the country.

* * *

To Kate's delight, *the darling buds of May* decorated the gardens, orchard, and woods of her estate in leafy Hertfordshire.

After her morning ride, Kate returned to the manor through a stone arch that led into the stable yard. She patted Scheherazade's glossy neck before she strode through the west door which led into the most frequently used wing.

Every time Kate came back to the peace at Missendene, her spirits rose. Built with two wings added to the main part in the reign of Henry VIII, the manor had naught to do with either her ancestors or her husband's. Unencumbered by the Sinclair's past, she could do whatever she pleased with Missendene and its portion of ancient forest. When she bought it, she willed the property to her daughter with the assumption she would find her. The next thing she did after purchasing it was to furnish an apartment for her missing child.

Oh, the joy of making Missendene perfect for her girl.

She sighed. What of Charles? If he ever visited the manor, she hoped he would appreciate it. Missendene lacked the grandeur of Sinclair Place but it had a charm of its own which the larger property did not possess.

In her mind's eye, Kate saw her son riding out over the Chiltern Hills on a bright spring day like today. Deep in thought, she entered the house and approached the main staircase. A lackey stepped forward to open the fretwork wooden gate, which prevented either her own dogs or those of her guests from bounding up the stairs to the first and second floors.

Kate hurried upstairs. She hastened through her dainty parlour, furbished with white painted wooden panels and upholstery in pastel hues, and entered her snug bedchamber.

"Jessie, where are you?" she called. "Make haste, country air has given me a hearty appetite, the like of which I never experience in foggy London. Indeed, I am so sharp set my stomach rumbles vulgarly."

Her face wreathed in smiles, Jessie bustled through the dressing room door. "I have laid out your pink and white striped satinet gown and your pink silk petticoat my lady, but you didn't tell me which stays you wanted to wear. I suggest either the pink satin ones fastened with your ruby buckles, or the white velvet ones fastened with pearl buckles."

"The pink ones, 'tis too warm to wear velvet."

How did Charles fare? At the thought of her son being beaten, she shuddered.

Startled, Jessie's hands jerked the laces of Kate's bodice. "My lady?"

"'Tis naught."

"A glass of apricot cordial?" Jessie suggested.

"No, I have told you 'tis naught."

"To be sure it is not, my lady,"

"Don't lace me tightly, we are not in town."

"Very good, my lady."

What would she do without dear Jessie's devoted ministrations along with her motherly ways?

Jessie drew the laces through the last holes at the bottom of the bodice and tied them into a neat bow.

Kate sat at her dressing table. She tried to force her thoughts away from her children and studied her reflection. No need for rouge today, country air had brought a glow to her cheeks. With a rustle of crisp silk and the swish of satinet, she rose, still preoccupied.

Someone rapped on the door.

Jessie opened it.

"There's a gentleman to see you, my lady," said a lackey.

Kate's heart beat faster. Captain Howard? Rumour said he was visiting his brother, whose estate lay not far away. In spite of her high heels, she hurried forward to the narrow landing.

"Who is the gentleman?" Kate asked.

"He said he has come from London to speak to you about an urgent matter." The lackey offered her silver salver on which a pasteboard card reposed.

She read the card. Mister Milton! Had he brought bad news concerning Charles? "I will receive him immediately."

"Very good, my lady."

Why had her brother-by-law's chaplain come? Was something amiss with Charles? Did he have a message from George? She would find it difficult to eat until she knew what brought Mister Milton here.

Kate perched on the edge of a chair facing the door of her parlour. Her jaw clenched until it ached.

Mister Milton entered, neatly garbed in a black broadcloth suit, its severity relieved by white linen bands at his throat, his clothes and his inquisitive air brought to mind a dapper magpie. Kate extended her hand. Mister Milton bent his head, presenting a close view of his modest, white-powdered wig, and kissed the air above her hand. "Countess, I trust I find you in good health."

"Yes, yes," she replied impatient for news of her boy. "But Charles, is all well with him?"

Mister Milton coughed harshly. "Very well indeed, my lady," he said when he caught his breath. "His situation is much improved."

130

Kate relaxed. "Please sit, and tell me what I may do for you." She indicated the sofa opposite her chair.

To avoid creasing his coat, Mister Milton arranged it before he sat.

"A glass of wine to refresh you after your journey." Kate rose to pour him a glass of red viana.

"Thank you, my lady, you are most gracious," he said and coughed again.

"You are mistaken. I dislike servants with prying ears in constant attendance. I prefer to perform simple tasks myself." After filling two crystal glasses she handed him one.

Kate sank onto the edge of her chair. "Please tell me what I may do for you," she repeated.

Mister Milton cleared his throat, then sipped some wine before he placed his glass on a low table, supported at each end by pairs of gilded wooden cherubs. He tilted his head a little to the right. "I am here out of my sincere attachment to the earl, whom I have known since the day of his birth. Lord Sinclair possesses a singularly sweet nature. He is kind and intelligent. No words can express how glad I am that his tutor, who treated him with unnecessary harshness, has been dismissed."

Kate pressed one hand to her heart. "Thank God."

He ignored her interruption while wiping his forehead with his handkerchief. "Until recently, I offered his lordship consolation. Indeed, on occasions, I took the liberty of reminding the earl that when he reaches his majority he can sever his connection with anyone who has ill-served him."

Bright colour, which indicated anger unbecoming to a gentleman of the cloth, rose in Mister Milton's cheeks. "However, when Mister and Mrs Sinclair planned to betroth his lordship to their eldest daughter, I knew the match would not do. Some time ago, I decided it is my duty to broach the matter with you."

Kate doubted this was the sole reason for his visit, for he knew she had no authority or influence in respect of Charles. Nevertheless, her lips twitched at the memory of her son's words.

"I amuse you, my lady?"

"Charles told me the girl has a pudding face."

"Most apt. She is also pudding-brained."

Mister Milton's lack of Christian charity regarding Charles's cousin, and his laugh, made her like him all the more.

While Mister Milton sipped some wine, she thought he looked unwell, but waited for him to come to the point of his visit. "My lady, after your husband's death I remained in the Sinclair household for your son's sake." He looked pointedly at her hands clenched on her lap. "There is no cause for alarm. I came to tell you I have no doubt your son's situation will continue to improve, but I have resigned my position." He twirled the stem of the wineglass. "Do you remember that during your incarceration in the country, your husband gave his grudging consent for me to visit you, to offer your ladyship spiritual consolation?"

"How could I forget your kindness?"

"At the time, I admired your strength of character," he continued as though she had not spoken. "After you met your son for the first time, I harboured no doubt that your influence caused Mister Sinclair to reconsider the nature of his lordship's future education." Mister Milton cleared his throat yet again. "To tell the truth, I must admit my abhorrence of excessive corporal punishment. I confess I encouraged the earl, albeit in a roundabout way, to wait on your ladyship."

Eyes moist, her heart moved by such devotion to her son, Kate sniffed. Although life's vicissitudes had taught her to suppress her sensibilities, sometimes she found self-control almost impossible. She applied a handkerchief to her nose. "What will you do now?"

"By God's mercy I have a small inheritance sufficient for my needs."

"No need to scrimp, sir, I can make provision for you. The vicar of Missendene parish church, a very old man, died recently. The living is still vacant. Will you accept the position of the new incumbent? The stipend is generous."

"Yes, I thank you for your kindness."

Her butler entered the room. "Dinner is served, my lady."

After Kate inclined her head to the butler, she opened her mouth to address Mister Milton again. "The kindness is yours for I know you will deal gently with your flock. Shall we dine?"

Mister Milton looked down at his clothes.

"No, don't protest," Kate said. "You need not change your attire."

Instead of rising and offering his hand to escort her to the dining room, Mister Milton remained seated. "Countess," he commenced, "I must tell you something. I promised your late husband not to divulge the truth to you, yet, since his death, I have laboured long and hard with my conscience. When I overheard your son tell his uncle that for as long as he could remember he dreamt of meeting you, I knew I must confide in you." Another

133

fit of coughing overtook him. When it finished, he gulped the rest of his wine.

"You are unwell, sir," she said, genuinely concerned for his health.

He waved his hand. "No, no, the dust on the journey irritated my throat."

Simon entered the room. "My lady, Captain Howard has arrived. Will you receive him?"

"Yes, and he may dine with us."

Kate stood, eager to see Edward. Although she had decided to rebuff him, she could not do so.

Boots on the wooden staircase. Kate smiled when she heard Captain Howard's voice.

She sprang to her feet when he entered the room. What brought the captain here? How handsome he looked, in spite of a smudge of dirt on his left cheek. Fire ran through her veins. Never had any other man quickened her blood as Captain Howard did.

"Forgive my intrusion, milady," the captain said. "I was returning to London from my brother's house when a wheel parted company with my coach."

"Are you hurt? Was anyone injured? What of your horses?"

"Only the coach is slightly damaged, milady."

"You must put up here until it is mended."

Even if he had not been welcome she would have honoured the obligation to offer stranded traveller hospitality for the night.

Mister Milton coughed yet again, this time more gently.

"Ah, you have not been *formally* introduced." Kate smiled. "Captain Howard, Mister Milton, the new incumbent of Missendene church. Mister Milton, Captain Howard."

"My pleasure to meet you, sir," Mister Milton said.

The gentlemen exchanged bows.

What had Milton been on the verge of telling her? Something to do with his conscience and her late husband?"

"With your permission, my lady, I must withdraw to doctor myself." He bowed and left the room.

Chills ran up and down Kate's spine. Other than her boy, she could only think of one thing in connection with her that might cause Mister Milton to search his conscience. He knew where her daughter was. Her pretty parlour receded. A grey mist formed before her eyes. Would she faint? Kate swayed. On the edge of consciousness, she took deep breaths. She had never fainted and would not allow herself to do so now. "Milady, you are very pale, allow me to support you." Edward put an arm around her waist.

The proximity of his tall, muscular body sent tingles along her spine. "It is nothing, sir. I shall now do well enough."

Released, Kate lowered herself onto a chair.

"May I?" Edward asked, his hand poised above one of the small bottles of viana.

In spite of her anxiety to receive news about her daughter—if that was what plagued Mister Milton's conscience—she composed herself. "Captain Howard, how remiss of me not to have offered you a glass of viana." She pushed herself to her feet. "Allow me, 'tis my pleasure to serve you."

She poured wine for him, conscious of unseen energy, as powerful as a magnet's, drawing her to him.

Her hands trembled. At such a time, surely only an unnatural mother would be conscious of an attractive man.

"Please allow me to pour some for you, milady, I think you need a restorative."

Kate sank back onto the chair and accepted the drink, but her hands were unsteady, and she spilled some onto her petticoat. Immediately, the captain took the glass from her while she dabbed at the stain with her handkerchief.

Gertrude flung open the door. "What's afoot, Daughter. The hour grows late. I have been waiting to dine for more than a half-hour." Her eyes narrowed. "How clumsy you are. You have ruined your expensive petticoat."

Kate's cheeks burned.

"Clumsy is a word I would never use to describe your daughter," Edward said.

Mister Milton returned. "I trust I don't intrude."

"No, you do not," Kate assured him.

Gertrude glanced at the gentlemen. "Captain Howard, good day to you," she said belatedly.

"Good day, Mrs Corby."

Gertrude stared with palpable curiosity at Mister Milton. "Introduce me, Kate!"

"Allow me the pleasure of introducing Mister Milton, the new incumbent of Missendene Church. Mister Milton, my mother, Mrs. Corby."

"How secretive you are," Gertrude grumbled, "you did not tell me you had found a replacement for the late vicar."

"I did not think the matter would interest you." Kate tried to exercise patience. "'Shall we dine?'"

136

"May I have the privilege of escorting you, Mrs Corby?" Mister Milton asked.

Gertrude simpered and then went to his side.

"Milady," Edward said and held out his arm.

Kate rested her hand on his smooth broadcloth sleeve.

They proceeded in silence to the dining room where Kate did scant justice to the meal.

"My chop is tough and this chicken is overcooked," Gertrude complained. "You must forgive my daughter for her poor table, gentlemen."

Kate frowned. She set an excellent table. Her mother's ungrateful complaints were ill-founded.

"Speaking as one who has endured rations at sea, I find naught to complain of," Edward said. "In my humble opinion, this meal is fit for princes."

"I agree," Mister Milton said. "We must always thank the Lord for His bounty and remember the poor are always with us."

"Don't worry about your new parish, Mister Milton," Kate reassured him, "Leftover meats and other food are distributed to those in need, some of whom gather at the gates, but I want to help much more and shall be grateful for your suggestions."

"My dear lady, you are to be commended. I shall be happy to discuss other ways in which you can assist unfortunates." Mister Milton forked a morsel of chicken into his mouth.

Captain Howard inclined his head toward her. She gazed into the depths of his dark eyes. A frisson ran down her spine. Conscious of her blushes, she looked at her plate.

Kate struggled to eat. What had happened to her appetite? Bother Jessie, in spite of her instruction, the woman had buckled her stays too tightly for her to partake of her food in comfort. No, she should not blame Jessie for her lost appetite. She must make an effort. If she followed her instinct to push her plate aside, it would be a signal for the lackeys to clear the table before the others finished eating.

Ever aware of her surroundings, Kate looked up at the ceiling. How many meals had been consumed beneath it? She squared her shoulders. Although nothing could alter her past, she dreamt of a happy future in which her son and daughter sat at her table.

"Are you not hungry, Kate?" Gertrude asked. "You have not eaten enough to satisfy a mouse."

Kate forced herself to eat some buttered turnips. Their unique flavour caught in her throat. How could she sit here with a semblance of calm while, like the poor who came daily to the gates of the manor, her daughter might be in dire need? She faced Mister Milton. "When you are settled in the vicarage, I will consult you. 'Tis my intention to provide footwear and warm clothes for the poorest in the parish and to found a school. Education, my dear sir, provides the key to alleviation of suffering."

"How revolutionary, Daughter," Gertrude said, when she could make herself heard above another bout of Mister Milton's coughing, "if common folk were educated, who would serve us?"

Determined not to be drawn into yet another petty argument with her mother, Kate turned her head to look at Captain Howard. "You are observing the shields, banners, and arms on the walls. They are those of the previous owner of Missendene, who supports the claim of the second King James's son to the throne. After I bought the manor, I intended to replace them with oil paintings."

"A good idea, they would look well here," Edward said.

"Or some tapestries," Gertrude suggested.

Kate nodded and thought of her children. To buoy her spirits, she must believe that one day they would live under her roof. For now, she should rejoice because Charles's cruel tutor had been dismissed. Her appetite returned with her optimism. Although the clergyman did not look well, she was impatient to cross-question him. At the time of the twins' birth he served as her husband's chaplain. More than likely, he could give her an important clue as to the whereabouts of her girl.

Chapter Eleven

After Kate dined, she and her mother left the captain and Mister Milton to enjoy some brandy. However it was not long before they joined her in the parlour, where she and her mother were discussing the replacement of furniture that dated back to the reign of the first King Charles and earlier.

Kate greeted them with a smile. "As you see, gentlemen, Missendene does not bustle like my London house. Other than playing cards, I have little entertainment to offer, but if we are fortunate my mother might agree to sing for us. For now, Mother, perhaps you will show Captain Howard my collection of paintings in the minstrels' gallery. He is an accomplished artist, so I am sure he will appreciate them."

Edward blinked, but as always his manners were punctilious. He offered his arm to Mrs Corby.

"Captain Howard," Gertrude began, "I hope you will share your knowledge with me. My daughter praised your paintings so they must be superlative."

"You flatter me, Mrs Corby. I only dabble with the brush."

"You do far more," Kate said, anxious for the captain and her mother to be gone. Since his arrival she had been struggling with her impatience to question Mister Milton about the reason for his visit and her duties as lady of the manor.

The captain smiled—perhaps in appreciation of her words—and then led her mother out of the room.

Sick with mingled apprehension and hope, Kate could not prevent her lower lip from quivering like that of a small girl who was about to cry. She took a deep breath before she spoke. "Mister Milton, come to my closet where we can be private." She frowned. "You look unwell. Perhaps you took a chill on your journey. Would you care for a hot toddy?"

"Yes please, my lady, you are very kind."

* * *

Kate and Mister Milton sat by the fireplace in the closet, furnished with a desk and a pair of wing chairs on either side of the hearth, while he sipped his toddy.

"Please tell me what brought you here, Mister Milton?"

The reverend gentleman looked around as though nothing in the world interested him more than the jewel-coloured Oriental rug.

"Will you not unburden your conscience, sir," Kate cajoled.

Mister Milton smoothed his waistcoat. "My lady, I regret that I have nothing of importance to tell you."

Kate rose to light more candles to dispel the gloom. "I beg you not to prevaricate. Earlier, you declared you have something you must tell me. You told me you promised my late husband not to divulge the truth. You also explained that after his death you laboured long and hard with your scruples."

He glanced at her. "My words were ill-judged."

141

"Maybe they were, but having spoken them you should speak out instead of torturing me."

"My lady, I know better than to break a confidence. I shall pray for forgiveness for having been tempted to do so."

Lord above, trying to extract information from him was as difficult and painful as trying to extract a tooth. Her heart beat uncomfortably fast. "I beg you to tell me if your promise concerns my daughter."

Mister Milton shifted his position and surveyed the book-lined wall behind the desk.

"Come, come, sir, please unburden yourself. In the past you expressed sympathy for my plight. You even indicated you believe I am innocent of my late husband's charge of adultery."

Colour suffused the clergyman's unnaturally red cheeks. "His lordship believed you were unfaithful to him."

"I was not," Kate said, still desperate for any information Mister Milton could provide. "I never cuckolded my husband." She controlled her urge to pace up and down the closet. "Do you not think I have suffered long enough?" Her heart pounded. "If my girl lives, what of *her*, an innocent deprived of her rightful position by my husband's cruelty? For pity's sake, Mister Milton, tell me if you know where I can find my daughter."

Again he studied the carpet, his mouth pressed into a narrow pink line.

The closet seemed to spin around. Kate closed her eyes. Why had she convinced herself Mister Milton had good news about her girl? Perhaps he did not. She opened her eyes. Why did he avoid looking at her?

She shivered and gazed out of the window. A mass of pewter-coloured clouds obscured the sun. In contrast to the dull sky, the colour of the grass stretching from the manor to the woods deepened to emerald green.

Should she summon a lackey to light a fire in the grate? No, flames leaping high in the chimney and spreading their warmth could not alleviate the chill in her heart.

Perhaps Mister Milton would confess if she asserted herself instead of pleading. "Well, sir, I believe you lie. I think you have knowledge of my daughter's fate."

The gentleman's hands trembled on his lap. "God might strike me dead if I break my word," he said and coughed violently.

"I doubt He will. No more prevaricating. Out with the truth!"

"Although I could not be party to your husband's evil, even now my promise binds me."

She shuddered. Evil? What evil? What had her husband done with their daughter? Maybe an appeal to Mister Milton's better nature would bring the desired result. "Have you no compassion? Can you not imagine the fears besetting me on my child's behalf?"

Mister Milton studied the moulded ceiling.

"Come, come, sir, do you not think I have the right to know the truth?"

The reverend gentleman looked at her full in the face. "Yes, I have always thought so. Concealing it troubled me greatly. Until recently, I believed you were indifferent to your children's fate. I now perceive it is not so, therefore, since you press me so hard, I will tell you the truth. His lordship accepted the first born twin as his son and gave orders for his daughter to be drowned like an unwanted kitten."

Wanting to howl, Kate gasped for breath. She knew her husband had been a wicked man, but never had she imagined how evil he had been. Bile rose in her throat.

His eyes moist, Mister Milton continued. "I followed the lackey who was ordered to commit the murder. With the power of the church invested in me, I threatened him with eternal damnation if he carried out those orders. At first, terrified of his master, the fellow refused to hand me the infant. However, I insisted on baptising her. He agreed, put her in my arms, and then followed me to the church. After the baptism, I sent the man on his way with the promise that Christ, who suffered little children to come unto him, would bless the lackey. I also told the man I believed Lord Jesus would overlook his lie when he told the earl the infant was dead."

The thought of her daughter's murder had terrified her. Now, having discovered the child lived, the relief was indescribable. She swallowed as she leaned forward. "Where is my girl?" she demanded between bitter tears for the lost years and joy at the possibility her daughter might soon be found.

Again, the cleric shifted on his seat. "Your husband swore those who knew you bore twins to secrecy."

Anger boiled within her. She wanted to curse him. He could have saved her from years of suffering during which she did not know if her child lived or died. "Don't try my patience! Did you not tell the lackey ordered to murder her, that Christ would forgive his lie to my late husband? Do you not think Christ will forgive you for breaking your promise to the earl?"

Mister Milton straightened his back. "I hope He will," he said and drank the rest of his toddy. "Ah, that has revived me."

At long last, she might be able to clasp her daughter in her arms. "She lives? My girl lives?"

"I believe so," he said.

Her fists clenched. "What do you mean by saying 'you believe so'?" she sputtered.

"My lady, you are distraught, shall I pour you some wine?"

She pressed her hand to her throat to still her pulse. "No wine, thank you, but please tell me whatever you know about my daughter."

He smiled for the first time since they entered her closet. "When I baptised her, she cried loudly as the devil quit her mortal flesh."

"What name did you give her?"

"Amanda, which means fit to be loved. Your husband judged her unfit to be part of the Sinclair family. I judged that in Lord Jesus Christ's sight she is worthy of love."

Tears welled in her eyes. "Thank you, I can never repay you for your compassion. You not only saved my baby's life, you also gave her a beautiful name." Kate took a deep breath. "What provision did you make for Amanda after her christening? Where is she now?"

"First, I found a wet nurse for her. The woman was one of my parishioners, a poor widow whose husband and babe died within days of each other. I sent both your daughter and the woman to my cousin, Tabitha, in London. Poor Tabitha's marriage had not been blessed with children. I knew she would welcome Amanda with joy and hoped her indulgent husband would permit her to keep the babe."

Kate rose. "I will set out for London immediately. I cannot wait to meet my daughter and thank your cousin for taking care of her."

The cleric shook his head.

"What?"

"I regret to inform you Tabitha died four years ago and her husband died two years later without making provision for Amanda in his will. His heir saw no reason to support your daughter and sent her to a workhouse."

"If she is still there, I shall rescue her." Fearful for her girl, Kate pressed her right hand over her heart. "Where did your cousin live?"

"In Bishopsgate, two doors from The King's Head."

"To which poorhouse was my unfortunate child sent?"

"The London Workhouse. I assure you that it really is a sanctuary for impoverished children where they are educated and trained to earn a living."

Kate sank back against her chair. "I *must* rescue her. Mister Milton, I shall return to London at first light. Tell me what Amanda looks like." Even as she put the question, she knew the answer. Charles had described his twin sister as a feminine version of his own image.

"Dressed in identical clothes, Amanda and her twin would be as alike as two butterflies of the same species." He cleared his throat. "Well, not quite,

Amanda is more petite than her twin. At least she was when I last saw her."

"When was that?"

"Shortly before the death of Tabitha's husband."

Kate clenched her fists. "And you did not see fit to find out whether she lived or died at The London Workhouse or to make other arrangements for her?"

"While employed by Mister Sinclair, my time was not my own." He sighed. "I wanted to care for Amanda but did not have the means. Besides, how would I have persuaded the governors of The London Workhouse to release her into my custody?'

Kate sent for Jessie.

"Pack immediately," Kate ordered her tirewoman when she hurried into the room. "We shall return to London tomorrow."

Jessie curtsied. "My lady."

After Jessie left, Kate put further questions to Mister Milton. She treasured his answers, which described a spirited child as intelligent and sweet by nature as Charles, a daughter any parent could be proud of—at least, any parent other than Amanda's odious father.

Kate shuddered. For a moment, she imagined the sickly sweet scent of the earl's aged body permeated the parlour. Her mouth turned down at the corners. If his ghost lurked near her, how incensed he must be to know Amanda lived. She trembled, shaking her head, denying the possibility that the girl had died in the workhouse. No, she must not think thus.

She tried to convince herself she had much to live for. Charles was happier since the cruel tutor had been dismissed. She must believe she would soon be reunited

147

with her daughter. She ached to clasp Amanda in her arms.

"Mister Milton, you must accompany me to London and identify my daughter."

"As you please, my lady," he said in a faint voice.

She looked at him. His forehead perspired and his cheeks were very red. "Another toddy?"

He stood. "No thank you." He tottered. "Please excuse me, I am feverish."

Kate sprang to her feet. "Take my arm, sir. I shall send for the doctor."

Chapter Twelve

After his tour of the gallery, Edward took a long walk before supper. Later, he listened to Mrs Corby sing in her beautiful soprano and applauded her enthusiastically.

"Thank you," Mrs Corby fluttered her fan. "Will you not join me in a duet, Captain? 'Twould pass the time."

Edward obliged her. Yet all the while, he remained conscious of Kate's tension. "Will you not favour us with a song, Lady Sinclair?"

Kate shook her head. "After hearing my mother sing, I fear I would disappoint you."

Gertrude sat a little straighter. "Shall we play cards?"

Time passed until Kate, who showed little interest in the game, put her hand in front of her mouth to conceal a yawn. "I crave your pardon, Captain. My mother and I keep country hours. I suggest we partake of some sack posset before we retire for the night." She gestured to a lackey.

The servant fetched the rich mixture of hot spiced sack and eggs to which sweetened, scalded cream had been added. He spooned the potent mixture into silver cups from a posset pot engraved with the Sinclair coat of arms.

Several cups of the hot beverage warmed Kate's blood. She hoped the sack would numb her senses and ensure a good night's repose.

"Shall we retire?" Kate asked. She did not wait for an answer, but instead made her way to the foot of the stairs where she picked up a candlestick.

"Make sure the fires are out and all the candles snuffed before you go to bed," she ordered the butler.

* * *

Edward followed Kate and Gertrude up the narrow stairs. After he bade them goodnight, he ascended a flight of stairs which twisted and turned up to the third floor. He entered his bedchamber, yawned, but did not unbutton his coat. He was curious. Why had Kate's eyes sparkled and smiles come readily to her lips this evening, only to fade and leave her on the brink of tears. What caused such a change? Edward turned around and made his way toward her apartment.

On the second floor a door opened. He watched Kate, candlestick in hand, walk along the corridor, her shadow keeping pace with her along the panelled walls. She opened a door and crossed its threshold.

"A word with you, if you please, Lady Sinclair."

Kate spun around. "Captain Howard, what can you want of me at this hour of the night?" she asked without a trace of the flirtatious manner she flaunted in London.

"Milady, this evening you veered between tears and laughter."

"You are impertinent, sir. My private joys and sorrows are not your concern."

Her proud reticence did not cause him to think less of her.

Kate's taut jaw relaxed. "My apologies, I am not ungrateful but my business is not yours and—"

"Indeed," he broke in, "although every great lady has many private matters to consider, never forget I will always be ready to serve you."

"You are too kind, sir."

"I am trustworthy and hope you will always feel free to confide in me."

Kate glanced along the corridor. "Please leave, sir. Think of the scandal if we were seen here alone at this hour of the night."

"Yet you once offered to receive me alone at your levee."

"And you refused for propriety's sake. What of the rules of etiquette now?"

"You don't seem to be the type of lady who is concerned with them."

"Is that so?" Kate asked, opened a door, and stepped across the threshold into a bedchamber. The captain followed her before she could shut the door.

"Do you really want me to go?"

She hesitated.

"I want to talk to you." What, he wondered, would she do if he refused to leave? She was not strong enough to force him out of the bedchamber, and if she summoned servants, they would be sure to gossip.

"Very well, a quick word if you must."

The candle flickered. Kate lit those in the candelabra on a low table. The pretty bedchamber, with its light blue wallpaper sprigged with pale pink roses and the dainty china figurines on the mantelpiece, blossomed by candlelight.

Kate shut the door and turned to face him. "What do you want, sir?"

"I want to protect you."

She sank onto the padded window seat.

Flickering candlelight illuminated her face. "You are little more than a boy. How can you aspire to protect me?"

Moonlight streamed through the windows, combining with the candlelight to bathe Kate in its glow. Never before had she appeared more beautiful or more distant. He knelt and raised her cold hand to his lips. "I am younger than you in years but not without experience."

"With my sex? Oh, I believe you. With your cozening ways and handsome face, you must have enjoyed many dalliances."

"Enough, I am neither a rake nor a greenling. I am a sailor hardened in battle, a man tested at sea. A sailor eager to know you intimately and assist you."

Kate's narrow nostrils widened as she drew in a deep breath. "Do you think you have said anything which I have not heard other men say since my husband died?"

He kissed her hand again before he raised his head to look deep into her eyes. "That is as may be, but I vow none of them spoke those words with such sincerity."

Her hand remained quiescent in his. Did she look at him more kindly? By candlelight he could not be sure.

"Captain Howard, I appreciate your desire to help me, but I don't know what you want of me. Do you seek a scandalous liaison or marriage? A liaison is out of the question. As for marriage, I am appreciative of the honour you do me and hope my refusal will not give you pain."

Edward tried to decide whether an amused gleam lurked in her eyes. "You have not pained me because I did not mention marriage."

"You are arrogant." Kate withdrew her hand from his clasp.

As the captain stood he smiled down at her. "No, not arrogant, merely a poor fool who is fascinated by you and set afire by your intelligence and beauty."

"You might be fascinated but I hope this does not mean you will attempt to force kisses on me."

He sighed. "Is that what your gallants do? I promise I am cut from a superior cloth." He raised her chin with his thumb. "Maybe you *would like* me to kiss you but I am not sure whether or not I *want* to kiss you."

Kate rose and stared into his eyes. "You don't want to kiss me?" A frown creased her forehead.

"If I decide I wish to, it will be at a time of my choosing."

"Oh!" she exclaimed, presumably indignant because she was unaccustomed to being spoken to thus.

The wretched man's eyes filled with amusement.

"One day, milady, you will burn for a man, and all the signs indicate that I will be that man." The captain lit more candles and then sat by the marble fireplace with a surround carved with cherubs holding bunches of grapes. "You are to be congratulated on so charming a bedroom."

She ignored his comment. "You are mistaken."

"Do you not think it is charming?"

"Captain Howard, you *know* I did not speak of the bedchamber. Y-you are presumptuous."

Kate pressed her hand to her throat. "I furnished this room for my daughter. Now, you must excuse me. I am tired. If you wish to remain here you may, but please snuff out the candles before you retire."

She turned to leave.

He crossed the small space between them. "Milady."

Kate turned again, this time to face him, her eyes widening. "What?"

The captain indicated the bed. "I am sure I could please you if you want me to."

"I know there is no pleasure to be found in bed with a man. And I cannot understand why men want to bed a woman unless it is to get her with child."

He laughed. "When did I speak of bedding you?"

Her cheeks flamed by candlelight. "You...you implied—"

Now the expression in his eyes sobered. "I am sorry for teasing you, but my dear countess, most men and women make love to experience joy."

Kate shrugged. "What joy is to be found? Or rather, if there is joy, I assure you it is not for me. Oh, don't smile at me thus! If you knew me better, you would expect nothing of me. Be warned, my mother accuses me of breaking hearts."

"Milady, I have naught but a good opinion of you. Say no more. I am sure you will like everything about me when we are better acquainted."

"Odds bodikins, must you have an answer for everything?"

He laughed.

"You are a romantic fool," Kate said, but her eyes glinted as though she, too, was on the verge of laughter.

"Romantic, but no fool, my lady." He left the room before she could make further protests.

* * *

Kate sank onto the window seat. How bold the captain was. Not only bold, at times he seemed percipient. Nothing had prepared her for his effrontery. Most gentlemen were not so bold. No, that was not true. She shuddered at the memory of Stafford. Edward possessed far more finesse than any of her other gallants. She tried to dismiss him as no more than a callow young man and failed.

Many men had proposed marriage to her and had also sworn they loved her. In addition, the blind fools promised to make her happy. She had always thanked them for the honour bestowed upon her by their marriage proposals, and then dismissed them with the knowledge her fortune attracted them as much or more than her person.

Why could she not dismiss the captain with the ease she dismissed all other gentlemen?

Kate swung her legs up onto the window seat. She looked out across the moonlit knot garden with its potted orange trees, one in the centre and others at each corner of every bed. During the years her husband incarcerated her, she took pleasure in growing herbs and working in the still room. It might be pleasant to give up town life to settle here with Amanda. She would busy herself with her daughter's welfare, books, correspondence, trade, and the simple pleasures of country life. She covered her face with her hands. Dare she hope to be reunited with the babe she birthed over twelve years ago?

She must face facts. For all she knew Amanda might have died. No, Charles was certain his twin still lived. As soon as possible she would rescue Amanda. Even if she did not find her daughter, the years until Charles came into his inheritance would pass swiftly while she filled them with all the entertainments London offered. No need to think of the captain. No reason to ponder the sensation the touch of his lips on hers aroused when they first met and he had given her a brief, formal kiss. Shivers ran up and down her spine.

Kate shook her head. Nothing would ever persuade her, the Countess of Sinclair, an acknowledged beauty in absolute control of her fortune, to either enter into an illicit liaison or remarry. She stroked her lips with her forefinger. Even in the unlikely event of changing her mind about remarriage, why wed a much younger man?

Her thoughts dwelt on the captain, a gentleman unlike any other she had ever known, who seemed far older and wiser than his years.

A light knock on the door. She opened it. Edward stood before her, the expression on his face remorseful.

"May I come in? I think everyone is asleep but cannot be sure and it is inadvisable to be seen in conversation at this hour of the night."

"You should have thought of that earlier," she said, but opened the door wider to admit him. "Why have you returned?"

He closed the door. "To make my apology, in the hope you are not angry with me. I could not sleep uncertain as to whether or not all is well with you, milady. I trust my desire to make love to you will not shock you, but I am nothing less than honest in all my dealings."

"Please say no more."

A deep crease appeared between his eyebrows. "What is amiss?"

"Nothing," she said before the urge to confide in another human being overcame her. "That is, there is wonderful news, but I scarce dare hope."

"About your daughter?" He crossed the room in a few swift strides.

After years of keeping her own council, the temptation to unburden her heart to this sympathetic young man was too great. She nodded.

"That is wonderful."

"Yes it is. It feels like a miracle."

Her words flowed until she finished revealing everything Mister Milton had told her. Even as she did, she marvelled at the strange alchemy between herself and the captain.

"I shall come to London with you and assist in every way I can."

Oh, she liked him, really liked him better than any other gentleman of her acquaintance.

Had he enchanted her? Her cheeks burned. She considered him a friend and…and what else? A very kind, charismatic gentleman or…or more?

Chapter Thirteen

Kate stretched and yawned. She could not tell the hour until she parted the curtains around her bed. Yet she did not open them. In the privacy of the dark, she hugged herself out of joy, which warmed her from head to toes. Amanda survived infancy. Soon she would be reunited with her girl and then they would make up for the years of enforced separation.

A door opened. Jessie must be on her way to awaken her.

Raised voices disturbed her. "What is ado?" she demanded, annoyed by the commotion.

After Kate thrust back the quilt, she hurried into the adjacent closet.

Scarlet-cheeked, Jessie turned to face Kate while pointing at Mrs Corby. "My lady, I cannot obey two mistresses. I have told your ladyship's mother, *you* pay my wages, so I follow *your* instructions, not hers."

Kate frowned. *How vexatious!* Why must her mother provoke Jessie today of all days?

"Lady Sinclair," her servant commenced. "You know it's not my habit to grumble, yet when Mrs Corby gave me a list of errands before complaining of the way you arrange your hair, my flesh and blood couldn't put up with it."

For how long, Kate wondered, could she endure living with her mother, who never gave her affection or uttered a word of praise and even criticised her to the servants.

"Kate," Gertrude snapped, "why do you appear in public with plaits around the crown of your head? They look ridiculous. A properly trained tirewoman would coax you into arranging your hair in a more fashionable style."

"Begging your pardon for speaking freely, my lady," Jessie began, her forehead beaded with perspiration, "my blood boils when Mrs Corby criticises your manners and modes."

"Silence!" Kate held up her hand. Although she allowed Jessie—who had shared many of her sorrows—some freedom of speech, her tirewoman must curb her tongue when they were not alone. "Silence," she repeated in a softer tone. "Jessie, you will make my head ache."

Aware of her mother's provocative nature, Kate sympathised with the woman. Besides 'twas both ill-bred and unkind of her mother to vex the servants, most of whom dared not answer back for fear of losing their positions.

"Please allow me to speak, my lady. Isn't Mrs Corby forever asking me to run errands, as though I've time to serve both you and her?"

Despite her much loved servant's cause for complaint, it would be improper of Kate to criticise her mother to any servant.

Flushed with anger, Gertrude plopped onto a chair. "Are you not going to reprimand your woman?"

"In due course," Kate said slowly.

Her mother's eyes glittered with palpable anger. "Dismiss her for being rude to me."

Tears rolled down Jessie's plump cheeks. "It's all very well for folk living on their daughter's charity to complain and grumble *and* criticise until they drive a body mad. They don't know what it's like to earn their daily bread." A sob caught in Jessie's throat before she continued. "You wouldn't dismiss me, my lady. Didn't I stay with you when the earl—God rot his soul—imprisoned you? Didn't I comfort you? Wasn't I with you when the twins were born?"

"Twins? You had twins? When?" Gertrude shrilled.

Aghast, Kate pressed her hand to her throat.

Jessie's face paled. "I'm sorry, my lady. Seeing as I kept your secret for these twelve years past, I don't know what came over me," she mumbled, busying herself moving cushions and rearranging Kate's china ornaments.

Bright colour flooded Gertrude's cheeks. "You wicked woman! You committed adultery."

Kate caught her lower lip between her teeth. A mother should be the first to think the best of her own, but *her* mother was too selfish to ever think of her children's needs.

Jessie banged open the shutters and clattered the fire irons while muttering, "My lady never cuckolded him. What's more, Mrs Corby, you shouldn't believe that stupid old wives' tale."

"Be quiet, Jessie, you have done enough harm," Kate ordered.

Her tirewoman sucked in her plump cheeks. "I'm so sorry, my lady, I really am. I should have cut my tongue out before I spoke of your secret."

"Leave us," Kate ordered. "The damage is done."

160

"I'll fetch your chocolate, my lady," Jessie said and scurried out of the parlour.

Kate looked at her mother full in the face. "We must part company."

"What? You prefer *that* creature of yours to me? A creature more in your confidence than I am?"

"Please say no more and don't pretend to care for me. You gave me away when I was a babe and now you always believe the worst of me."

Fingers interlaced so tightly that her knuckles gleamed white beneath podgy flesh, her mother pressed her hands against her chest. "I did not want to part with you, but our means were limited. Your father persuaded me you would have a better life with your uncle and aunt. Anyway, what do you know of my suffering on your account after you were handed over to them?"

Was it possible that her self-centred mother grieved for her as deeply as she did for Amanda? Kate gathered her wits. This was not the time to weaken. Since her mother came to live with her, they rarely took pleasure in each other's company. Indeed, most of the time, they were at odds. "Whatever the case, Mother, until my husband died, I scarce knew you. When I took you in, we were strangers. Since then you have constantly complained and criticised. Now you have carped at my Jessie until you drove her distracted, which is why she was indiscreet."

"But it seems *that* woman knows all your secrets. You are cruel not to have confided in me. Twins, indeed!"

Kate realised Mother was jealous of Jessie. Her breath caught in her throat, but she did not reproach herself for being honest; after all, her mother was little more than a stranger in whom she had not wanted to confide. "Yes, Mother, twins. Charles, whom you have seen at a distance, and a daughter taken from me at birth by my husband, both of them begotten by him, regardless of whatever you think." Again, she gathered her wits. "Let us be sensible, it will not do for you to continue to live with me."

"What?"

Kate ignored her mother's startled question. "I shall lease a house in London for you. I shall also give you an allowance sufficient for you to employ a companion, go out and about in town, go to Bath to take the waters, to visit any other place you wish, and to dress in the height of fashion."

Again, her mother attempted to speak. "No, don't protest. My mind is made up. Moreover, if you speak to anyone about my lost daughter, I shall cut you off without a penny." Kate narrowed her eyes. "For the moment, you will remain here at Missendene Manor while I return to London."

"You are heartless."

"If that were so, I would not have taken you in after my brother refused to tolerate you under his roof. What is more, if you drove his wife as demented as you have driven Jessie, I don't blame him."

Gertrude wiped tears from her eyes. "My children are cruel."

Kate did not respond to her mother's accusation and forced herself to ignore the tears. "You may wait on me occasionally and I shall wait on you," she said, aware of her duty toward her parent.

"What will my friends say?" Gertrude shrilled.

What of them? In Mother's book of life, other people's opinions were more important that her family's. Well, at least it would ensure her mother told no one about Amanda.

Kate shrugged. To end the conversation, she rang the hand bell.

Within moments, a lackey answered the summons.

"Tell my bailiff and steward to attend me in the book room in an hour. Order my coach as well as the fargons for most of my servants and the baggage. I am returning to London."

Astonishment flared in his eyes, for he was but young and partially trained. He bowed. "Very good, my lady."

"And inform Captain Howard he is welcome to travel with me."

"The captain departed at daybreak." His face flushed. "Your butler said he left a note for you."

"Please fetch it."

Left? After his declaration of love, the captain departed without thanking her for accommodating him, or making his farewells in person. How could he be so rude?

Instead of the youngster, Simon brought the note. Disappointed and upset by the captain's unexpected desertion, Kate ripped the seal apart and read.

Milady,

Believe I am ever at y'r service. I have therefore proceeded to London to assist y'r ladyship in y'r search. I shall seeke Hinchcliffe's advice about the matter deare to y'r Hearte and wait on you there three days hence when I believe that by the Grace of Almighty God you will have reached London.

163

Y'r servant,
Edward Howard

How kind of him to exert himself on her behalf. Kate hoped, whatever the outcome, they would remain friends for as long as they both lived. Her cheeks grew warm. Could they ever be more than that? No. Impossible. She truly had no taste for…for dalliance.

* * *

Every mile of the journey increased Kate's impatience to visit the workhouse. Each one brought a new fear of Amanda suffering from neglect and mistreatment. However, because of a broken bridge, the coach did not clatter over the cobbled streets of London until dusk on the fourth day of her journey. Due to an overturned dray blocking the road, darkness had descended by the time she reached her house. By then it was too late to set out to rescue her girl from the possible diet of bread and water, daily beatings, and even worse—thoughts of which flashed through her mind all the way to town.

Maybe Hinchcliffe or the captain had written to her. Heedless of heavy rain, Kate sprang from the coach. A lackey bounded up the steps to knock on the door. As soon as it opened, she hurried to her closet where her correspondence would be on the desk.

Darkness, total darkness. Kate groped for the hand bell and tapped her foot while she waited for the candles to be lit by a servant.

The closet flowered into light. Letters and cards lay on her desk. Without pausing to remove her damp cloak she sat to flip through them. *Good, a letter penned in the captain's hand.* She held her breath, broke the seal, and read.

Milady,

I have visited The London Workhouse where I ascertained the following. With the understanding that the utmost discretion must be employed, I did not speak Amanda's name. I merely sought to set y'r ladyship's mind at reste concerning the chyldrens' well-being.

Y'r Ladyship is not to feare y'r daughter is ill-treated. Although a female chylde's life in The London Workhouse is not fitting for A Lady by Birth the lyttle ones are treated kindly.

When the church bells sound the hour of six in the morning, the chyldren rise. At half past the hour they attend Prayers after which they partake of a hearty breakfast.

At seven of the clock, twenty of the neatly clad older girls either knit stockings, spin both wool and flax and wind silk or besides stitch their own clothes and those of the younger chyldren.

Ah outrageous image. An earl's daughter should not be obliged to perform menial tasks.

Kate caught her lip between her teeth, imagining her daughter's fair head bent over such tasks. Dear God, were those older girls really kind to her, or did they pinch her behind closed doors, and take her share of breakfast? On the other hand, Amanda might be considered as an older girl.

In addition to those skylls necessary for the chyldren to earn their living when they are old enough for an apprenticeship, they go daily to the schoolroom to study arithmetic, reading, and writing for one hour.

At noon the chyldren dine after which they may play until the bell sounds the hour of one. They then work until six of the clock after which they attend Prayers in the chapel, partake of supper, and play until they retire. On Sundays they labour not. Instead they receive religious instruction and attend services in the chapel at eleven and six of the clock.

Twenty chyldren sleep in a ward, which their nurse is responsible for. A nurse told me she cleans the ward, makes the beds, mends her youngest charges' clothes, and ensures the cleanliness and neatness of each chylde. Indeed, they must wash their persons and brush their hair daily, besides which their nurse applies a small toothcomb to each girls' hair three times a week.

The nurses are clean, God-fearing women much attached to their charges.

Kate cursed the man who sent her child to The London Workhouse. Then she read through the lines again, blessed the nurse who had taken care of Amanda, and decided to reward her.

As for sustenance, the lyttle ones fayre better than poor chyldren who fend for themselves on the streets. For dinner they are served boyled beef or mutton and broth together with bread three days a week. On Mondays, Wednesdays, and Fridays they partake of bread, cheese, and butter, and on Saturdays pease pottage, rice milk, ferminty or other pottage. For supper they have broth or milk pottage with bread.

I will conclude by assuring Your Ladyship the provisions are weighed every week in the presence of some of the committee, the members of which also take great care to ascertain the servants keep good hours and none of them abuse the defenceless lyttle ones in their charge.

I have requested Hinchcliffe to hold himself available to attend your business. If y'r ladyship will be good enough to acquaint me of the place and time you wish to meet with us, a note sent to me at Mrs Radcliffe's house will suffice.

I remain y'r ladyship's humble servant,

Edward Howard

A long, drawn out sigh escaped Kate. How her girl must have suffered when banished from home to the workhouse. Did she cry at night for her foster parents? Did she ever long to find her real parents? When did she last see Mister Milton? Did she wonder why he came not to see her?

Kate forced herself to breathe slowly. Soon she would be reunited with her girl. First thing on the morrow, she would deliver Amanda from the London Workhouse and then take her to Missendene. In the peaceful countryside, she and her daughter would become acquainted, making up for the twelve years of their separation.

Kate pursed her lips while she penned a letter to the captain. She thanked him for his efforts on her behalf and asked him to wait on her in the morning, assuring him her return to town had not yet been announced in the broadsheets, so she would not hold her levee. After a moment's reflection, she wrote to Hinchliffe with a request to present himself first thing on the morrow.

* * *

Church bells rang out ten times as Edward approached Kate's London mansion. A flower girl came up to him. "Buy some violets fresh picked for yer lady, sir. Only a penny a bunch."

He removed a shiny coin from his purse and handed it to the girl.

She pressed a posy into his hands. "Thank you kindly, sir, may God bless yer kind face."

Edward's footsteps slowed when he neared the flight of freshly scrubbed front steps, before which a milkmaid, perched on a three-legged stool, milked a placid black and white cow.

Kate's lackey, Simon, stood near the animal's head—a full pail of milk at his feet—noticed him, and bowed. "Captain Howard?"

"Your mistress asked me to wait on her." Deep in thought he pressed his lips together. Kate's widowhood ensured her independence, which she exercised to her advantage. Would the decisive, somewhat stubborn lady, accept advice from him? If not, would she take it from Hinchcliffe? The milkmaid stood and balanced her stool on her head. She indicated a second pail. "Milk's ready."

Simon handed her a coin before he looked at Edward. "I shall knock on the door for you, Captain, before taking the milk to the kitchen."

Conscious of his boots sullying the steps, Edward ascended them while Simon descended to the basement.

Edward waited for the door to open. If Kate permitted, he would protect her, even at the cost of his life—if it were ever necessary. A cough alerted him to

Hinchcliffe's presence. The man bowed. "At your service, Captain Howard."

The black painted door opened. "Come," Edward said to Hinchcliffe.

Edward hoped Kate's expectations would not be tarnished by reality. He handed the violets to the butler. "Please give these to her ladyship and inform her that Mister Hinchcliffe and I seek the honour of a few words."

Today, if he guessed correctly, Kate's lengthy toilette would have been completed long before the hour at which her usual morning levee would commence. If he were not mistaken, she would want to set out for the workhouse after an early breakfast.

The lackey admitted them to a small anteroom on the ground floor. "Gentlemen, please wait here."

Edward stood with his feet apart in front of the fireplace. Why did Kate tug at his heartstrings as no other woman ever had? Her beauty, coupled with his lust, formed a powerful combination, but his interest in Kate was more complex. He not only admired her, she had earned his respect. *Gallant* described her. Yet one did not expect to find that quality in a female.

Hinchcliffe sat on the sofa opposite the fireplace. "Might one ask if her ladyship wishes to give me further instructions concerning her daughter?"

"It is possible."

"You may depend on my total confidentiality. My livelihood relies on it, Captain Howard."

Edward hesitated while he marshalled his thoughts. "Yes, to be sure I can depend on your absolute discretion. It is why I recommended you to Lady Sinclair."

"You have some particular interest in her ladyship's affairs?" Hinchcliffe probed.

"This way, gentlemen," a lackey interrupted.

* * *

While Kate waited for Captain Howard and Mister Hinchcliffe in the green salon, she scrutinised the captain's portrait of her at the same age as Amanda. Did her girl really look thus? Well, she would soon know. The door opened. She turned around.

"Captain Howard and Mister Hinchcliffe," the lackey announced.

She raised her eyebrows. "Good day to both of you."

Hinchcliffe bowed low. "How may I serve you, my lady?"

She regarded him for a moment. When they first met, Hinchcliffe—a middle-aged gentleman of medium stature—assured her of his ability to remain incognito in most situations. Noting his unremarkable features and plain attire, she still had no reason to disbelieve him.

Kate crossed the floor and sank onto a chair. "Captain Howard, please be seated." She indicated a chair opposite her own on the other side of the marble fireplace. "You, too, Mister. Hinchcliffe, sit yourself down."

Careful not to crease his steel-grey coat, Mister. Hinchcliffe lowered himself onto a chair while she addressed her lackey. "Pour wine for each of my guests and then leave."

170

She waited for the servant to withdraw before she addressed Hinchcliffe. "Mister Milton, a gentleman in Holy Orders, informed me my daughter is at The London Workhouse. Unfortunately, he is laid low with a fever from which the doctor predicts he will not recover for three weeks or more. Therefore, he is unable to come to town to identify Amanda. However, I shall deliver her from the workhouse this morning. Therefore, I no longer require your services."

Edward put his empty glass down. He leaned forward, hands on his knees. "Lady Sinclair, I know how anxious you are to be reunited with your child, but in my opinion you would be unwise to visit the workhouse."

She stared at him. "Why?"

"Reflect for a moment," the captain said. "You are a well-known figure and the subject of reports in the broadsheets. To visit such an establishment without due consideration will attract attention I am sure you wish to avoid."

Kate clutched a fold of her petticoat. "What do you suggest I do?"

"First, allow Mister Hinchcliffe to ascertain your daughter is still there."

Still there? The possibility that Amanda would not be had not occurred to her.

Edward turned his head to face the agent. "How do *you* think her ladyship should proceed?"

Hinchcliffe stroked his upper lip with his forefinger before he spoke. "Lady Sinclair, I agree with Captain Howard."

"Of course she is still there," Kate snapped, sick at the thought Amanda might not be. "I am sure the committee would not allow a girl to go into service at such a young age."

Captain Howard rose, stood behind her chair, and rested his hands on her shoulders. The warmth, seeping through her gown, calmed her. "There is the possibility Lady Amanda succumbed to illness," he said gently.

Kate stiffened. She turned to look up at him. He had voiced her worst fear. She stared at the green wallpaper which resembled watered silk. At this moment, it reminded her of a heaving ocean threatened by storms. Although tears filled her eyes, Kate blinked them away and summoned her courage. "Don't mince your words, sir, you mean Amanda might be dead, but you are wrong. I am sure you are wrong." If she told them she believed Charles, when he said he would know if his twin had died, surely the captain and the agent would look askance at her.

In the mirror above the mantel, Kate saw the captain bend as though he would press a kiss on the top of her head. He did not. Instead, he nodded at the agent.

Hinchcliffe coughed before he spoke. "Lady Sinclair, should Captain Howard be right, and if the purpose of your visit to the workhouse becomes public knowledge, impostors will claim to be Lady Amanda."

Kate's hand gripped her fan. After Mister Milton told her the truth about Amanda, she had tried to thrust every unpleasant possibility to the back of her mind. Her shoulders slumped. Where was the confident, decisive lady who traded on equal footing with men? Her hand crept to the bunch of fragrant violets pinned to her stays.

"My apologies, Captain, I forgot to thank you for the posy."

172

"My pleasure. Should I purchase a basketful next time?"

"No, no," she replied, her thoughts elsewhere.

Edward removed his hands from her shoulders and returned to his chair.

By tomorrow, her return to town would be common knowledge. On the next day, she would be expected to make the best of her appearance and hold her levee. Kate fingered her hair. Though her mother's comments about her hairstyle stung, she did not intend to alter it. How shallow of her to think of her hair at such a time. Yet for once, only once, could her mother not have shown compassion?

What to do or say? How unlike her to lack concentration and be unsure of how to act. She focussed on her dilemma. "Hinchcliffe, I will tell you all I know about my daughter and you may make inquiries. In the meantime, I shall become a patroness of The London Workhouse. As a patroness, surely no one will question my motivation for visiting it and making enquiries concerning the children's welfare."

Edward shook his head. "You must be patient. Suppose someone connects you with Hinchcliffe's visit. No matter how good he is at his task, there is always a risk. Imagine the unpleasant gossip and speculation if you gave the ton and the broadsheets cause for suspicion."

"I agree with Captain Howard," Hinchcliffe said.

She pressed her hand to her throat. Only her iron will kept her seated instead of allowing her to pace up and down. "Both of you are over-cautious."

Hinchcliffe's head bobbed up and down. "Perhaps we are too wary, but I advise you to take no risk,

173

however small. My lady, will you not trust me to maintain my discretion while making every endeavour to find Lady Amanda? Now tell me whatever you know about her."

While Kate complied, she glanced at the captain from time to time. "Yet I cannot think my daughter is the young actress the actor mentioned. She is not yet fourteen, so I doubt the committee would have allowed her to leave the London Workhouse."

When she finished, Hinchcliffe frowned. "Mister Milton's description of Lady Amanda is very helpful."

Kate indicated the picture painted by the captain. "Perhaps that is a portrait of the child we seek."

Hinchcliffe smiled. "I hope this matter will have a happy conclusion. I doubt not, that if I grease some palms, it will not be difficult to find your daughter— presuming she still lives." He bowed. "Give me leave to depart and be about your business."

The door closed behind the man.

Kate swallowed hard. "Captain Howard, when I awoke this morning, I hoped I would be reunited with Amanda today. Now, after waiting for more than twelve long years, you and Hinchcliffe say I must be cautious." She waved her hand at him. "No, please don't explain your reasons again. Both of you are right, yet it is hard, extremely hard, when all I want to do is to find my girl."

Edward stood, grasped her hands, and drew her up into his embrace.

To her amazement, she remained quiescent in his arms, resting her head on his shoulder. How long they stayed thus she knew not, but she allowed herself to be comforted by the faint scent of the sea that clung to his coat and the spicy toilet water that filled her nostrils while she leaned against him.

Amanda. Kate scarce knew how to contain her impatience until Hinchcliffe reported to her. She would ride in the park, her thoughts her only company. She withdrew from Captain Howard's arms. "Thank you for your good advice."

Chapter Fourteen

After their consultation with Hinchcliffe, the countess left the green salon before Edward could bow. Extraordinary to have held her so close with compassion not tinged with lust. Even more strange to realise how vulnerable Kate was. Although, when they first met, Edward discerned her sorrow, he had not suspected the depth of her grief. He could paint her a hundred times and each picture would reveal a different aspect. And each aspect would depict her allure. He whistled low. Perhaps, like the legendary sirens whose sweet songs enticed seamen to their deaths, her fascination was dangerous. Maybe it demanded too much of him.

With slow footsteps, he made his way to the front door. Simon opened it and the wind buffeted Edward as he crossed the road. On the other side, he gave the boy a penny for sweeping his path clear of debris. Someone clapped him on the back. He swung around to look at his friend, Captain Lindsay's, face.

"What brings you to London?"

"While my ship, *The Heart of Oak*, is being refitted, I received orders to report to the Admiralty. What of you? Will there be a court martial?" Keith Lindsay, with whom he had served when they were lieutenants, frowned. "If there *is* one, and you are judged guilty, nothing could be more unfair. You alone found the courage to put an end to that brute of a

176

captain's bullying. Discipline, there *must be* aboard ship, but not that which amounts to a licence to murder."

How he missed the sea, the feel of his feet on the deck, his excitement when he spied a distant sail knowing not if it were friend or enemy. "Shall we repair to a coffeehouse?" Edward asked.

"Yes, but which one?"

"Mariners. Who knows, we might meet old friends there."

Lindsay doffed his hat to a girl who was followed by a lackey laden with parcels. She sniffed. He looked the other way.

"As pretty a piece as ever I saw." Lindsay chuckled.

"What about that girl in Folkestone to whom you vowed eternal love?"

"Unkind of you to remind me. What of you? Have you met anyone to tempt you into the parson's noose?"

Marriage? Did he want to marry Kate?

Lindsay roared with laughter and slapped him on the back. "Hesitation from you, of all men. Who is the fortunate lady?"

"You are mistaken."

"Am I? And there I was thinking you looked lovesick." He sighed. "Well, it would not be a bad thing for *me* to be lovesick. My mother insists it is time to tie the knot. The problem is that I don't like any of her candidates for the position of Captain Lindsay's wife and, alack, I have few acquaintances in London to introduce me to suitable ladies."

Edward laughed. "After our visit to the coffeehouse, wait on my godmother, Mrs Radcliffe,

177

with whom I am putting up. There is little she enjoys more than matchmaking."

"No maypoles. No squinters," Lindsay warned.

"Of course not." Edward hailed a hackney. "Mariners," he instructed the driver.

* * *

A gust of wind urged Edward and Lindsay forward through the door and into the noisy, smoke-filled coffeehouse. They made their way to the counter which was presided over by a good-looking female.

A flirtatious gleam appeared in her eyes. "What's your pleasure, gentlemen?"

Edward handed her four pennies. "A bowl of coffee apiece."

She indicated a lad of some ten years or more dressed in breeches, full-sleeved shirt, and apron. "He'll serve you."

Edward seized Lindsay by the arm and guided him to a bench to prevent his friend making advances toward the woman. "Don't venture down that road unless you would welcome the pox."

They sat facing the fire, above which lidded iron pots of water hung from hooks. The boy soon set bowls of steaming coffee on the trestle table before them. Edward laughed at the expectant look on the child's face. "A penny for your trouble."

The coin disappeared into a pocket before the boy darted off to serve another customer.

Edward sighed.

"Want to be back on board?"

"Yes, the wait is interminable but my uncle, Admiral Rooke, will see me right."

"All very well for those with grand connections," Lindsay teased.

Edward laughed as he punched his fist playfully.

Equally playful, Lindsay parried the blow.

Oh it was good to be with an old friend.

Lindsay pointed to one of the many frames hanging on the wall. "A lock of mermaid's hair," he mocked. "And look at the horseshoes. One would think one was in a farrier's shop." He eyed a shelf. "Do you see those pills and potions? Nectar from the East to rejuvenate a man. I am surprised they don't claim all those remedies are as infallible as the Pope."

"Howard, Lindsay, as I live and breathe."

They looked up at an elderly man—with a turban on his head—who wore a rust-coloured banyan. Both of them stood to salute the senior officer. "Captain Dennison," they choroused.

"Nay, lads, I've retired. I live nearby with m'married daughter. Sit yourselves down. No need to salute." Two gentlemen on the bench opposite Edward and Lindsay moved to make room for Dennison. "Boy," he shouted. "Coffee laced with rum." He gazed at Edward. "Heard about your trouble, m'lad. Can't condone insubordination. I ran a tight ship but none called me tyrant. Never did approve of bullies. Well, who knows better than the two of you? Those were the days."

Edward retained a soft spot for the old man who had always encouraged him to set his sights high. "Indeed they were, sir."

Captain Denison eyed the fine glass lantern, inadequate to completely illuminate the coffee shop. "More light is needed, I can scarce see." He peered through the tobacco smoke. "By my faith, there's young Manners. Now he's a likely lad. What's he doing in London?" He waved to attract Manners's attention.

The lieutenant made his way to them and saluted.

"What news?" Edward asked.

"I am on shore leave, after serving on *The Dauntless*, one of a fleet of frigates which escorted merchant ships through the Mediterranean and back. French privateers attacked us. They sank *The Swift* before a favourable wind came up. Damnation to the Froggie king, say I."

"Amen," Lindsay seconded.

Edward's stomach rumbled. "Lindsay, shall we go to an ordinary, to partake of meat pies and ale?"

"By all means," Lindsay said. "Good day to you, Manners."

The lieutenant saluted and made his way back to his friend.

Edward stood and touched his hat. "Captain Dennison, will you join us?"

"No thank you, my boy, m'daughter expects me to take m'victuals with her."

* * *

In the street, Edward took several deep breaths to clear his throat of pipe smoke. "There is a tolerable ordinary on the corner."

180

"Good." Lindsay eyed a fashionably dressed girl on the opposite side of the road. "Now there's a sight for a man after ten months at sea. What do *you* say?"

"I have naught to say on the subject. Come on, I am famished. By the way, please don't ogle the ladies at my godmother's house." He laughed and slapped Lindsay on the back. "You are like a volcano. Let us hope some ice maiden does not quench your fire."

No sooner did he speak than he remembered Kate garbed in white with diamonds at her bosom, in her ears, and hair. "I beg your pardon?" he said, after realising Lindsay spoke to him.

"I swear London becomes noisier each time I visit it. A man cannot hold a proper conversation. I assured you I will do nothing to displease Mrs Radcliffe."

Edward smiled. Perhaps his godmother would bring Jane Martyn to Lindsay's attention, instead of continuing her attempt to interest *him* in the young lady. For the moment, only the fascinating, indomitable Lady Sinclair, who skilfully disguised her vulnerability, interested him.

* * *

Edward finished his pork pie, cheese, and potted onions, then pushed his platter aside.

After paying the bill, he stood looking down at his friend. "Shall we go to my godmother's house? By now her salon will be crowded. She is sure to scold me if I don't attend."

His friend wiped his mouth with his kerchief. "Lead the way."

A brisk walk took them to Mrs Radcliffe's house. When the front door opened, they were assaulted by a babble of voices. Edward and Lindsay handed their capes and canes to lackeys before ascending the stairs to the salon, where Edward could hardly help noticing many feminine eyes appraising them.

For a moment, Edward—with Lindsay by his side—stood still, glancing around the salon, made light by many windows and mirrors. "Come," he said, leading his friend past portraits of magnificently dressed personages, to the sofa where his godmother held court.

"May I present my erstwhile shipmate, Captain Lindsay?"

The captain bowed, flourishing his handkerchief so low that it nearly swept the floor.

"Welcome, Captain. Are you related to Lord Lindsay of Stoke?"

"His third son, madam."

"Ah, I remember him well. Why does he not frequent town anymore?"

"He is too devoted to his estates to venture into the metropolis."

Frances Radcliffe patted the sofa. "Do sit next to me and tell me about your dear mama. If I am not mistaken she is the daughter of the late Sir Hugo and Lady Mellors."

"That is correct, madam."

Edward stifled his amusement. Without doubt, after his godmother established that Lindsay's lineage was impeccable, she would introduce him to eligible young ladies.

A chortle escaped Sir Newton, who stood behind the sofa looking down at Mrs Radcliffe. Edward guessed the gentleman understood her questions were a preliminary to matchmaking.

Frances fluttered her fan. "Surely, Captain Lindsay, your parents will come to town to introduce your sisters to society."

As though he seemed confused by his hostess's rapid questions, Lindsay hesitated before he replied. "Alas, madam, I have no sisters, but I do have three splendid brothers, two of whom are married."

Frances glanced from Lindsay to Edward. "Have you heard the shocking news about the Martyns?"

Had his godmother given up hope of interesting him in Mistress Martyn and decided to introduce her to Lindsay? Yet, if the news were scandalous, why should she do so? He scrutinised her anxious face. "What has happened?"

"The Martyns are distraught. Their daughter has disappeared."

Startled, Edward continued gazing at his godmother. "I am sorry to hear that."

Frances dabbed tears from her eyes before she surveyed the salon, glancing from one pair of curious feminine eyes to another. "Have you met Miss Hargreaves, Edward?" She stood. "Come, you must put all thought of Mistress Martyn out of your head."

In spite of her words, Edward sensed his godmother's distress and patted her on the back. Where could Mistress Martyn be? His mind drifted to the day he had met the young lady. After his godmother introduced them for the first time, Mistress Martyn followed the gentleman dressed in puce into the garden.

What was his name? Ah yes, Lord Kershaw. *Could his lordship have anything to do with her disappearance?* Although his godmother had failed to kindle his interest in the heiress, he hoped no harm had befallen her. It was not uncommon for wealthy women to be kidnapped and forced into marriage.

The fan fluttered again. "Edward, don't dawdle. Captain Lindsay, please give me your arm."

With Sir Newton at his side, Edward followed his godmother through the fashionably dressed throng. Torn between amusement and irritation, he assumed Miss Hargreaves must be another heiress.

According to his godmother, before he took up residence in her house, the salon had never been so crowded with eligible young women. "Nothing," she had declared, "is more likely to attract visitors than a handsome bachelor with means sufficient to support a wife."

Edward sighed, bored by mothers who all but flung their daughters at him. Would these matrons be so eager to secure him for a son-by-law if they ever studied a newspaper or concerned themselves with any matter outside of fashion and gossip? Should his uncle fail him, as the result of a court martial, he might be discharged from service or even worse.

A quarter of the way across the salon, a buxom woman tapped his arm with her fan. "Captain Howard, allow me to introduce my daughter."

He had no interest in the unfortunate horse-faced girl, primped out in pale pink silk, unflattering to her sallow complexion. The mother gripped his arm to prevent him from following Lindsay and his godmother.

For a moment, Sir Newton regarded him enigmatically. Then he bowed to mother and daughter before he sauntered after Mrs Radcliffe.

"Shall I have the pleasure of seeing you at Lady Ancaster's rout?" Edward asked the young lady politely while easing his arm from the woman's grasp.

"Yes, Captain. I look forward to it." The young lady simpered.

She seemed pathetically grateful for his attention. Her mother beamed. The lady's aggressive manner was not the girl's fault. He made an effort. "I shall look forward to seeing you there." Before either lady could say a word, he retreated. At a safe distance, he sighed. Society contained as many perils as storms at sea.

He had made his escape only to be accosted by yet another mother, a tall thin lady who introduced her daughter—a girl so young she looked as though she would be more at ease learning her lessons than in this spacious salon. He remembered thinking Mistress Martyn would also be more at ease in the schoolroom.

After a third lady grabbed his attention with militant determination, Edward wished he had stayed at the coffee house. He remembered a lepidopterist with a cabin filled with specimens from remote parts of India. At the moment, he felt like some rare butterfly pursued by the intrepid gentleman. Well, he must be careful not to be netted by a determined female.

"Ah, there you are, Edward," Frances said. "Miss Hargreaves, allow me to present Captain Howard."

Watched by her proud parents, the dainty brunette curtsied in response to his bow. Edward concealed a grin at the sight of Lindsay, who stared at Miss Hargreaves and moistened his lips with his tongue.

He looked more closely at the young lady, gowned in apricot satin and ivory silk, a pretty enough girl with a porcelain complexion and dusky curls. But in his opinion, no female outshone Kate.

After his godmother introduced his friend to the young lady, he tapped Lindsay's arm. "Come up to my rooms, there is something I wish to show you." He inclined his head to Mrs Radcliffe and Miss Hargreaves. "Please excuse us, ladies."

Conscious of his godmother's annoyance, he dragged Lindsay to the door, their progress continuing to be interrupted by matchmaking mamas with hopeful daughters. When they finally escaped to the spacious, marble-floored hall, Edward found he could breathe deep without the cloying scent of so many competing perfumes and pomades irritating his nose.

Lindsay looked at him reproachfully. "What is important enough to drag me away from so many charming ladies?"

"Nothing. I did not wish to rouse false hopes of matrimony in some maiden's bosom."

His friend chuckled. "Miss Hargreaves is shapely, is she not?"

"Is she?"

Lindsay raised his hands in protest. "Don't tell me you are indifferent to the ladies. Why, I remember that raven-haired beauty in Gibraltar."

Edward shook his head, aware of the servants whose gossip might reach Kate. "I would prefer you not to mention such matters here."

"Very well, but if you have no objection, I shall return to the salon."

"As you please. And do call again. I am sure my godmother will make you welcome. I daresay we will meet either at the coffeehouse or our club, if not at the Admiralty."

Chapter Fifteen

Kate sat behind her desk, sorting her correspondence into separate piles: bills, letters concerning business, letters from friends, letters begging either for her patronage or money, as well as invitations to balls and other entertainments. Heaven above, she needed a secretary. She summoned her steward.

"Ah, Browne," Kate greeted her tall servant, clad in his habitual black.

He bowed low, revealing the top of his neat periwig. "I am at your ladyship's service."

She handed him the pile of bills. "Please settle these accounts immediately. I don't care to keep the tradesmen waiting."

"Very good, my lady."

"The bill for wax candles is exorbitant."

Browne looked past her at the window.

She frowned. "The servants are to be supplied with tallow candles. However, in accordance with their usual prerequisites, they may have the stubs of the wax ones. Remind them I am no fool. I can estimate how many candles are required each month."

Browne inclined his head. "I shall attend to the matter."

Alone, Kate stifled a groan. She could not banish thoughts of Amanda.

In spite of her eagerness to find her daughter, she must not withdraw from society. It would give rise to the speculation about her reason for doing so. Kate leafed through the invitations. Should she attend Lady Ancaster's soiree? Yes, perhaps Edward would be there. Would he admire her new periwinkle-blue gown and matching petticoat? Dear God, why did she care so much for his opinion? She had never been one to shilly-shally and now thoughts of Edward reduced her to being no better than a foolish girl dreaming of a handsome man.

Captain Howard's unfashionably tanned face filled her mind. Kate realised she enjoyed his friendship more and more as time passed. She dipped her crow's quill into a monogrammed silver inkpot to pen an invitation for him to dine with her and attend the theatre on Monday. She would sink her fear for Amanda's well-being into the pleasures of London life. Long ago, the uselessness of repining on her sorrows had impressed itself upon her. A lady must always present a cheerful face to the world.

Kate put down her quill. Perhaps she would meet the captain when she rode in the park. Her laugh filled the closet. What would the gossips think of her new habit, a turquoise one trimmed with gold and cut even more daringly than the scarlet which provoked criticism from staid matrons?

A letter from Hinchcliffe. After she read it, Kate stared out of the closet window. Amanda had disappeared. Hinchcliffe had written that either she had been abducted or she had run away from the workhouse. But if her girl had not been abducted, why did she run away from the workhouse where she was supposedly well looked after? Edward must have been mistaken about the kindness with which the orphans were treated. More than likely, someone had mistreated the child, so she absconded. Kate dabbed her eyes with her handkerchief. It would do no good to brood. She knew each London parish resembled a village where no stranger went unnoticed. Therefore, if her daughter lived in London she would be found. No need to think Amanda suffered a cruel fate; perhaps she had sought the protection of some person known to her before her foster parents died. Kate straightened her shoulders. She decided to instruct Hinchcliffe to pursue that line of inquiry.

Her jaw clenched; she could not, would not, sit at home fretting and worrying.

* * *

Although she did not encounter Edward during her ride, he arrived at her house before dusk. He strode into her closet, filling its feminine daintiness with the odours of leather, pomade, and spicy toilet water.

"My lady, good day to you. I trust I find you well."

"Good day, sir, indeed you find me in good health. Please be seated and tell me what brings you to my door at this hour."

"Tomorrow is Sunday. I thought you might care to accompany me to morning service at the London Workhouse."

"Is it possible? Am I allowed to do so?"

"Yes, my godmother tells me it is fashionable. The commissioners—ever conscious of their need for funds—permit visitors to attend their chapel on the

Sabbath. Who knows, there might be an opportunity to enquire about Amanda in a circuitous manner."

Kate looked at the clock. Oh, if only 'twere not too late to purchase comfits from a confectioners. She rang the hand bell.

Simon, his wig not quite straight, hurried into the closet, caught sight of his reflection in a mirror, and set the wig to rights.

"I beg your pardon, my lady?"

"I must speak to my cook. I want her to prepare at least four trays of sweetmeats, as she did at Yule for the tenants' children at Missendene," she said, as breathless as an excited child. "And I want her to make two trays of gingerbread dusted with ground cinnamon and ginger. Tell her to use only the best quality breadcrumbs."

Simon swallowed. Kate struggled to hide her amusement. Perhaps cook's ill temper scared her tall, strong servant.

After Simon withdrew, Kate clapped her hands. "I shall distribute the sweetmeats in person and scrutinise each child's face. Although my visit will have a dual purpose, I hope the poor orphans will be pleased with my gift."

Edward captured her hands and kissed the top of her head.

Surprised, she looked up at him. His eyes glowed. A crease appeared on his forehead. Wise in the way of amorous gentlemen, she released her hands. "Please be seated."

"Your enthusiasm is like that of a little girl awaiting a rare delight."

She looked at him through unshed tears. "It will be a joy and a privilege to tread the floor on which Amanda walked."

* * *

At ten of the clock, Kate sat beside Edward in her coach; the servants had loaded it with hampers of sweetmeats, shelled nuts, raisins, and her cook's famous gingerbread. Scarce able to conceal her impatience, she peered out of the window several times. Never before did a short journey seem to take so long.

Immediately after the coach drew to a halt, the groom let down the steps for Kate and Edward to alight. However, she did not wait for Edward to hand her out.

Inside, a girl wearing a dark green uniform, trimmed with scarlet piping, directed them to the chapel.

"Wait here with the hampers," Kate instructed her servants. "When the service is over, I will distribute the packages."

Kate stood near the back of the crowded chapel with its stained glass windows, an ebony crucifix, and silver vessels. The pure voices of young girls, rising to the dome, moved Kate to tears. Edward joined in the hymn but she could not summon her voice. Fortunate, she thought, smiling, for unlike her mother she was tone deaf.

She heard not a word of the sermon; instead, she scanned the children's faces beneath their white, peaked bonnets, tied under their chins with narrow bands. Here and there, curls escaped, or a curious girl stared at the wealthy visitors. *Where would Amanda have stood?*

With the other girls of her age? Kate tried to imagine her flaxen-haired, blue-eyed daughter standing with her back to the dark wood panelling.

So lost was she in imagination, Edward's light touch on her arm startled her. "Come, milady, the service is at an end."

She trembled with mingled anxiety and disappointment as she turned to leave. Most of the other visitors—many of whom she knew—recognised her and made way.

* * *

In the entrance hall, Kate smoothed her bodice with nervous hands while she waited for the children.

When the eldest girls led the others from the chapel in a column of twos, she and Edward gave a small bundle to each delighted child.

She smiled at a tall girl with curly red locks, a colour of hair frowned on by most people.

"How old are you, child?"

"Thirteen, nearly fourteen, madam."

"I thought so. What is your name?"

The young girl blushed—presumably because she was not accustomed to being singled out for attention. "Rose Bennet, madam."

"My lady," prompted an attentive instructress gowned in a grey uniform.

"My lady," Rose said.

"Is Rose a good student?" Kate asked.

The woman fingered her ear. "Yes, my lady. Although, as her red hair indicates she is quick tempered."

The colour in Rose's cheeks deepened. Resentment flashed in her eyes.

Kate sympathised with the girl. What must it be like to be an orphan, always in the company of others and at the mercy of personal comments from her superiors? She would do more than join the board of commissioners, she would employ this girl out of charity, and in the hope Rose knew where Amanda was.

"Child, my tirewoman grows old. She needs someone young and nimble on her feet to help her. Would you like me to employ you?"

The girl started. Hope dawned in her large blue eyes. "Yes, madam, I mean, my lady. I'd very much like to work for you and I'd serve you well."

"So be it, my steward shall arrange the matter."

Kate handed a bundle to the next girl in the line.

Even if Rose did not know where Amanda went after she left the workhouse, one of the other girls might.

Kate tried to think of every possibility. A dreadful thought popped into her mind. If Amanda had gone on the stage, she might have joined a band of strolling players. If so, she could be anywhere in the kingdom. Hinchcliffe must track her daughter before her own heart tore asunder.

* * *

Edward sat in his parlour, stockinged feet propped on a couch upholstered in gold velvet. He tucked a

194

matching bolster into the small of his neck and then closed his eyes.

Instead of taking his ease in his godmother's house on this pleasant morning, he longed to be with the fleet in the Mediterranean, or on the high seas, protecting British merchantmen from attack by the French. Damn the Froggies! Although England and France were not at war, Louis XIV raised no objection to acts of piracy by French ships of the line.

Edward frowned. Confound the Admiralty for its tardiness. How long would it take his uncle to restore him to service in the navy? He did not enjoy languishing on half pay. Well, he for one would not welcome the bloody business of war, yet when war came, as it must, surely he would be given command of a ship. The country would need every able-bodied, experienced officer. He tapped his fingers on the arm of his chair. If he served with distinction, he might be promoted.

Although inaction irked him, he hoped to triumph in another battle unconnected to the navy. "Kate, oh, Kate," he whispered, recalling her beautiful features. He twisted his cabochon ruby ring—a legacy from his late father—around and around his finger. What would Father have thought of Kate, whose poise was as fragile as thin ice? Like him, would his perspicacious parent have seen hints of the tortured woman behind the gay mask she affected in public?

Kate was the core of his heart's passionate desire. Each time he saw her, he read new anxiety in the taut line of her jaw. To divert his mind from thoughts of her anxiety and pain, he picked up the copy of Gomberville's romantic Mexican novel *Polexandre,* borrowed from his godmother's well-stocked library. Although he was not in the habit of reading novels, he had wanted to read this one since a friend mentioned that, on the evening prior to his execution, the first King Charles bequeathed his copy of the book to Lindsay's ancestor, the Earl of Lindsay. Thinking of the ill-fated king, Edward snorted with contempt for the Parliamentarians. What did their crime of regicide accomplish for the kingdom? In his opinion—little.

Edward turned the pages to find his place in the novel. Despite several attempts, he could not concentrate. An image of Kate's face replaced the text. The book slipped from his fingers onto the floor. What did he want? The answer came to mind. He wanted to expunge Kate's pain, to make her laugh like a carefree girl, and to give her the gift of joy, the like of which she had never experienced before.

A knock on the door jerked him from his thoughts.

"Come in," he called.

Newton entered, every inch The Exquisite, in pearl grey silk and a pale pink waistcoat embroidered with silver.

Edward stood and bowed. "Please sit, sir. Will you partake of a glass of muscadine wine?"

Poised on the edge of the seat, the good-natured gentleman accepted his offer. "Won't beat around the bush, m'boy, come to ask you about the Earl of Sinclair. You are close to the countess, so I thought you might want to know the youngster was pointed out to me dressed in a bodice and skirts in the streets of London." He shook his head. "Stap me, if I am not shocked."

Amanda! Had Sir Newton seen Amanda? "Oh Lord, surely you are mistaken, sir, if not it might have been a harmless prank."

Newton gazed into the golden wine. "Perhaps. We have all done reckless things when young. Unless—"

"Unless, what?"

"'Tis said we all have replicas of ourselves." He regarded Edward across the rim of his glass. "To be frank, although I said that I agreed with my friend and distracted his attention, I don't think it was Sinclair. I am almost certain that I saw a girl. True, she looked like the earl, yet despite of the same fair hair, blue eyes, and a similar build, in my mind the youngster was most definitely female."

Edward's mind raced to the obvious conclusion. "Where did you see her?"

"In Drury Lane, outside the Theatre Royal, in the company of a gentleman." Newton sipped the rest of his wine.

God save any young girl abroad in that area known for its bagnios, pimps, brothels, and gambling dens.

"You look shocked, m'boy. Is the coincidence of any significance to you?"

He must guard his expression. "Of course not, sir, I merely wondered if the girl is one of those unfortunates forced into a life of prostitution."

"You are blunt."

"My apologies. I am in the habit of being forthright. Now, please humour my curiosity. What impression do you have of her?"

"She wore a gown gaudy enough for her to be a bird of paradise, but unlike such creatures, she did not mask her face with a vizard."

"And the man who accompanied her?"

The expression in Newton's habitually lazy eyes sharpened. "Do you know something about the girl?"

Edward shook his head. "Please humour me, sir."

"The old man wore plain black. He might be a man of the cloth. A tutor or suchlike."

Gentlemen garbed in respectable clothes were as likely as others to seek the services of any one of a multitude of child prostitutes. In order not to further arouse Newton's suspicions, Edward posed no more questions. "Some more wine, sir?"

"Yes, thank you. Tell me, do you think Lady Sinclair's husband banished her because that girl who looks so like their son, put a cuckoo in her nest?"

"Sir," Edward protested, aware of hot colour flooding his cheeks.

"No need to either redden up or get on your high horse with me, m'boy. I know you have a particular fondness for the lady, but in m'opinion, the girl whom I saw, resembles her ladyship too closely for it to be a coincidence."

Edward pursed his lips. Newton had made an obvious assumption, one more believable than the real explanation. He sought for a reply worthy of the fencer of words seated opposite. "Did you not say everyone has a double, Sir Newton?"

"Not sure I believe it. Question is, shall I mention the matter to the countess?"

"If I were you, sir, I would not."

Newton, a connoisseur not only of fashion but also of *objets d'art*, picked up a silver snuff box set with a ruby. "A pretty trinket. Yours?"

"Yes, one of the spoils of war from a Froggie captain."

"Those?" Newton asked, indicating a pair of oil paintings, the first of a frigate in a safe harbour, the second of the same frigate at sea.

"Take no notice of them. They are painted by an indifferent hand."

Newton rose to examine them. "In m'mind the artist has more than his fair share of talent. How much did you pay for them?"

"Nothing, sir."

Quizzing glass raised to his eye, Newton peered at the signature. "Yours. By God, m'boy. Knew you paint, never knew you were so talented."

"I amuse myself thus, to while away otherwise tedious hours at sea." An urge to once more paint Kate, not from memory or sketches, but in the flesh, seized Edward. He wanted to depict her in deep shadows, beyond which the sun poured its radiance on lush fields, and then if her fortune changed, in full sunshine.

Newton broke in upon his reverie. "Will be honoured if you agree to paint a seascape for me."

"Your wish is my command, sir."

"'Pon m'word, nice manners." Newton chuckled. "I understand why Mrs Radcliffe is fond of you."

Edward's nostrils flared.

"No need to take on, boy. Now, I must be on m'way before your godmother wonders what keeps me from her. She worries, you know, and it distresses me to see her disturbed."

"Yes, I know she frets, but tell me, sir, is she anxious about something in particular? Can I serve her in any way?"

199

"Yes, Mrs Radcliffe is desperate for that protégée of hers to be found. Mind you, I told her she might have misjudged the girl. Maybe Mistress Martyn has eloped. On the other hand, she stands to inherit a fortune. She might have been abducted. In either case, the matter preys on my dear lady's mind. It will not do, it really will not do."

"That young girl abducted? I hope not." Edward frowned. He remembered the young fop Mistress Martyn flirted with when using the language of the fan. Well, he for one did not blame the girl if she did not want to marry the charismatic, but questionable Fenton whom Mrs Martyn favoured.

Newton took a pinch of snuff and peered at him. "Who can say why the chit is missing?" he mused. "The Martyns are beside themselves. Glad I spoke to you. Look forward to you presenting me with my seascape."

"As I said, your wish is my command, but—" Edward began. He broke off. Useless to protest that he disliked painting from memory. In spite of Newton's amiability coupled with a good heart, he possessed an inflexible will.

Hand on the doorknob, Newton turned. "I forgot to tell you Mrs Radcliffe has completed her toilette. She expects you to join her in the salon." He gestured with his handkerchief, held between the thumb and forefinger of his right hand. "Don't protest. Whatever the lady desires, she must have. Make haste to join her, m'boy."

Chapter Sixteen

Immaculate in blue and white and every inch a naval officer, Edward entered his godmother's crowded salon.

From her seat on a sofa cunningly placed with its back to the window, Frances Radcliffe held her hands out to him. He clasped them and bent over to salute her on the lips. "I trust you are in good health, madam."

"Well enough. Well enough for a woman of my age. I must not complain."

He smiled at her, his artist's eyes appreciating her pale blue and blush-pink ensemble and her skilfully applied cosmetics. He bowed again. "You are as beautiful as ever."

She released her hands from his. Her ivory fan—painted with flirtatious beauties and their swains—fluttered. "You are mistaken, Edward. Beauty fades. Why else would I sit with my back to the light of day, if not to conceal the ravages of time?"

"Time deals kindly with you, madam. With the passing of years, your heart grows ever kinder."

Frances patted the sofa. "Sit by me."

"Godmother, cast your mind back to the day when you introduced me to Mistress Martyn, when a young man dressed in puce and cream visited you."

Surely his godmother would remember. She and Sir Newton took an extraordinary interest in the latest modes. They often whiled away the time with discussions of fashionable people's jewellery, snuff boxes, and clothes.

The fan stilled. "Ah, yes, young Lord Kershaw. Kershaw's late father was one of my suitors." She wafted her fan to and fro. "'Twas exciting after my parents announced my betrothal to Mister Radcliffe."

He sat beside her. "Indeed."

"My suitor, young Kershaw's father, threatened to blow his brains out if I refused to renege on the marriage contract with Radcliffe and marry him instead."

"If the father was as handsome as the son, I would understand if you were tempted."

"Not for a moment. The Kershaws come from old stock, but even then their estate was small." The fan stilled. Her eyes peeped at him over its half circle of ivory struts and painted silk. "Besides, he did not tempt me because, as my dear parents knew, Mister Radcliffe engaged all my affections."

The butler tapped his rod on the wooden floor. "Lady Sinclair."

Frances's lips compressed in a hard line before she rose and curtseyed.

Edward's chest tightened while he made his bow. Did his godmother dislike her ladyship, in spite of the sympathy she expressed over that unnatural marriage? Surely not. Doubtless his godmother's pursed lips indicated only disapproval of the disparity between his age and Kate's.

"Please be seated, Countess," Frances said after he and Kate greeted each other. "I believe you are acquainted with all my guests."

Kate extended her cane, ornamented with a knot of cream ribbons which matched the colour of her attire, and then rested her hand on its gold knob.

"'Fore God, madam," Newton said with obvious admiration and appreciation, "by carrying a cane, you emulate the gentlemen. The effect is arresting."

"If a gentleman may set the fashion by wearing a red hat, a lady may set the fashion by carrying a cane," Kate said, her eyes alight with laughter.

Newton executed an elaborate bow. "*Touché.*"

"You are too gallant, sir."

Frances coughed.

"Pardon me, madam," Kate began, "for taking up your devoted cavalier's time. I must greet old friends." She extended her hand. "Captain Howard, your arm, if you please."

Kate smiled at him. He yearned to kiss one of the enchanting dimples which had appeared on either side of her mouth.

He led her around the perimeter of the salon at a slow pace. She ignored the other visitors, indicating Mrs Radcliffe and Sir Newton with a graceful wave of her hand. "They are devoted to each other. I cannot understand why they don't marry."

Edward glanced back at his godmother and her beau. "Do you not know their sad tale?"

"Sad?"

"Yes, although it took place so long ago that most people have forgotten. My father told my older brother that Sir Newton wed a beautiful young heiress in accordance with his parents' wishes. One night, an accidental fire started in Lady St John's bedroom. She suffered dreadful burns which also scarred her face."

Kate glanced at Newton. "How dreadful, what happened to her?"

"The unfortunate lady lives in a house on Sir Newton's estate. She still refuses to receive anyone, even Sir Newton."

"Blighted lives with no heirs. How they must suffer," Kate murmured.

"Indeed, and unkindest of all, heartless gossips said he and his wife never cared for each other. They even claimed he might have set fire to her room to escape the marriage."

"Outrageous. My slight acquaintance with the gentleman tells me he is kind-hearted."

"Yes, he is. Unfortunately, slander lingers like a bad smell." He patted her hand which rested lightly on his forearm. "Shall we take a turn in the garden?"

Kate hesitated before she answered. "If you promise not to flirt."

He laughed. "If and when I decide to flirt, nothing will deter me. I refuse to dance either to *your* tune or any other lady's." He smiled to soften his harsh words.

Chapter Seventeen

On the morning after Edward had spoken to Kate about Sir Newton's tragic marriage, he stood by the window in his dressing room, thinking about Kate. He desired her with an intensity with which he had never desired any other woman. The thought of her in his bed seized his imagination with such violence that he shook with passion. He forced himself to take even breaths and regain command of his unruly body.

Kate rode roughshod over all her other gallants. He would not allow her to ride roughshod over him. It would be a novelty for her, which might earn him her respect.

With all the ardent desire of a stripling in the throes of first passion, he gazed down at the street hoping to see her. Rain pattered against the glass. Pedestrians hurried along. Wrapped in a midnight blue cloak and hood, she emerged from the house. As if she sensed him staring down at her, she paused for a moment and looked up in his direction, but he did not think she glimpsed him behind the windows veiled in thin muslin. A bearer opened the door emblazoned with Kate's coat of arms before she stepped into her sedan chair.

He watched the conveyance proceed along the road. Should he tell her he suspected the girl Newton saw in Drury Lane was her missing daughter? Yet suppose the child had been lured into prostitution? If so, would Amanda have sunk too low for redemption? What would Kate's reaction be if that were the case?

The wisest course would be to see if he could find out anything concerning Amanda's whereabouts, as well as also consulting Hinchcliffe about Sir Newton's comment.

He removed his coat, fetched his sketchbook, and sat at the table. Within an hour he completed a small drawing of Charles attired as a female. He would use it to pursue inquiries regarding the boy's sister. Although London had grown larger since his birth, it was still possible to trace someone. For the time being, he would search in the vicinity of Drury Lane. If fortune favoured him, someone there, in The Strand or possibly Covent Garden, Long Acre, or St Martin's Lane, would know the girl.

What of the other missing girl? A gallant impulse impelled him to sketch Mistress Martyn. For his godmother's sake, he might as well search for the missing heiress while looking for Amanda.

Poor Mistress Martyn! The most likely explanation was that she had run away from home to escape being bullied into marrying the libertine, Fenton. Edward would instruct the agent to ask if anyone knew of the Martyn heiress's whereabouts while searching for Kate's young daughter.

Edward tapped his chin with his forefinger. He wondered why the Martyns favoured Fenton's suit. It was deuced odd. After all, Mistress Martyn's expectations were substantial enough to attract more worthy suitors.

He set aside the sketch. Perhaps the Martyns were unaware of Fenton's dubious reputation. Surely they did not know he frequented male brothels in and around Covent Garden. In all probability, Fenton had charmed the mother, making her believe he was fit to wed Mistress Martyn. Did the ambitious woman have her heart set on her daughter marrying into the nobility? Well, if it were so, he was safe from his godmother's ploys. Despite Godmother's attempt to arrange his marriage to the young lady, her mother would not accept a mere captain as a son-by-law.

Perplexed, he shook his head. If Mrs Martyn desired her daughter to have a title, why did Jane Martyn hesitate to declare her interest in Lord Kershaw to her parents? Money? Most likely because their fortunes were unequal. One day the girl would be much richer than Kershaw.

* * *

Propped up by bolsters and pillows in linen covers, Kate sipped her morning chocolate. Thoughts of Charles and Amanda filled her mind. Suddenly, the drink tasted bitter. Kate could not partake of another mouthful. She tensed, asking herself if Rose the orphan might have information about Amanda's whereabouts. She shut her eyes, hoping against hope the agent would find her girl. While breath remained in her body, she would never give up the search for her daughter. Her throat constricted. She breathed with difficulty. What if she never found Amanda?

Kate put the chocolate dish on the silver tray. Another meaningless day without her children stretched ahead.

When she first put aside her black mourning clothes, her London levees amused her. Now, a tiresome waste of precious minutes, they wearied her. She considered discontinuing them. After all, she did not wish to encourage the attentions of any other gentlemen of Mister Stafford's ilk. Only Captain Howard interested her, and he infuriated her by refusing to attend her levees. Anyone might think he was a puritan.

Kate slid down in the bed. She rested her head against a pillow. Without her son and daughter, what should she do with the rest of her life? Spend her mornings entertaining men like Stafford? The prospect of interminable social rounds dimmed every bit of joy she ever knew.

The captain intruded on her thoughts. From the moment she first encountered him, he attracted her. Confused, she recalled the astonishing thrill running through her, from the tips of her toes to the nape of her neck, when Captain Howard's cool, silky lips touched hers in a formal greeting for the first time.

Without question, Edward Howard posed a threat to her peace of mind. He knew more about her than any other person. Little by little he had insinuated himself into her life so slowly that she had scarce been aware of it.

She rang the hand bell.

Her tirewoman came from the dressing room.

Kate indicated the tray. "You may take it."

In unusual silence, the servant obeyed and put it on a small, high table by the bed.

"Jessie."

"Yes, my lady."

"I shall not receive any gentlemen this morning."

"If you deny your gallants entrance, they will take offence," Jessie warned.

The rope of Kate's plait lay uncomfortably along her spine. She pulled it forward over one shoulder, untied the ribbon, and then freed her hair, releasing the delicate perfume of lavender, roses, and lily-of-the-valley. Would the captain admire her hair if he ever again saw it unbound? Would he comment on its scent?

Jessie rolled her eyes. "What excuse shall I make for your not receiving anyone?"

With perfected daintiness, Kate raised her shoulders. "I care not. Instruct the porter to tell them to go to the devil."

"My lady!"

Kate twitched the ruffles edging the sleeves of her night rail into place. "Oh, say I have the plague. It will send them scuttling to safety."

"I shall say you are so afflicted by the megrims that you need peace and quiet so you cannot receive anyone."

No, she neither needed peace and quiet nor the attentions of her admirers whose flattery bored her. She needed to divert her mind, but how? Foolish to be wearied by London life with its many distractions. Perhaps she should take the air in St James Park, wait upon friends, seek out the newest fashions, shop, and consult her mantua maker. If her mind dwelt on her children, she would turn mad.

"Bread and butter, my lady?" Jessie asked.

Kate shook her head.

"It's thin cut. The bread's freshly baked. The butter arrived from Missendene yesterday."

"Even a morsel would stick in my throat, Jessie."

"You don't eat enough to nourish a sparrow, my lady."

"Don't fuss over me."

Her tirewoman ignored the admonition and handed her a plate. "Mark my words, Lady Sinclair, if you don't eat more, you'll be little more than a skeleton before it's time for your winding sheets."

"Nonsense, stop scolding me. Take that bread and butter away." She frowned. "Please give me my hand mirror."

After Kate looked at her reflection, she ran her forefinger down the hollow of her right cheek. If she did not eat, she risked looking like an old hag. "Give me the bread and butter, Jessie." She forced herself to eat two slices of the fragrant bread and then drank chocolate laced with cream.

Irritated by her insistent tirewoman, she dabbed her mouth with a monogrammed napkin. "Satisfied, Jessie?"

"For now, my lady, if I may say so, I hope you'll sup well. To tempt your appetite, I suggest you instruct Cook to serve a broth alongside the meat and fowl. I know you're partial to broth. I also suggest you instruct her to make an almond pudding. It's always been one of your favourites. I daresay you would relish it."

"When you finish nagging me, Jessie, go and break your own fast." She changed her mind. . "No, stay for a moment."

Arms at her side, Jessie stood by the bed.

"You look tired. It is selfish of me to expect you to stay up at night, waiting to undress me when I return home."

"Don't worry about me, my lady. I sleep when I can."

"At your age, it is not good enough."

Jessie rolled her eyes. "Well, there's naught to be done about it. What would you do without me?"

"Oh, I could not manage if you retired from my service—like my old cook because I asked her to make gingerbread for the children at the London Workhouse."

Jessie clicked her teeth. "If you don't mind my saying so, Cook did not mind making it. She objected to your wanting it so quickly and having to stay up half the night to prepare it."

Perhaps her order had been unreasonable. Kate fixed her attention on Jessie. "It brings me back to the point I was making. You should not forgo your sleep, so I have employed a girl to help you."

"My lady, I can look after you as I've always done!"

"I hope you will continue to do so for many years. Nevertheless I shall rely on you to train her."

Back straight, her shoulders squared, and chin held high, Jessie sniffed.

"I know I can trust you to be kind to my protégée, whose name is Rose Bennet. She will arrive today from the London Workhouse." Jessie knew her so well that Kate did not want to arouse Jessie's suspicions concerning her reason for employing Rose. "Those to whom the Lord has given should share their wealth. I am now a patron of the workhouse. My intention is to help the unfortunate children, all of whom are somewhat pale. Small groups of them will visit my manor house in Surrey. I never go there so it should be put to good use. The children will benefit from a change of air and country food."

Jessie lowered her chin a little. "I'll take Rose under my wing because you want me to, although I can assure you I'm capable of tending to your needs. Now, with your permission, I'll go to break my fast."

"You have no reason to be anxious, Jessie. You are my most trusted and valued servant."

"Thank you, my lady."

Her tirewoman beamed at her and left the room.

Kate leafed through the latest edition of *The Gazette* scanning the advertisements.

"May Dew with the power to cure every Manner of unsightly Skin Eruption and restore the Bloom of Youth." She snorted. *Heaven help any poor fool who trusted a quack doctor.*

Kate read an advertisement offering a reward for news of Mistress Martyn. Tormented with anxiety regarding Amanda, she sympathised with the girl's parents.

She scrutinised an advertisement for an Almanac.

"*On Friday next will be published Dr James' Almanacs Bound in Red Leather, with Paper to Write at a cost to the Public of Three Shillings.*"

Kate took a deep breath. Some respectable authors of almanacs practised as physicians, astrologers, and clairvoyants. She would confer with a clairvoyant in the hope he could divine Amanda's whereabouts. *What was the name of the doctor whom Lady Rutherwycke consulted?* Her ladyship had explained that he not only produced a popular almanac, cast horoscopes, and treated the sick, but that he was also a respectable schoolmaster—although, according to her, he exercised supernatural powers. Kate searched her memory for his name and the title of his publication. Ah, yes, *Vox Stellarum*, by Francis Moore. She would send for him. Oh, the relief of the prospect of finding out something useful.

Without delay, she must pen a note to Lady Rutherwycke asking for Mister Moore's direction.

Kate swung herself out of bed, chose her red and white striped quilted nightgown, pulled it over her night rail, and then tied the sash. Careless of her loose hair and face, innocent of cosmetics, Kate went to her closet, where she surprised a maidservant.

The girl's cheeks flamed. "I beg pardon, my lady. It's my duty to dust this room."

"You may go, Sara."

"Yes, my lady, at once, my lady."

How old was the girl? Two or three years older than Amanda?

"Wait. Sara, are you well treated here?"

"Yes, yes thank you, my lady, it's very kind of you to ask. The new cook makes sure I have enough to eat."

"The previous one did not?"

Sara shook her head.

Kate frowned. "You may go, Sara." From now on she would ensure everyone in her household ate their fill.

After penning her note, Kate sealed it by pressing her seal ring into the hot wax. She toyed with the folded paper for a moment and then stood to ring the bell for a lackey.

Simon arrived wearing an apron. "Begging your pardon, my lady, I was bringing more coal up—in case the weather turns chilly again—when I heard the bell. I didn't have time to put my coat on."

Kate handed him the note. "Tell my foot page to deliver this without delay."

"Very good, my lady."

She approached the door which Simon opened.

"Thank you." She proceeded along the landing to the top of the long flight of stairs.

A discreet cough from below halted her. She looked down at Robert Tyrell, handsome in a suit of honey-coloured velvet which flattered his fair complexion. 'Pon her word, she was in no mood to speak with Tyrell.

"Were you not told I cancelled my levee?"

"Yes, but I have considerable powers of persuasion."

One hand behind his back, the gentleman bowed low before he ascended the stairs to the second floor from where she watched him with narrowed eyes.

Tyrell bowed again before he greeted her with a light kiss on her lips. "'Fore God, milady, your beauty rivals the rising sun. Egad, you need no paint or powder, frills or furbelows."

Although her nightgown covered her from throat to toes, warmth crept into her cheeks. "Please leave," she said in an icy tone, embarrassed to be caught *en déshabillé* in these circumstances. It was acceptable to receive a group of admirers in her bedchamber, but not acceptable to be seen elsewhere in her night attire. She collected her thoughts. "Mister Tyrell, my servants were instructed to admit no one."

Tyrell might have bribed her porter. If so, she would have a sharp word with the fellow.

"Leave? The sight of you sets me on fire and more than suffices to turn my thoughts to matrimony." He removed his hand from behind his back to hand her a bouquet of double white narcissi. "My tribute to you."

"Thank you, but please go now."

Tyrell knelt. He seized her hand, crushing her fingers with his leather glove.

"My dear Lady Sinclair, I beseech you to do me the honour of becoming my wife."

Her heart raced. In her mind's eye, she recalled her wedding night, picturing the leer on her late husband's gargoyle of an elderly face. Now, she wanted to run, to hide, but her feet seemed stuck to the spot, as they had been on that dreadful night.

At last, Kate managed to tug her hand free. "This is not the time or the place for a proposal. Besides, did you not tell me you will never marry?"

A lackey answered a knock on the front door. She heard Captain Howard's voice. Her lips mouthed his Christian name.

She stood frozen in time while Tyrell knelt at her feet.

The captain looked up. He bowed. Even from a distance, she discerned his mouth tightly drawn in a contemptuous line.

Edward doffed his hat. He bowed again, this time with elegant, but exaggerated slowness that expressed his disdain.

Hot with embarrassment, the fire of shame scalded her cheeks. What must he think?

Edward turned and left the house. She reached out as though her hand could summon him back.

Kate looked down at Mister Tyrell. "You forced your proposal on me. Please leave. You are no longer welcome in my house."

The gentleman rose, his small dark eyes glinted like a rodent's. "You lack backbone, milady. The minute a gentleman seeks to draw close, you flee."

What might she say to Captain Howard? How could she prove he had not seen her on the brink of taking leave of her lover? With passion drawn from the core of her being, for the first time in her life, Kate wanted a suitor to think well of her. It surprised her. Why did she not realise before that she was on the verge of falling in love with the captain? On the verge? No, she loved him. How shameful! She loved a youngster nine years her junior who deserved to take to wife, not a cynical older woman but an innocent young girl.

Mister Tyrell snatched back the posy. "I shall place this in more deserving hands."

What a mean gentleman. A flicker of amusement cut through her confusion.

He glared at her. "I think a fair wind blows in Captain Howard's direction."

Kate glanced at him again. "I don't understand you, sir."

"Oh, I think you do. A gentle breeze blew the captain into your house. The harsh east wind blew him away. Now, like a foolish girl, you want the west wind to blow you after him. What has he to offer? He has no title, no command, and his fortune compared to yours is paltry."

"What has he to offer?" she repeated after him. "It suffices for him to be Captain Howard."

"Really? You have my pity, for you are besotted by him."

He descended the stairs and without as much as a bow. A lackey closed the front door behind him.

Kate pressed her hand to her heart. In spite of the situation, she must confront the captain in his den to find out if he had any information about Amanda.

* * *

White-hot temper and outrage curdled Edward's guts while he knocked on his godmother's front door with unnecessary force.

Even from outdoors, Edward heard the sound reverberate throughout the house. The lackey, who answered his summons, looked at him and recoiled.

Edward breathed hard. Doubtless his face reflected his rage. He did not notice Newton until he brushed past him on the landing outside the salon, causing the elderly gentleman to drop his red hat, but Edward did not pause to apologise. Instead, he hurtled up to his rooms on the third floor.

He shut the door, threw himself down onto the padded window seat, and stared across the road at a silver birch, its bark dulled by a sky, darkened with steel grey storm clouds.

"Kate," Edward groaned. He buried his face in his hands. His wrath cooled. He shuddered. What a fool jealousy made of a man. Since he first met her, he understood Kate did not adhere to rigid social conventions, and he knew she enjoyed having a string of admirers to amuse her.

A reluctant laugh escaped him. Clad in a delectable red and white striped nightgown, Kate had been eccentric enough to stand at the top of the stairs with that fop, Tyrell, at her feet. What did it signify? Very little, logic told him. If the pair were lovers, Tyrell would have taken leave of Kate in the privacy of her bedchamber, not in full view of anyone who knocked on her front door.

Edward rested his unsteady hands on his knees. Kate had often made it clear she thought of him as a mere boy. Well, he was not a boy even if, at this moment, he deserved to be called one. Only a green youth would have judged a lady guilty based on scant evidence. In his heart he had not believed Kate and Tyrell were lovers. Jealousy prompted his ill-judged frenzy. Well, at least he was man enough to recognise it.

A knock at the door stole him from his thoughts. *Damnation!* "Come," he called.

Newton entered. "You seemed helter-skelterish, m'boy. Thought it best to find out if you want to hang yourself."

"Hang myself? No such thing, sir, I would never die for a lady." Confound it, he had unintentionally betrayed himself. He changed the subject. "Please accept my apologies for my rude behaviour, sir. I trust your prized hat suffered no ill effects due to my despicable lack of manners."

Newton sank onto a low chair opposite the window. Outside the sun appeared through a gap in the dark clouds. An errant ray streamed into the room, enhancing the pure colour of Newton's sapphire ring.

Blue, a colour Kate favoured in every shade. Pale blue which matched her eyes, forget-me-not blue setting off her fair complexion to perfection. His deep sigh forced all the air from his lungs. Oh, how he burned to touch Kate's satin smooth skin.

Newton lowered his hand. "Lady Sinclair is one of the loveliest women it has ever been my privilege to see."

"Yes, she is beautiful," Edward said before Newton could continue.

Newton held up his hand. "Spare me your praise of her, m'boy. Regard m'ring. The brilliance of its gemstones and the depth of its colours remind me of the Aegean Sea."

"I am regarding it," Edward said, unable to keep his impatience from his voice.

"Jewels enchant us. Collectors covet them as much as some men covet beautiful women. It is understandable, but a woman of Lady Sinclair's calibre is as dangerous as the sirens' songs of enchantment luring sailors to their doom. If m'memory does not play me false, Ulysses plugged his men's ears with wax before he lashed his body to the ship's mast to save himself. Perhaps you should plug *your* ears and wear a blindfold."

Edward suppressed his desire to tell Newton to avoid either indirect or direct criticism of Kate. "Please come to the point, sir."

Newton inspected his ring again. "I spoke forthrightly because you are an officer in Her Majesty's navy. You must not let yourself be 'all at sea' for the sake of a lady who is The Toast of The Town. Instead of plugging your ears, wear blinkers. In other words, don't look at her ladyship."

Edward tensed. Much as he liked and respected Newton, the gentleman had no right to meddle in his business. Although he had faced the enemy at sea without a tremor, his hands quivered. "Please don't interfere, Sir Newton, and please don't take offence when I ask you to keep your unsolicited advice to yourself."

He stood to pour two glasses of the expensive Italian wine his merchant supplied on the previous day. He handed one to Newton. "Tell me what you think of this Montepulciano, sir."

Newton sipped. "Mature, fruity but dry. Yes, I like it." He ruminated. "Wines should be mature, but a young man's ladylove should not."

Enraged heat scalded Edward's cheeks. Would nothing check Newton's presumption? He tossed back his wine. "Thank you for your advice, sir, I shall bear it in mind. However, her ladyship is not, to repeat your word, my ladylove."

'Swounds, until this moment he had not realised the depth of his entanglement with Kate.

Sir Newton laughed. "Well, m'boy, judging by the way you look at the fair countess, society believes you love her."

"If you were younger I would not be able to restrain my indignation."

"Yes, yes, you might challenge me to a duel for being impudent enough to warn you in respect of the lady. Bear with me. Why do you admire the countess?"

"Because she is Kate. Yes, she is beautiful but her beauty lies not only in her face and form."

"Stap me! I do believe you love the lady and are not, as Mrs Radcliffe thinks, infatuated." Newton sipped the rest of his wine. "I must order a case of this what-do-you-call-it from the wine merchants?"

"Montepulciano," Edward ground out.

"Well, m'boy, you know your own business best. I wish you success with Lady Sinclair."

"Thank you, sir, I am glad you understand."

A bitter smile twisted Newton's lips before he replied. "I understand only too well."

Jerked from his preoccupation with Kate, who coloured many of his waking hours, Edward pitied his godmother and her ever faithful gallant. Although they had loved for so long and so deeply, they could not marry. Yet, in all honesty, he envied their shared love.

"I must take my leave of you, m'boy. Mrs Radcliffe will be wondering where I am. She does not care to be separated from me for a moment longer than necessary." As though embarrassed by revealing more than he intended, Newton cleared his throat.

"Indeed," Edward responded, "I meant it when I said you are very kind, sir." He strove to express himself without seeming mawkish. "Doubtless a good fairy arranged for Mrs Radcliffe to be my godmother. What is more, after my father died, I wished she had also arranged for you to be my godfather."

"Oh, you did not need me, your brother seems pleasant enough," Newton murmured.

Unused to speaking of personal matters, Edward emulated the elderly gentleman by clearing his throat. "Although Giles was only twenty-five when our father died, he has ever been a splendid brother. There must have been times he wished he had not been saddled with a youngster, but though he was no more than twenty-seven when our mother died, Giles was particularly kind to me. Fate could have dealt me a much harsher hand."

His eyes moist, Newton patted Edward on the shoulder. "I would be proud to have a godson like you."

Newton sauntered out of the room. Edward smiled. If he and Kate ever had a child, he would invite Sir Newton to stand as godfather. His eyebrows drew together. Had a child? What was he thinking of? Marriage? Surely not! Although he wanted Kate in his bed it did not mean he wanted to *wed* her. Yet to win Kate's hand in marriage would not be a small feat. Edward sank onto a chair. Matrimony was not something he had envisioned in the near future. Perhaps he *should* force himself to steer away from her. No, only a coward would not seek to help a lady in distress, and he had always prided himself on his courage. He must help Kate to discover the truth concerning Amanda's fate.

* * *

Newton peered into one of the gold-framed mirrors hanging between candle sconces on the walls in the corridor. He adjusted his hat and smoothed the gold facing on the cuff of his silk-velvet coat. Satisfied with his appearance, he nodded to a lackey. The man, regal in his green and gold livery, announced him to Mrs Radcliffe.

She smiled at him. "See how industrious I have been while waiting for you?" She held up her embroidery frame. "I have embroidered half a violet on my handkerchief. Is it not pretty?"

He bent over to raise her hands to his lips. "Not as pretty as you, my love."

She blushed. "Lud, how you flatter me."

Sir Newton sat next to her on the sofa. Your meddling will not do. It will not do at all." He slid his arm around her waist and drew her a little closer.

Frances returned the embroidery frame to her mahogany workbox. She shut the lid with unnecessary force. "What is your meaning, sir?"

"Edward is not only a man full grown, but whether he knows it or not, he is also a man deep in love with Lady Sinclair."

"Bah."

"You may say 'bah' as often as you wish, my love, but his mind is fixed."

"Then I pity him, for I believe his love will lead to heartbreak." Frances snapped her fan open.

The fragrance of her perfume, a blend of orange, vanilla, and attar of roses, which always reminded him of her, enveloped him. "Not if he can persuade her to marry him, for I think he sees through her affectations and cares naught for her fortune."

Her fan fell to her lap. "My poor Edward."

"You are mistaken. If he loves the fatal widow as much as we love each other, and can persuade her to wed him, he is more blessed than we." He cupped her chin in his hand, taking care to prevent his rings biting into her tender flesh. Careless of the neat arrangement of his wig's grey curls, he kissed her.

Chapter Eighteen

Kate lay in bed, the ribbons of her nightcap tied coquettishly beneath her right ear. She beckoned Rose with one hand. With her other hand, she fingered her long plait arranged to fall over her left shoulder.

Rose hurried to the bedside.

"Sit yourself down. Read to me child, before my levee begins." Kate handed Rose *The Gazette*, while simultaneously addressing Jessie. "I shall wear my violet gown with the lavender silk petticoat and stays."

"My lady, have you forgotten a gentleman tore it when he stood on the train of the gown?" Jessie tutted. "Clumsy man! As though your ladyship didn't pay a lot of money for that taffety from India."

Kate wanted to be alone with Rose, who had arrived on the previous day. However, she did not want to further exacerbate her devoted tirewoman's hostility toward the orphan. "The tear is only a small one, Jessie. First go and break your fast and then mend the gown."

"I am not hungry, my lady. Rose may eat while I lay out another gown instead of the one you've chosen."

"Jessie!" Kate's voice brooked no disobedience.

"As you please, my lady," Jessie said sulkily.

Kate raised an eyebrow. "I do please." She waited for the door to close behind her disgruntled tirewoman. "Rose," Kate said, "see if there is anything about a Mistress Martyn. If there is, read it to me."

The girl turned the pages. After a few moments, she read an advertisement offering a reward for information which led to Mistress Martyn's whereabouts.

"Rose, it is a dreadful thing for a young girl to run away. Who knows what evils might befall her. You must feel for your friend who ran away from the London Workhouse."

Rose shifted on the gilt-legged chair. She stared at the floor as though nothing in the world interested her more.

"Have you nothing to say, child?"

"I asked her not to go but she didn't listen to me. Amanda's very stubborn."

Kate tensed. "If you know what she planned, please tell me. There are wicked people only too eager to prey on a young girl's innocence."

"I don't know where she is. Shall I read some more to your ladyship?"

Kate sighed, breathing in the aroma of rosemary added to the fire in the hearth. Unlike most people, she did not practice the economy of not lighting fires when spring arrived. As for the servants, she paid them well regardless of the inconvenience of cleaning hearths and hauling wood and coal up the stairs. She could not endure cold, so for as long as a chill remained in the air, she kept her house warm.

She looked up above her bed at the blue canopy which was embroidered with brightly coloured silks. "Rose, would a gold coin persuade you to tell me all you know of your friend's plans?"

Rose shook her head. "No, because I don't know anything."

If the girl did know something in connection with her friend, she was not going to admit it. "Very well, Rose, but should you remember anything, please tell me. Now, go and break your fast."

Irritated by her lack of success, Kate got out of bed. She thrust her feet into a pair of dainty mules decorated with seed pearls. She stalked around the room and at last paused by the window. More rain! It would not deter her. Whether or not Captain Howard kept his promise to accompany her, she would attend the play at The Haymarket.

In the immediate future, she intended to visit every theatre in London in the hope of Amanda appearing on stage.

Her strength of mind and will had carried her through many previous difficulties. No obstacle would deter her from her quest.

No news from the agent. Could Hinchcliffe have communicated with Captain Howard? He might be reluctant to admit he had nothing to report concerning Amanda.

* * *

"You sent for me, Captain?" asked the butler, who appeared out of breath after climbing three flights of stair

"Yes, Perkins, I know you are well-informed, so I hope you can help me."

The man puffed out his narrow chest.

"Where does Lord Kershaw reside?"

The elderly man raised an eyebrow as though he could not believe Edward did not know. "At Kershaw House in King's Square."

"Ah, only a step away from here. I am obliged to you."

Followed by Perkins, Edward made his way to the front door, which a lackey opened for him.

"It's wet outside, Captain. May I suggest a sedan chair?" Perkins asked.

"Sailors take no notice of drizzle."

* * *

It was only a short walk to Kershaw House. Soon, Edward stood in the rain looking up at the imposing structure. Built some ten years after The Great Fire of London, it was similar to all the other dwellings around the square. The more he considered the matter, the more convinced Edward became that he would find the answer to Mistress Martyn's disappearance in this house.

He rattled the doorknocker. A shabby lackey responded. Edward handed him his card. "Captain Howard presents his compliments to Lord Kershaw and begs for a few minutes of his time."

"His lordship isn't at 'ome to visitors."

The man attempted to close the door. Edward shoved his booted foot over the threshold.

The lackey scowled. "Please 'ave the goodness to remove your foot. I want to shut the door."

"No," Edward said firmly. "I am determined to see your master. If necessary I shall use force."

227

"Now, now, sir, it's more than my position's worth to admit you." The impertinent lackey leered. "'Is lordship's on 'is 'oneymoon. 'E's not receiving visitors at this hour of the morning, though it's a queer kettle of fish if you ask me," he said in a low voice.

"Firstly, I did not ask you. Secondly, although his lordship is on his honeymoon, I still wish to see him."

If the ill-trained, over-familiar manservant had anything in common with the rest of the servants, Kershaw must be impoverished. If not, he would not tolerate such service.

"You can't see 'im."

Edward removed a purse from his coat pocket and extracted a silver coin. "Stand aside. What is your name?"

"Jem, sir." The lackey stared at the new-minted silver coin.

Edward took a step forward. "Stand aside, Jem."

Jem opened the door wide enough for the captain to enter the house. As Edward went inside, he dropped the coin into the fellow's rapacious palm.

Seeking lost damsels promised to be an expensive business. If Kershaw had not married the young lady, it would cost a pretty penny to have the sketches of Mistress Martyn printed and circulated. However, any expense would be worthwhile if it eased his godmother's fears over the young lady's well-being.

As for Kate, his beautiful Kate, she was all but out of her mind with anxiety regarding her daughter. Every penny he spent, regardless of whether he found Lady Amanda and Mistress Martyn or not, would be worthwhile, for he could then rest assured he did his best to trace their whereabouts.

While Jem shuffled off to announce him, Edward looked around the dusty entrance hall. By God, he might be an enlightened naval officer, but any lazy rating who failed to scrub the decks until they were spotless would receive a tongue lashing from him, if not worse. Judging by the dirty steps leading up to the house, as well as the state of the hall, he deemed Kershaw to be in desperate need of a wife. If Mistress Martyn had married the young whippersnapper, she might be the very one to put everything in order. After all, from an early age, tradesmen's daughters were trained to be good housewives.

A sneeze—doubtless the result of the dust—heralded Jem's return. "His lordship can spare a moment or two of 'is valuable time. May I take yer 'at and cloak?"

Edward smoothed the folds of the impeccably cut broadcloth. He did not care to risk his cloak being hung in some musty corner. "No, thank you."

"'As you please, sir," Jem said, his manners improved by the bribe.

The footman ushered the captain up a flight of narrow stairs, along a corridor in sad need of redecoration, and into a small, panelled dining room with black mould in one corner.

Lord Kershaw remained seated. "Sit yourself down, Captain Howard." He eyed him warily before he spoke again. "I think we met at Mrs Radcliffe's house. I am indulging in a late breakfast. Will you partake of some?"

He understood why any young lady would be charmed by Kershaw's elegance of dress, large grey eyes, polished manners, and splendid chestnut-brown wig. He inclined his head.

Edward noted a half empty dish of coffee at a second place setting opposite Kershaw. A bite had been taken from a thickly buttered roll on a plate next to the dish. By his faith, he would not chance the results of consuming so much as a mouthful in this grubby establishment. He ignored Kershaw's offer of breakfast and fired a long shot. "My congratulations on your marriage to Mistress Martyn, but I must apologise, for I fear my unexpected arrival alarmed your bride."

Kershaw's eyes blazed. "How the devil?"

"Do I know you married Mistress Martyn? Call it a fortunate guess."

"What else could a nobleman do?" Kershaw demanded. "Her dragon of a mother insisted on her marrying Fenton, a man steeped in vice. Would you have allowed the lady you love to marry such a creature?"

"No." Edward wished Mrs Corby had spared Kate the cruel fate of marriage to the late Lord Sinclair. After he dusted a chair with his kerchief, he sat at the table on Kershaw's right. "Instead of marrying the lady out of hand, I would have spoken to her father, man to man."

"Mister Martyn does not rule his house. The fire-belching dragon does," Kershaw said, pitching his deep voice higher than usual. "Whatever I said, Mrs Martyn would not have believed me."

"Did you address her?"

"No." Kershaw looked away from him. "You don't understand. Mrs Martyn is enamoured of Fenton's artificial charm and the prospect of his inheritance of an enormous fortune and a title." Kershaw rocked backward and forward on his chair. "Well, right or wrong, the deed is done. My angel and I are married."

Command of youngsters at sea alerted Edward. What was Kershaw concealing?

"May I ask how old you are?"

"What has my age to do with my marriage?"

"If you have trustees, I imagine it has a great deal to do with it."

"Yes, well, now I am married, they have no authority."

"Ah, one presumes that according to your father's last will and testament the trust ended either when you reached a certain age or when you married."

"Yes, you are right." Kershaw sighed and fiddled with a fork before looking at him full in the face. "Now that I am a married man, I am determined to use what little I have to put my estates, such as they are, in order."

"Commendable." In spite of his lordship's sincere reply, Edward resisted the rude temptation to suggest he start with the order for his house to be scrubbed from attic to basement.

Kershaw gulped some coffee. "Confound you. I cannot imagine why you are concerned with my affairs."

"Your affairs are not my concern. Mrs Radcliffe's are. My godmother took a fancy to your wife, who is her distant relation. She frets over your bride's safety and is blaming herself for introducing your wife into society, thus putting her at the risk of falling into the wrong hands."

"Do *wrong hands* refer to me, sir?" Kershaw sprang up. "Did you insinuate my angel will come to harm with me?"

"Only if your sole reason for marriage is to come into your inheritance and to also gain a fortune through your wife."

The young man sank onto his chair. "Breaking the trust is only part of the matter. I love my bride and hope for a long, happy life together."

Edward stood. "A word of advice, act like a man. Have the courage to face Mister Martyn in his den. Mrs Radcliffe told me your name is an old and honourable one." He observed the neglected room. "Who knows, if you are honest with your father-by-law about—shall I say—Fenton's proclivities, he may welcome you into his family in the role of his daughter's saviour. What is more, he might give her a generous dowry in order for her to live in the comfort to which she is accustomed."

"There is a reason why I cannot take your advice," Kershaw gabbled.

"What is it?"

The young man drummed his fingers nervously on the table. "A Fleet marriage. At the time, it seemed the best course of action."

"How could a clandestine marriage—probably conducted by a defrocked clergyman or some other rascal—have seemed advisable? In any decent person's opinion, Fleet Registers and marriage certificates are not worth so much as the paper they are written on. Besides, under the law, in the event of death, they don't entitle either husband or wife to benefit from each other's property, and their children cannot inherit."

Jane, her face the colour of whey, tiptoed out from behind a screen decorated with a classical scene as dingy as the depressing surroundings. "My lord, did you know?" she asked Kershaw. "Is it true?"

"No need to worry, my love. The man who married us is a genuine clergyman."

A pair of naïve babes, Edward thought, restraining a mocking laugh. "Take my advice, Kershaw, retire to the country, find a respectable woman to chaperone your wife, and then arrange for a genuine clergyman to tie the knot."

Jane burst into tears. She ran to the window, the farthest point in the room from Kershaw. Edward followed her. "Stop crying," he said sternly, under the circumstances unable to decide whether to address her as Lady Kershaw or Mistress Martyn. "Take my advice. If you and your bogus husband confess to your father, I am sure all will be well. He bowed. "Your servant, madam."

* * *

After Kate alighted from her sedan, she turned to cross the road. She intended to visit an acquaintance who went to the theatre four or five times a week and could name all the players. She warned herself to be discreet. Yet again, she rehearsed her most important question. "Are there any new stars treading the boards?"

A flutter of pigeons' wings overhead caused her to look up. Shocked, she pressed her hand to her throat. As bold as a miller's shirt, Captain Howard stood at the window of the opposite house with Jane Martyn.

Scarce able to believe the evidence of her eyes, she stared at the pair. Her breath came fast.

Careless of her skirts touching the multi-shaded, pudding-shaped cobbles, she turned around, hoping the captain had not seen her.

Indignant because she loved an unworthy man, she seated herself in her sedan chair. "Home," she ordered the bearers.

Kate drew the curtains to block herself from view. She sank back onto the seat. Oh she was naught but a dog-in-a-manger. What was wrong with her? She was too old for the captain; she even wanted him to marry a girl with a flawless reputation. Yet she had not believed him capable of deceit, which might lead to the ruination of a naïve young lady.

What of Mistress Martyn's morals? An assignation with the captain did not speak well of her character.

Infuriated, Kate plucked at her expensive lace bertha. When she first met the captain, Mrs Radcliffe had just introduced him to Mistress Martyn. Only a fool would fail to realise the man's godmother favoured a match between him and the heiress, even though her rank in society was inferior to his. Nothing wrong with it, nevertheless, Edward should not meet the girl clandestinely.

Her chest hurt. Kate released a slow breath. She would send a note, addressed to the captain, to Mrs Radcliffe's house, to inform him she would wait on him at three of the clock.

This very day she would tell Edward, she did not need his help to find Amanda. No, it would be foolish. Her bitter laugh rang out. Why should she expect the captain to be better than any other man? Though she was disillusioned and furious, she would still use him in her quest to find Amanda.

"Good day, Perkins," Kate said, much later, to Mrs Radcliffe's butler. "Is Captain Howard at home?"

"I shall enquire, your ladyship."

Kate pressed her lips together and glared at him. "He is expecting me," she said, with the assumption the captain had received her note.

Instead of waiting downstairs, she followed Perkins' tall, thin figure to the third floor, determined not to be fobbed off with an excuse.

Perkins rapped on a panelled door. He waited for a moment, cast a look of disapprobation at Kate, and then entered the captain's parlour. Kate followed, scarcely giving him time to announce her.

With a paintbrush, Edward gestured to his shirt tucked into a pair of shabby, broadcloth breeches. "You catch me at a disadvantage, Lady Sinclair."

"Did you not receive my message?"

"Is it three of the clock? Forgive me. Engrossed in my painting, I lost all sense of time."

Kate edged around the room to look at an exquisite depiction of a seascape, bordered by frozen wastes and illuminated by a pale sun. "How beautiful!"

"Thank you, I am working on this seascape for Sir Newton, using some sketches I made in the far north." Edward wiped his brush on a rag.

"How may I serve you, milady?" He cleaned his hands on a linen cloth. "Please be seated."

She eyed the chairs and window seat, all cluttered with books, paintbrushes, broadsheets, and a telescope besides other objects.

The captain removed several items and a small drawstring bag from a comfortable, old wing chair by the hearth. "Will you sit there, milady." He picked up his knee-length broadcloth vest, put it on and then addressed Perkins. "A glass of Canary wine for milady."

"And for you, sir?"

Edward shook his head. He picked up a coat as faded as his breeches. "I would ruin better clothes when I paint," he explained to Kate.

Perkins handed the countess a glass of wine full to the brim. "Will that be all, sir?"

"Yes, thank you."

Perkins left the room, shutting the door behind him.

"Has Hinchcliffe communicated with you?" Edward asked.

"No, surely he would report to you concerning Lady Amanda, not to me."

"Yes, if he were the bearer of bad news. He might decide to leave it to me to break it to you."

Fear gripped her heart. She put her glass down on an old table with rickety legs. The table wobbled. The glass fell over. Wine seeped into a portfolio. "How clumsy! I apologise." Kate hoped his work had not sustained much damage. Picking up the collection, she examined the contents, admiring the bustling drawings of London life, its people, and the River Thames. She turned her attention to another sketch. Her body tensed. "Is this how you visualise Amanda?"

Edward nodded.

His skilful hand captured the innocent face of a young girl before she was ready to embark on womanhood. "You really do believe she bears a close resemblance to Charles?"

"Why should I doubt it when Mister Milton confirmed it?"

"May I have the sketch?"

"Of course you may."

Kate rolled it up.

He handed her a frayed bit of crimson ribbon with which to tie it.

"Thank you, Captain, I shall treasure it."

She looked down. Mistress Martyn's sketched eyes stared at her. Kate's breath caught in her throat. She indicated the drawing with her hand. "You have a particular fondness for this lady?"

The captain stood behind her chair and bent over her. His warm breath fanned her cheek. To her surprise, she did not feel threatened by his close proximity. "If I am concerned about Mistress Martyn, is it of any importance?"

To judge by how close he stood to the young lady when she saw them framed by the window, his fondness for the girl was most particular. Well, his godmother would be pleased if he married the chit. No sooner did the thought flit through Kate's mind than a swift onslaught of jealousy took her by surprise, bringing blood rushing to her cheeks. She *really* did not want him for a husband, so what did she care if he kept a mistress, and why should she care who he married?

The captain rested his hands on her shoulders and kissed the top of her head. "Have you nothing to say, my lady?"

Her anger crystallised. "What should I say?" she asked in a hard tone of voice.

"Surely you are not jealous of Mistress Martyn." His deep voice held a hint of laughter.

Until now, Kate prided herself on her strength of character and indifference to men. She silently cursed the heat still flooding her cheeks, doubtless turning them to an unbecoming scarlet.

The captain removed his hands and stepped around the chair to face her, his dark eyes alive with amusement. "I drew your daughter in accordance with my imagination. I also drew Mistress Martyn with the intention of having both drawings printed and circulated in London and, if necessary, further afield in the hope they would lead to finding both young ladies."

The hypocritical liar. Could he really be base enough to have persuaded the girl to become his mistress? Incensed, she sniffed. Of what possible interest could insipid little Jane be to her?

Kate stared at a landscape on the opposite wall. If she did not need him to help her find Amanda, she would cut him out of her life.

"You are extremely quiet, milady."

"Why circulate Amanda's portrait in London? Why do you think Amanda lives here?"

"Kate, I may call you Kate may I not, for you once gave me permission to address you thus? First, the actor referred to a young girl who looked like you. Then Sir Newton told me he glimpsed Charles dressed as a female in Drury Lane."

Due to the pain of his deceitfulness and her acute anxiety over her daughter, she ignored his use of her name. "Impossible, Sir Newton must have seen Amanda."

"I agree."

"What else did he tell you?"

"Only that he thought he saw Charles in female attire walking in Drury Lane with a gentleman clad in black. More than likely, Sir Newton saw a girl with only a passing resemblance to your son," the captain said gently.

"Is *that* all?' Kate asked, determined to remain aloof from the captain's charm and obvious sympathy. For her pride's sake, he must never guess she loved him. "Well, it is more than I knew before. Did Sir Newton notice where the girl went with the man?"

"No, but I will sketch another picture of Lady Amanda for you to give to Hinchcliffe. He may use it to advertise in the newspapers. In the meantime, I shall have it copied. He and I shall arrange for it to be circulated."

Kate sprang to her feet. "Thank you, Captain Howard." In accordance with her custom when she was upset, she pressed her hand to her throat. "I will also search for her. Even if I have to walk every street and knock on every door in London, I *shall* find her."

"No."

"You overreach yourself, sir. You have not the right to forbid me anything."

"I know, but you must not expose yourself to the danger of being snatched off the street and held either to ransom or forced into marriage for the sake of your fortune."

Her heart fluttered in response to the captain's quiet tone. Unlike the other men who courted her, she almost believed the captain really did care for her, in spite of what she had seen at that heart-stopping moment through the window.

"Please allow me to continue to serve you, milady. If your daughter lives in London, she shall be found, but you must be cautious."

Kate did not voice the words that sprang to her lips. "What do I care for danger when my child is at risk?" She caught her lower lip between her teeth. Common sense won, for her children's sake, she must not put herself in jeopardy

The captain released her hands. "My brave girl."

"I am a woman, not a girl."

"True, but you look far too young to be the mother of twelve-year old twins." Captain Howard refilled her glass of wine, and then held the rim to her lips.

He stood so close that she breathed in the comforting scent of his sandalwood toilet water. "Please drink." He rested his free hand lightly on her shoulder. "You are uncommonly pale."

With the hope of finding Amanda, she relaxed a little, somewhat comforted by his kindness.

Was he a cheat? Kate stiffened her spine. The captain must be. Although he knew Mistress Martyn's whereabouts, he had told her he drew the chit's portrait as an aid to discovering her location. Oh, why did she allow him to become her friend? Despite all, while careful to keep the expression on her face impassive, she could not suppress her desire to put her head on his shoulder and draw on his strength. Never in her life had she known affection. Her wrongs filled her mind.

Kate sighed. The faces of her innumerable suitors floated before her eyes. Even Tyrell, who swore he never wished to marry, had proved himself to be no better than the rest of them who only wanted control of her fortune. Edward? What did he *really* want of her?

Why should a handsome young man, with more than enough to live on, interest himself in her, if not for her wealth? She sank onto a chair.

The captain knelt. He took her cold hands in his warm ones. If he had not held them so tightly in his reassuring clasp, she would have withdrawn them.

She closed her eyes. Heavens above, if Amanda had turned to prostitution to support herself, she would have adopted the custom of masking her face with a vizard. Her eyes opened as though of their own volition. In that case, Sir Newton would not have noticed her resemblance to Charles. For now, she hoped against hope her girl was safe.

Kate's heart pounded. Blood drummed in her head. She must return home. The mysterious Doctor Moore might have sent a message. The sooner she consulted him, the better. "Captain Howard, please let go of my hands. 'Tis time for me to return to my house."

He stood, raised her hand, pressed a kiss on her palm, and folded her fingers around it.

She recoiled, alarmed by a gleam in his eyes.

"Hold the promise of my kiss until we meet again. Trust me to do everything I can to help you find Lady Amanda."

Trust him? Would she ever have faith in him again?

Kate's eyes opened a little wider. Was he devious enough to keep Jane Martyn as his mistress and at the same time plan to marry her? Outrageous! If they found Amanda, she would rid herself of the captain's attentions.

How she longed to meet Amanda and become acquainted with her likes and dislikes. Oh, when she found her, she would do everything in her power to compensate for the deprivation Amanda had suffered. Her son and daughter would always be her most important treasures.

* * *

After Edward escorted Kate to the front door and bade her good day, he returned to his rooms where he sank onto the chair she had warmed. A trace of her perfume fragranced the air. If only she was as sweet as she was unconsciously sensuous. Come to think of it, why the deuce did Kate remain so aloof when she spoke to him?

Edward poured a glass of wine from the bottle on the table by his paint-spattered chair. Legs stretched out, his feet propped on the fender, he drew a deep breath. Like a resolute knight of old, he was determined to rescue his damsel in distress and claim his reward.

He grinned. His Kate was no timid damsel longing for the arms of a strong man. Edward sipped his wine, rolling it around his mouth before he swallowed. She had been polite, but showed no enthusiasm when he explained his plan to distribute pamphlets. She only revealed emotion when he requested her *not* to search in person for Amanda. Any man who took on such an independent lady would struggle to be master in his own house. Lord only knew the challenge Kate presented. Would he ever be able to break through her reserve?

For a moment, he had suspected she was jealous of Mistress Martyn. A ridiculous thought. Why should so proud a lady be jealous of the chit? Rich though her father might be, the runaway's fortune was only a fraction of Kate's.

He twirled the stem of his empty glass. How could he destroy her barricades? He poured another glass of wine. A ship at sea, buffeted by a contrary wind, tacked to throw her head-sails aback. Perhaps he should change course. Until now, he had pursued the beautiful countess and remained at her beck and call. From this moment on, he would not frequent her company, in the hope she would veer to chase him.

Of course, to put about against the wind on an opposite tack in the teeth of strong gales, was dangerous. Some contended turning the head of the ship twenty points of the compass instead of twelve, was far too dangerous. He chuckled. So be it. Kate, a barque of rare grace, with inflexible square sails, did not respond to him, so he must change tactics. However, before he put them into practice, he would approach her on Mistress Martyn's behalf. It should put an end to any unjustifiable jealousy Kate might harbour.

Chapter Nineteen

"Doctor Moore," Simon announced, his colourful livery in bright contrast to the visitor's sober black velvet.

Kate looked up from her book at the doctor, whose white periwig framed a face like the full moon.

"Good day to you," Kate said from her seat on a couch opposite one of the tall windows in the green salon.

The doctor, one hand on his silver-headed cane, the other holding the drawstrings of a black bag, advanced toward her. He paused some three feet away to bow low.

When he straightened his back, Kate pointed her furled fan at one of a pair of chairs placed at right angles to her couch. Gladdened by the possibility of receiving information about Amanda's whereabouts, she cleared her throat. "Please be seated. A glass of wine?"

The doctor settled on a chair. His pink mouth crinkled into a smile. "You are most gracious, my lady, a glass of wine would be very welcome."

"Is there aught you require?" she asked Dr Moore after Simon served the wine. She looked at him, slightly afraid of the answer.

"A table, only a table."

Simon fetched a small rosewood table of medium height from the farther side of the salon and put it in front of the doctor.

Doctor Moore sipped some wine and then rolled it around his mouth. "Excellent," he murmured.

"Aught else, sir?" Kate asked.

"No, thank you, my lady."

With a gesture of her hand, Kate dismissed Simon.

Moore leaned back in the chair. "How may I serve you, Countess?"

Should she come straight to the point, or could he divine the reason for her summons?

His eyes keen in the morning sunshine that streamed through the window, Dr Moore drew his eyebrows together. "You hesitate to give your heart to a naval man whom you believe to be a cheat. The prospect of either a liaison or remarriage terrifies you, my lady." He stared at something behind her. "You want to know if a ship has gone down at sea and if all its crew has drowned. So far there is no need for fear. It is delayed by unseasonable storms."

She stared at him, as shocked as a country girl at a fair. How did the doctor know about Captain Howard and the panic he aroused in her? How did he know of her anxiety concerning *The Star of The East*, in which she had shares? In truth, it should have berthed over a month or more ago, even if it had encountered gales.

His words were incredible. Perhaps he might have guessed the thought of an intimate relationship with a man terrified her. Gossip might have informed him that Captain Howard was now her most persistent suitor, but how could he know she fretted concerning the ship?

Her business interests were very carefully guarded. She trusted her agent to be discreet.

The doctor's eyes seemed unfocussed on his surroundings.

"Your greatest desire is to have both of your children under your roof."

She shrank back. Only four people in the world— other than the midwife and a few well-bribed servants—knew she gave birth to two children.

Doctor Moore chuckled. "You are amazed, a not uncommon reaction. Shall I tell you more?"

Now that his eyes focused on her, Kate nodded, frightened and a little spellbound. Could the doctor be a warlock? Did such creatures exist? The first King James had believed they did. She crossed her fingers behind her back.

Moore put his glass down on a low table next to his chair. "You have no reason to fear me, Lady Sinclair. With your permission, before we proceed, we shall recite The Lord's Prayer and the twenty-third Psalm. I shall then invoke a circle of protection around us to keep malicious entities away."

Malicious entities? Who were they? Thank the Lord he was not a warlock. Most likely he was a wizard who practised white magic. There had been such a one, who charmed the horses, when her uncle still had some left in his stable. Besides, a warlock would not bind himself with a cross on a chain around his neck, and she doubted he would recite the prayer and Psalm all Christian children learned in their nurseries. She had allowed fear to overcome her by not applying common sense. Before she summoned the doctor, she should have investigated him but had been too impatient to delay her consultation.

Without further ado, Moore knelt. Self-conscious, Kate copied him. She folded the damp palms of her hands together and joined her voice to his.

The prayers completed, they rose. The gentleman took a black silk cloth, embroidered in silver with the signs of the zodiac, from his bag. After he spread it over the table, he placed a crystal ball on a silver stand in its centre. "Shall I commence, my lady?"

"I thought you would cast my horoscope."

"I will, if you so desire, but it will take some days. With your permission, I shall consult my crystal. No need to fear."

So great were her expectations that Kate scarcely took breath. She nodded in fearful anticipation.

"Very well, Countess, but even if I put a question to you, please don't speak while I seek the answers you require." Dr Moore bent forward. He passed his hands over the crystal before staring into its depths. His eyes glazed. His voice became deeper and huskier. "In spite of your rank and enormous wealth, you have suffered greatly. I see two babes. They must be twins. How alike they are. A boy and a girl. It is true, is it not? No, don't answer. The boy resides with harsh relatives. The girl is in London, lodged near…near Drury Lane. I see a fair maiden between eleven and thirteen years of age. Am I right? Yes, I am sure I am. She sings as well as her grandmother. This girl has graced the stage on several occasions. She plans to earn her living as an actress. If she does, she has no reason to fear." He shifted and then peered into the crystal from another angle. "The iron spikes at the front of the stage will protect her from any lusty men in the audience who might try to storm it."

Her daughter on the stage leading the immoral life of an actress, subject to lewd eyes—not to think of the bad company most actresses encountered in the world of theatre. The room seemed to spin around but stilled when the doctor spoke again. "I see a gentleman with a paintbrush in his hand. He is of great assistance to you. Don't fear the gentleman, Countess. He will never harm you. My lady, you have experienced much fear, have you not? From this day forth, try to rest easy. All will end well."

Perspiration beaded the doctor's forehead. He frowned. "I see a golden lion's head."

His eyes no longer glazed, he looked at her. "The crystal has cleared. It will reveal no more." Kate handed Dr Moore a heavy drawstring purse. "Thank you, my lady." He passed a handkerchief across his face. After a minute or two he returned the crystal and cloth to his bag. Finally, he stood. "Please don't hesitate to summon me again if you require my services." He bowed, his face expressing nothing other than good humour and kindness. "No, don't ring for a lackey to show me out. I am capable of opening and closing the door."

Kate managed a courteous smile. "Thank you." For what she thanked him, she was uncertain. Hope? Perhaps. Reassurance about Edward? Certainly. Reassurance about her girl? Although the doctor had not given her the exact details of Amanda's whereabouts, she would search for her daughter in theatres in Drury Lane

"Sit quietly, my lady, and compose yourself in this beautiful room. Like a calm sea, it exudes the tranquillity you need."

After making his bow, Dr Moore stepped quietly out of the salon.

Kate stared at the sea green wallpaper and shivered. She rested her head against the back of the velvet upholstered couch.

In spite of the doctor's advice, she could not still the thoughts tormenting her mind.

A golden lion's head? Perhaps, the name of an inn, a tavern or a goldsmith's called The Golden Lion? Somewhere, did a painted sign displayed in the street, depict the creature? She wished Dr Moore's crystal ball gave exact information such as: At the Sign of the Golden Lion in King Street.

Kate stood, impatient to redouble her efforts. Why had she not asked the doctor if her search would succeed? For fear he might say it would not? Yet he had claimed all would be well. With agitated steps, she paced across the wooden floor, her hands gripped tightly together behind her back. Her agent must scour London. She would instruct him to ask the coachmen and hackney drivers who knew London well, to tell him where there were representations of the king of beasts. Amanda would be found. With that thought, Kate's nervous steps ceased. Her chest relaxed. She took deep breaths.

It would be a little while before she could take the doctor's advice and compose her mind.

Simon entered the salon. "My lady," he commenced in an uncertain tone. "Captain Howard asks if he may speak with you."

"Show him in. After you pour wine for us, you may leave."

* * *

"Milady, did I see Doctor Moore leave your house when I approached it?"

Kate stood opposite Captain Howard with her back to the wall. She willed herself not to reveal the joy that arose in her at the sight of him. Nevertheless, she still suspected him of paying court to Mistress Martyn. Yet, she would go to any lengths to prevent him from knowing her treacherous heart softened whenever she saw him.

Why must he look at her so intently, almost as if he sought to infiltrate her guard? "Yes," she replied, "Dr Moore waited on me."

"Why?"

Kate plopped onto the couch. "I am surprised you know the doctor."

"I have not been introduced to him, but I recognised him because he is a well-known figure. However, you have not answered my question."

Unused to discussing her private affairs—although the captain knew more about them than anyone else— Kate found his question difficult to answer. "As you say," she agreed lightly, "he is famous in his own way. Curiosity led me to invite him to wait on me."

"I think you are being less than honest. Come, come, confess. You consulted with him in order to help you find Lady Amanda."

Confound it, could the man read her thoughts? "If I did?"

"You had nothing to lose."

Edward sipped his wine while he watched her so intently she schooled her face to reveal nothing of her inner turmoil. Should she confide in the captain?

"My lady, surely I have proved you can trust me. Did Dr Moore give you any clues concerning Lady Amanda's whereabouts?"

She nodded. "The doctor confirmed she is an actress. He also said she lives near Drury Lane and claimed she would be found where there is a golden lion's head." Hand pressed to her throat, she looked down at her lap. "Truth to tell, he astonished me. He spoke of things he could not know through either gossip or the broadsheets. Matters known only to me."

She was grateful to the captain for accepting her words without argument.

"Drury Lane, milady," he said thoughtfully after a moment or two. "That information narrows the search. It seems Newton did see Amanda. As for the golden lion's head, would you like me to mention it to Hinchcliffe?"

Kate looked at the captain's oil painting of Amanda. She never baulked at her fences on the hunting field, nor would she fear Hinchcliffe's possible scorn when she admitted she had consulted a clairvoyant. "Yes, Captain Howard, you may tell Hinchcliffe. But what will he make of it?"

"His opinion does not signify, the only thing which does is finding Lady Amanda. And now, I have a favour to ask you."

"A favour of me?"

"Yes." Edward put his empty glass down. He stood and then scrutinised her face. "You are shivering." He glanced at the hearth. "Shall I light the fire?"

Anxiety, not cold, caused her shivering. "No, please don't go to so much trouble." In spite of her anger over the captain and Jane Martyn, she could not help welcoming his concern which wrapped her like a warm quilt. "No trouble." Edward knelt. He struck a flint to ignite the kindling in the grate. The seasoned pine logs soon caught fire. They filled the room with fragrance.

Kate inhaled, invigorated by the scent.

Captain Howard rose. He studied her face. "Are you unwell?"

She shook her head.

"My lady, sip your wine. It will warm you."

He sat next to her. In a moment of weakness, she longed to rest her head on his broad chest. Only yesterday in the park, she overheard a young matron tell her friend, "When I confide in my husband and he puts his arms around me, my troubles become unimportant." What would it be like to be comforted in the captain's arms? She cleared her throat to mask her emotion. "Captain Howard, you mentioned a favour."

"Yes, in a delicate matter which requires the utmost discretion."

Her curiosity aroused, Kate studied Amanda's portrait instead of the temptation of the captain's broad shoulders and muscular arms.

"My request touches on Mistress Martyn's good name."

Her jealous hand shook. Several drops of wine spilled onto her harebell blue petticoat. She fumbled for

252

her handkerchief and dabbed the Italian silk. "I hope Jessie can remove the stains." She summoned a haughty tone. "I apologise. Domestic matters cannot be of interest to any man."

"Why are you distressed?"

"You are mistaken. I am suffering from nothing more than ennui."

He raised an eyebrow. "I beg your pardon for not believing you."

Kate put her glass down. She forced herself to laugh in spite of the jealousy churning in her stomach. "Lud, did you compromise Mistress Martyn's honour?" Her voice sounded hollow even to her own ears.

Captain Howard sprang forward. He gripped her hands. "Look at me." His eyes flashed. "Why do you pretend you are a cold, heartless creature willing to believe the worst of me? What purpose can it serve?" He looked into her eyes for a long moment. "Oh, I don't deny past liaisons, but what have I done to make you think I would ruin an innocent?"

"Think of me as you please, sir, I care not for any gentleman's opinion, not even yours." Conscious of her lie, she shrugged in a well-rehearsed gesture designed to charm, although, due to her tender feelings for the captain, she found it difficult to pretend indifference. "Come to the point, Captain Howard. You spoke of Mistress Martyn. Whatever you tell me, you may trust my discretion."

"Thank you for your assurance. Mistress Martyn's parents are distraught, and I know Mrs Radcliffe frets about the young woman. So, to put her mind to rest, I acted on my suspicions."

"Which are?"

"Mistress Martyn ran away because she feared her mother would bully her into marrying Fenton."

If she could have escaped marriage to the earl all those years ago, how different her life would be. She might be a happy wife and mother wedded to a gentleman of Captain Howard's calibre. Lord, did romance lurk in her heart? How ridiculous.

"Captain Howard, I don't understand why Mrs Martyn set her heart on Fenton marrying her daughter."

"It does not take much intelligence to assume the man wants Mistress Martyn's fortune. He set out to charm the mother and succeeded."

"What a coil. Can the foolish woman not see through Fenton's wiles?"

"It seems she cannot."

Kate broke a brief silence. "Am I right to presume you know where Mistress Martyn is?"

"Yes, in order to have the blessing of the church, the foolish chit agreed to a Fleet Marriage. She is now at Kershaw's London house."

"'Pon my word, who would have suspected that whey-faced creature of being so lost to propriety? Yet, to have resorted to such a solution, how she must have suffered!"

How foolish she was to have suspected him of duplicity and worse. Kate sipped her wine before she put a question. "Captain Howard, what is the favour you wish to ask of me?"

"To visit Mistress Martyn and persuade her to return to her parents, after which I hope she and Kershaw will marry, this time with the blessings of the church. Should Mistress Martyn refuse to leave

Kershaw, I would like you to explain their daughter's situation to the Martyns."

"Upon my soul, sir, you wish a great deal. Why do you want *me* to speak to them?"

"For one thing, I suspect they will listen with more respect to a countess than to a mere naval officer. For another, I am keen to put my godmother's mind to rest." The captain cleared his throat. "I gave Kershaw sound advice, but doubt he will act on it. He and his Fleet wife remind me of a pair of frightened children lost in the woods through their own folly."

Kate twirled the stem of her empty wineglass while she marshalled her thoughts. "I admire Mistress Martyn's courage." She sighed. "I wish I had fled before my marriage. Yet, where could I have found sanctuary?" She caught her lips between her teeth for a moment. "Useless to dwell on my past. As for Mister Martyn, I am not acquainted with him." She shook her head. "'Tis useless, I am sorry, but to speak to him in connection with his daughter's situation would be impertinent. One may only hope your *children in the woods* will come to their senses and marry in church."

The captain opened his mouth to speak. Kate raised a hand. "Don't try to persuade me to change my mind. It would do more harm than good." She smiled. "If Mister Martyn rejects his ewe lamb after he knows the truth, I daresay Mrs Radcliffe will help her."

He sighed. "Maybe she will. My godmother has a kind heart. Perhaps she could arrange for the foolish couple to marry in the country and then announce the event in London."

"Some more wine, Captain Howard?"

"No, thank you, the bottles may be small but their effect is regrettable if consumed in large quantities."

Kate watched the logs crackling in the hearth. She wondered if Amanda was warm and comfortable or cold and in distress. Did she ever wonder who her parents were? Did she weep at night without anyone to comfort her?

"Milady, let us hope you will soon be reunited with Lady Amanda," the captain said in a soft voice.

Ill at ease with the captain, who seemed able to divine her thoughts, Kate bent her head to prevent him seeing her face. In spite of her efforts to contain her emotion, a few tears rolled down her cheeks. Captain Howard brushed them away with his thumb. Kate flinched a little, although his touch did not repulse her. She recalled that, for the first time in her life, her blood stirred when he gave her a conventional kiss of greeting when Mrs Radcliffe introduced them.

"My lady, please don't cry. It is not for a countess of such strong mettle to weep. Tears from a lady such as you upset a man."

She choked back a sob. "Forgive me, for I am not given to being a watering pot."

"I would never describe you thus. In fact, I admire your fortitude." He patted her hand. "Take heart, I believe Sir Newton saw Lady Amanda in Drury Lane. I also believe the actor, who spoke of your double, saw her on the stage. Moreover, I am sure you will find your daughter."

"I pray so. But, sometimes I think she is lost forever." Kate dabbed her tears away with her handkerchief.

The captain slid his arm around her waist. Her body tensed and she tried to draw away. Panic rose from her belly to her throat. "Release me!"

His arm tightened around her. "Why? Are you too proud to accept comfort?"

Although only minutes before, she longed to rest her head on his chest; she now shuddered.

He withdrew his arm. "Kate, surely you cannot believe I will take advantage of you."

Freed from him, she breathed more easily. "You called me Kate."

"So you have reminded me before."

"It was when I wanted to set you up as one of my flirts. Well, no matter, I prefer it to Katherine. You may call me Kate if you wish."

"You may call me Edward, but if you no longer want me to be one of your flirts, what *do* you want of me?"

"To be my friend," she lied, for he was much more than a dear friend.

"As you well-know, I am *already* your friend," Edward drew out each word as though oddly reluctant to say them. He patted her back. "Try to keep your spirits up. Already, there are responses to the pamphlets which are being distributed."

Of their own volition, her eyes widened. Perhaps Captain Howard's pamphlets, printed with her girl's portrait, would have a happy result.

Kate peered through her lashes at the captain's profile, appreciating his firm jaw, tanned complexion, straight nose, full upper lip, and a slightly thinner lower one. Folly to look at him so. Could she overcome the disgust of the marriage bed her late husband instilled in her? Kate sniffed. What was she thinking? On the day the earl died, she vowed no other man would ever shackle her.

Captain Howard faced her and looked deep into her eyes as though he sought to plumb their depths. "May I kiss you? Although I am your friend, I desire to be much more."

Frightened of his masculinity, Kate shook her head. She summoned every ounce of will to compose a carefree answer. "No matter how hard he pleads, I allow no man to kiss me."

"Is your sobriquet 'the fatal widow' deserved? Do you know men break their hearts over you?"

"I hope not, I have never set out to hurt anyone."

Light burned in his dark eyes. Would she drown in the intensity of his gaze? She stood and reached for the hand bell to summon a lackey.

With a lithe movement, Captain Howard sprang to his feet. He seized the silver bell and put it aside. "Kate," he murmured as he rested his hands on her shoulders. "You married a despicable old lecher, who misused you. You don't believe men and women can pleasure each other and women can reach ecstasy."

She shrugged, unable to believe unspeakable acts with her husband could ever result in rapture. Maybe more fortunate women experienced rapture but she was sure she could never ever do so.

With a hint of mischief in their depths, the captain's eyes scrutinised hers. "Kate, unlike your satyr of a husband, I would never misuse you. To the contrary, I would treasure you, while doing all I could to make you happy."

His hand moved from her shoulder to the back of her head. His strong fingers invaded her hair.

"No," Kate cried out.

"Trust me, no matter how much I desire you, I will never give you cause for fear."

"As I previously pointed out, you are arrogant."

His hand cradled her head more firmly. "Not so, merely a poor fool besotted by you."

She tried to turn her face aside. He cupped her chin with a gentle hand.

"Look me in the eyes, Kate. If you can say, in all honesty, you have never, ever wanted me to kiss you, I will release you and never importune you again."

Faint with a combination of curiosity and fear, she opened her mouth to reject him but could not force herself to speak.

Kate ran her tongue around her dry lips. "Edward," she whispered.

"You spoke my name." He smiled with great tenderness, released her, and stood completely still. The length of his lean, powerful body almost touched hers. In spite of an instinctive resistance, it overpowered her senses.

"Although I will not force a kiss on you, Kate, please take pity on me and kiss *me*." His persuasive voice seemed to come from a distance.

She could not make herself look away from him. Her lips quivered. He inclined his face forward. Like a woman in a trance she kissed his lips, which she realised were greedy for her submission.

"Kate." He laughed. "We can deal far better than that."

Edward's mouth covered her own. His kiss did not threaten. As its intensity increased, slowly, very slowly, her fear began to decrease. Almost against her will, her lips parted. His tongue, delicately provocative, moved around their inner edges. A thrill gathered in the pit of her stomach. Kate's hand crept to the back of his head, her fingers entwined in his thick hair.

Edward gathered her in his arms. His mouth left hers, leaving her bereft of his ability to please her. "Now do you believe that you have naught to fear from me?"

Unexpectedly shy, Kate buried her cheek against the smooth broadcloth covering the captain's chest.

"Look at me. One day, maybe you will love me."

Kate tried to look, but could not force herself to do so. She shook her head. "Think you there is no more to love, than a kiss, Captain Howard?" She stepped away from his embrace.

Scarce able to believe she had permitted such a liberty, she turned around, all of her old apprehension rising. "Good day to you, sir, a lackey will show you out." Unable to say more, she fled to her bedchamber.

After Kate drew the curtains at the window, she concealed herself behind them on the window seat. She had never imagined so sweet a kiss, never imagined so gentle a man. Her forefinger stroked her lips. What did Edward think when she fled like a naïve schoolgirl? How could she face him again?

She put her hands to her burning cheeks. A smile curved her mouth. Although she had not confided in Edward, he understood her husband had mistreated her. Her hand covered her breast which bore a tiny scar from the earl's yellowed teeth.

260

Chapter Twenty

Bathed in spring sunshine, blind and deaf to nods and greetings from several acquaintances, his mind in turmoil, Edward headed for his godmother's house.

He acknowledged raw desire had surged through him the first time he saw Kate. As a gentleman should, he always suppressed it when they flirted. While they had exchanged banter, some mysterious alchemy flared within him. Since that fateful day, Kate never ceased to attract and intrigue him.

His lips curled inward. The Countess of Sinclair, with the voluptuous curves of a pagan goddess and the face of an angel, deserved his comparison of her to an Ice Queen when, dressed in white and sparkling with diamonds, he accompanied her to the theatre soon after they met.

His mouth relaxed. The gentleman for whom Kate thawed would be fortunate. Edward intended to be that gentleman. For a moment he could have sworn she responded to his kiss. What would it be like to teach her the art of love?

Edward banished the image of their bodies powerfully entwined in mutual lust. He came to a halt. No, not lust, love. Lud, what did he want of the countess? Unbidden, the word "marriage" came into his mind. He steered away from the thought of the parson's noose, a gold ring on Kate's slim finger, coupled with sacred vows.

He walked on. How sweet and innocent were her lips, as though she were completely untutored in love making. Of course, she was. Without any explanation from Kate, he understood her oaf of a husband had terrorised her. What would it be like to awaken her trust and teach her that a generous lover put the needs of his beloved first? He must be patient and woo her tenderly in and out of his bed, coax her into unfolding her petals like a flower responding to the sun, until her eagerness to share matrimonial bliss matched his.

Another frightening word: matrimonial. Was he or was he not, ready to be shackled? He whistled low when he reached his godmother's house. Should he carry out his plan to ignore Kate, in the hope she would miss him and then as a result seek him out? Until now, he had been at her beck and call. From now on, unless he received news of Amanda, he would be cool, in an attempt to pique her burgeoning desire for him. Whether the fair countess realised it or not, she was not as indifferent to him as she seemed to believe.

Edward laughed. Kate had said she wanted him to be her friend. Yes, he would stay her friend, but he intended to be much more.

At that moment, to his astonishment and bewilderment, he realised he would do almost anything to make her happy. If they married, perchance they would have a child. Not to replace Amanda and Charles in Kate's affections, but to grant her the joy of motherhood which she had not experienced in her first marriage. They would not only share the bliss of the matrimonial bed, but also the day-to-day companionship of happy lovers who relished each other's company.

And what of Kate's children? He liked young Charles and had no reason to believe he would dislike Amanda. In any event, he would not be a heavy-handed step-father. At sea, he enjoyed the company of youngsters. He did his best to guide and teach them with a firm but sympathetic hand. In his experience, kindness reaped the best results.

He breathed his love's name and then laughed so loud and joyously that people stared at him as though they questioned his sanity. He smiled gleefully. Kate's obvious jealousy when he mentioned Mistress Martyn boded well.

A street-hawker's cry caught his attention. "Daffodils and gilly flowers. Who will buy my sweet fresh flowers?"

Edward beckoned to the woman with a basket on her head. The fresh blooms perfumed the air. He purchased all of them together with their basket.

Relieved of her burden, the woman winked. "For a lady, are they, sir? She's a lucky lass to net a handsome gentleman like you."

Already, he had broken his decision not to be constantly at Kate's command. His laugh mocked himself. Who would have thought he, a resolute officer in Her Majesty's navy, would be rendered indecisive by a bewitching female?

Simon answered his knock. Edward handed him the basket. He wanted to tell the lackey to deliver them with his love, but could not, for it would not be seemly.

Edward could scarce believe he was seriously considering marriage to the beautiful countess. He sighed. Even if he succeeded in winning her love, why should she wed a younger man whose fortune did not match her own? In their milieu, marriage was a matter of land and property, not love.

He looked past Simon to the stairs, which Kate was descending, attired in her riding habit. She frowned.

Was she angry with him? After all, she *had* run away after he kissed her.

Edward retrieved the basket from Simon and held it out to Kate. "With my devotion," he ventured.

"You are too kind, Captain. The flowers are beautiful."

Although the countess did not look at him, the frown disappeared as she descended the rest of the stairs. Was she cross? Was she pleased to see him? Perhaps embarrassed? Her cheeks bloomed as pink as a rose.

Edward claimed a conventional fleeting kiss of greeting, aware of a shiver running through her slender frame. "Are you going to ride in St James Park, my lady?"

Kate nodded.

"Shall I join you there?"

"Yes, no, that is," she dithered.

"I shall seek you by the canal within the half hour, sooner if I can." Once more, he knelt metaphorically, at her feet.

A faint smile encouraged him. He stepped aside to allow her to go down the steps to the street where a groom held Scheherazade and a roan gelding's reins. Edward hurried after Kate. He cupped his hands to receive her foot, in order to help her mount her mare. Kate arranged the full scarlet skirt of her riding habit and then looked down at him seeming to have a multitude of questions in her eyes.

Edward smiled. "Please don't be anxious, my lady. The sea has taught me patience. We shall do our best to find Lady Amanda." His tone was too quiet for the groom to overhear.

Scheherazade whinnied.

"Off with you, Countess. Your lovely lady is eager to be away."

He watched Kate ride down the cobbled street followed by the attentive groom mounted on the roan. Kate's riding habit was a blaze of red and gold in contrast to the pale buildings. Edward smiled. She attracted no less attention than Newton when he sported his red hat.

* * *

Kate drew rein, looked across the grass sward, and saw Edward approach the canal on horseback. Sunlight intensified the blue of his coat, his red sash, and the glitter of gold braid and buttons. One after another, several carriages halted, their occupants beckoning to the captain. Each time, he doffed his beaver hat and smiled at match-making mamas and their daughters, dressed to emphasise their good points. A pang sharp as broken glass pierced Kate.

A fair-haired lady, gowned in sage green and primrose yellow, walked toward the captain. She raised her face. He smiled and shook his head. The girl gesticulated. He dismounted and greeted her with a conventional kiss, before bowing to her mother.

Kate snorted. Scheherazade side-stepped but she brought the mare back under control. She glared at

Edward, who was greeting a black-haired, simpering beauty.

For the first time, Kate realised the extent of Edward's popularity. Although he did not have a title, the main branch of his family had a long history of serving at sea. His maternal grandmother was a marchioness. His brother was a baron. So far as she knew, he possessed a not inconsiderable fortune, supplemented by his half pay and an allowance from his affectionate brother. No wonder the mothers of unmarried daughters regarded him favourably.

Assailed by a fierce twinge of jealousy, Kate clicked her tongue. Scheherazade's ears pricked. Absent-mindedly, Kate patted the mare's neck, most of her attention still focussed on Edward.

Marriage to a man nearly ten years younger would invite trouble. All too soon, he might weary of his elderly wife and turn to younger women. Unlike the swan on the canal, which glided after his mate, men were unfaithful creatures. As a result of her experience with her husband, who had been faithful to his brace of mistresses but not to his wife, infidelity would be intolerable if she ever married again. She grimaced. Society, the church, and the law, dictated women must submit to their husbands, no matter how unreasonable their demands. Men expected to be masters in their own homes. "Marriage," she concluded for the umpteenth time, "is an unenviable state not to be wished on one's worst enemy." Yet she knew women who seemed to be happily married. They welcomed their husbands with a smile and their eyes shone when they caught sight of them.

Why was she thinking of marriage to the captain? What was amiss with her? Not by word or deed had the captain indicated he wanted to marry her, even in the unlikely event of him proposing. "Walk on," Kate ordered Scheherazade.

* * *

Edward, too polite to ignore the auburn-haired young lady, caught a glimpse of Kate's scarlet habit. He touched a corner of his hat. "Good day to you," he said to the girl.

He remounted. Spurring Dark Lady forward, he caught up with Kate halfway along The Mall.

"May I say you look enchanting?"

"Do I?"

Again, he wondered if the memory of his kiss angered her. "Shall we ride by the canal, milady?"

"No, the hour grows late."

"Not so late that we must leave the park. Am I to assume you don't want my company?"

She made no reply. He forced himself to smile. Had that passionate kiss cost him her favour? "Allow me to escort you home before I visit the inn. I must find out if there are any more replies to the pamphlets about Lady Amanda."

"You are more than kind, sir."

"You know full well I shall serve you with every means at my disposal," he said, conscious of her glare.

"Thank you."

In spite of his intentions not to do so, here he was again, running after a lady who seemed not to care as little as a flick of her fingers for him. The wind most definitely blew from the wrong direction.

In silence, they rode back to her house, where he refused to accept her dismissal. Instead, he accompanied her to the green salon. Alone with Kate, he put a hand on either side of her waist and stared down at her. "Now," he said in a tone as frigid as the one she used earlier, "please be good enough to tell me what the deuce causes you to use me so harshly." He raised an admonitory hand. "Please don't tell me my kiss brought about the change in your behaviour. I shall not believe it. In fact, I am sure you enjoyed our kiss."

A pair of startled blue eyes gazed up into his. Her mouth formed a surprised 'O'.

"One day, milady, you will enjoy my second kiss even more," he promised.

Chapter Twenty-One

Kate stared at Captain Howard, whose tall frame cast a shadow on the walls of the green salon. She narrowed her eyes. Horrified by the audacity of his provocative assurance that his second kiss would be more enjoyable than his first, coupled with the amused gleam in his eyes when he said so, she moistened her lips with the tip of her tongue. Maybe another kiss would be enjoyable. An unfamiliar sensation inched its way upward from her toes. Innumerable tingles, like tiny bubbles of champagne, burst in her veins. Beyond logical thought, she raised her chin.

The ability to speak deserted her. She gazed into the captain's compelling eyes. He rested his warm hands on her shoulders. Thrills of excitement ran up and down her spine. She focussed on his mouth—the attractive deep pink of a healthy young man.

Edward's eyes laughed at her. "Unless I propose marriage to you, perhaps I will not kiss you again."

Marriage? *Although he seemed to be teasing her, the last bubble of desire burst. Her mouth twisted. She shuddered. Perspiration beaded her forehead.*

"Kate?" Every vestige of amusement left his eloquent eyes.

She stiffened her back. "'Twill never be of use to ask me to marry you. I am determined to live and die a widow."

"Why?"

Captain Howard continued standing close to her. The spicy perfume of his soap, his toilet water, and his pomade, assaulted her senses. He put an arm around her. With his fingers, he traced the line of her spine beneath the armour of her bodice and stays. "Why?" he repeated, his voice low and insistent.

Kate understood him well enough to know he would not leave until he dragged a satisfactory answer from her. Resentment swelled. He had no right to demand a response, no right to make her want him to kiss her again. She withdrew from his embrace.

"Marriage is abhorrent to me. I would prefer a blood sucker of a leech in my bed, to a husband."

Captain Howard roared with laughter. "You are nothing if not honest. Will I ever recover from your comparison of me to a leech?"

Indignant, she glared at him. "Your *amour propre*, by which I mean your self-love and vanity, are no different to that of every other man who has courted me. You assume you can persuade me to love you against my will." Her deliberately harsh words terminated his laughter.

"My apologies, milady, if I led you to believe I am a suitor with marriage in mind."

"Captain, don't play a game of words. In all honesty, I have been led to believe that you want to marry me. Is it your intention or not to propose marriage to me?"

She took so deep a breath that, restricted by her stays, her breasts ached. Or was there another reason for them to do so? Dear Lord, what was amiss? How could she have put such an indelicate question to

Edward? It was not for ladies to raise the subject of marriage to a suitor.

Kate caught her lower lip between her teeth. Even when the captain mentioned marriage, his amusement made it plain he did not have that in mind. The only possible conclusion was that he lusted after her and did not intend to seek the blessing of the clergy. She pressed her hand over her heart to still angry tremors.

"Perhaps I implied I would ask you to enter into holy matrimony. How remiss of me to forget whether I have or not." He frowned as though rueful. "No, I remember, I did not." Laughter danced in his dark eyes.

Outraged, Kate sniffed. "Don't trifle with me, sir."

Edward held up his hands, palms toward her in a gesture of surrender. "I am too frightened of you to dare. However, please satisfy my curiosity. Tell me if you compared your *late husband* to a repugnant leech?"

"Good day to you, sir," Kate snapped, infuriated by his amusement and her own betrayal of letting him know about her fear of surrendering to any man.

He stepped forward. His firm hands clasped her shoulders again. "Kate, don't use your late husband as a gauge to judge all men. I have never ill-used any lady. I shall never mistreat you." His eyes gleamed in the frame of his thick, dark lashes.

She trembled. Edward gently massaged her shoulders. "You did not enjoy marriage to an unpleasant old man but you might take pleasure if married to the right gentleman." His eyes searched hers. "And I mean a *gentle* man in every sense of the word."

"Enjoy?" she snapped. "There is no enjoyment in the matrimonial bed for unfortunate females."

He laughed low. "You are mistaken, my lady, but for the moment I am becalmed, however I promise you I shall come about."

Was he toying with her—like so many men—in an attempt to make her want to share an illicit bed? Did she truly desire no more than his friendship? Driven off course by conflicting emotions, she fled from his company, ashamed. Before she met him, she never suffered from such indecision.

* * *

Deep in thought, Edward rode back to his godmother's house, heedless of a chill wind swirling debris around his legs. Although his heart overflowed with compassion, he did not allow his mind to dwell on the horrors of Kate's legal bondage to a self-seeking old husband.

So much for his plan to woo Kate slowly, coaxing her into matching his desire. He must change his plan. Well, on numerous occasions he had battled stormy seas to bring his ship safe to port. Rueful, he knew he must either run before the storm ahead, or triumph over it. Yes, he would ignore Kate to see if it brought her about.

* * *

In her cosy closet, furnished with a desk, neglected sewing box, bookshelves, and a pair of comfortable wing chairs, Kate slipped off her shoes and stretched cold feet toward the fire.

She read a few lines of Congreve's novel, *Incognita,* before the book slipped out of her hands and onto her lap. It was unfair to keep a suitor on a proverbial string; yet, every time she thought of the captain, her pulse fluttered.

She sprang up. Who was on a mythical string? She or Edward Howard? She scowled. No doubt about it, she was the one dangling during the last ten days, since she glimpsed him enjoying dalliances while she hoped for his attention in the park or at the theatre, routs, or balls.

A knock. Had the captain returned? Kate smiled, impatient as a romantic young girl about to see her lover. "Come in." She placed the novel on the low table by her chair. All impatience, she looked at the door.

Simon held out a silver salver on which reposed a letter.

She took it and returned to the chair by the fire. She broke the seal and began to read, trying to make sense of the letter from her mother.

"*You will be surpliced...*" (Surpliced? Mother had not learned how to write neatly.) "*...to know Mister Milton and I are bothered and will nuns it soon.*" (Nuns?)

She gave up her attempt to decipher the scrawled lines written too close together. Without doubt, something momentous had occurred. But of what significance was Mister Milton's surplice? Had Mother undertaken the task of sewing a new one for the gentleman and realised she was unequal to the task? And what did her mother have to do with nuns?

One thing remained clear. Mother penned the letter in a state of great agitation. Kate's frown deepened. By now her mother should have been housed in London with an increased allowance. She had ignored her for too long. Despite any conflicts and differences of opinion, duty demanded she care for her impoverished parent.

She sent for Jessie and while waiting, tried to decipher the letter again and attempt to interpret another phrase. Something about the hens not laying. Strange, it was unlike her mother to interest herself in the barnyard.

"You sent for me, my lady?" Jessie asked from the doorway.

"Yes, come in and close the door, 'tis unseasonably cold for late May."

Kate's fingers stroked the velvet armrests of her chair while she reached a decision. "Pack without delay. Tomorrow we leave for Missendene."

She would miss the sight of Captain Howard while she was out of town.

"For how long will we stay there, my lady?"

"Maybe a week or more."

Her tirewoman bobbed a curtsey. "Is there anything else, my lady?'

"No, you may go."

Kate penned some notes in which she expressed her regrets for her inability to attend several social engagements. Her crow's quill hovered above a fresh sheet of paper. Should she inform Captain Howard of her imminent departure? Yes, she should. In her absence, he might receive a genuine reply to the pamphlets he had circulated apropos to Amanda's whereabouts.

She brushed away a tear. In her bleakest moments, she doubted her daughter lived. Each time the agonising thought insinuated itself into her mind, she tried to dismiss it. Moreover, Charles had assured her he would know if his twin sister had died. To preserve her sanity she must cling to the hope that her girl was alive and well.

* * *

No sooner did Kate step inside Missendene Manor than her mother swept down the broad staircase in a swirl of silks and lace. Gertrude held her daughter tight and kissed her on the cheek. "My dearest child, I can never thank you enough."

With little enthusiasm, Kate returned her mother's kiss before disengaging. "I have no idea why you should thank me." She pulled her cloak around her and eyed the butler. "Why is there no fire in the hall? 'Tis unseasonably cold in here. I would not be surprised if a late frost strikes and ruins this year's fruit crop. 'Pon my word, I am chilled to the bone. I sent news of my arrival so I trust fires have been lit in my chambers."

The butler nodded. "Yes, they have, my lady."

"Good, I shall retire to them, but I am sharp set. I wish to sup within the half-hour."

"My dearest child," her mother spoke again.

Kate narrowed her eyes. It was out of character for her mother to address her affectionately. What could be amiss? "Yes, yes, Mother, you have already said you cannot thank me enough for coming here in answer to your letter, but please excuse me for now. You may explain while we eat."

She turned. Aware of her cloak swirling around her, Kate sped up the stairs, one hand on the carved banister. Inwardly she cursed the impetuosity which brought her to Missendene out of concern for whatever ailed her mother when, in fact, Mother's cheeks glowed—an indication that the country air suited her.

A lackey opened the door to her private parlour, furbished in her favourite pastel pink and light cream. She nodded, pushed back the hood of her cloak, and stepped across the threshold.

Jessie hurried from the bedchamber to unfasten the ribbons at Kate's throat and to help remove the outer garment.

"Pour a glass of cordial for me," Kate ordered the tirewoman.

Standing before the fire, Kate rubbed her cold hands together to warm them.

Jessie handed her a small glass. Kate stared into the golden liquid, raised the glass to her mouth, and sipped some of the pungent contents. "Ah, apricot, my favourite. Thank you, Jessie."

"Do you want to wear your apple-green gown and matching bodice or the cream tapsiel silk gown with your blue and cream striped petticoat and the cream bodice?'

"The cream and blue. The green and silver one is too ornate to wear at supper with my mother."

"And Mister Milton," Jessie informed her. "It seems the gentleman's very much at home here."

"Is that so? Well, I shall be glad to know what Mister Milton's surplice has to do with my mother. I think embroidering dainty handkerchiefs is more to her taste than stitching a surplice."

Someone knocked on the door. Jessie admitted three lackeys, each of whom carried two large wooden pails of hot water.

Her tirewoman bustled into the bedchamber where a portable bath stood before the fire.

Kate sipped a second glass of cordial and nibbled a biscuit dotted with poppy seeds.

The lackeys departed.

"Come, my lady, your bath is ready." Jessie glanced at the small, half empty bottle.

She knew her tirewoman feared her sorrow for her children might drive her to seek consolation from strong drink. "Don't look so worried, Jessie, I have no intention of tippling until my nose is red as a cherry and my complexion ruined."

"I am glad to hear it, my lady."

Kate stepped into the bedchamber.

Behind a tall screen, painted with a summer landscape of idyllic pastures through which ran a stream, Kate washed away the dust of the journey in lavender perfumed water.

In less than a half-hour, she leaned forward to scrutinise her reflection in the mirror. She patted the wisp of lace secured to her head with a pair of hairpins tipped with sapphires and then glanced at her left hand. It still bore her wedding and betrothal rings. On impulse she removed them, longing to throw them away, but the betrothal ring was a Sinclair family heirloom. One day, Charles might want to give it to his wife. However, her wedding ring, a symbol of humiliation, belonged to her. She would toss it into the dung heap with intense satisfaction.

"My jewel box, Jessie."

Free from the last vestige of her husband's bondage, Kate smiled and selected a sapphire ring, slipping it onto her finger. Despite her widowed state, to leave the third finger of her left hand bare would give rise to unwanted comments.

In the mirror, she saw Jessie's reflected smile and nod of approval.

"Your sapphire earrings?" Jessie suggested and handed them to her mistress.

* * *

Kate entered the great hall. With pleasure, she inhaled the delicious fragrance of beeswax candles, mingled with the scent of pine logs burning in the fireplace, and smiled. In accordance with her instructions, the servants had stripped the walls of the ancient banners, polished the oak panelling and floors, removed the cobwebs and repainted the ceiling.

Mister Milton led her mother into the great hall where the Lord of the Manor had feasted in times past.

"Lady Sinclair." Mister Milton looked pale and somewhat plumper. "I trust we have not kept you waiting."

"No, you are in good time." Kate took her place at the head of the table. "Mister Milton, please sit on my right. Mother, please be seated on my left."

Lackeys served a variety of cold meats, crusty bread, butter, and cheese. Last of all, a lackey put a sallet—which Kate had ordered her cook to serve with every meal—on the table.

"Wine, Daughter?" Gertrude suggested. "Wine to toast us?"

"To toast you? Why?"

"Did you not receive my letter?"

"Yes, Mother, but your scribble was unreadable."

Gertrude blushed. She looked at Mister Milton, her eyes soft and luminous by candlelight. "Oh, I thought you came in response to it, Daughter."

"I did. I thought you were ill, but it is obvious you are in the best of health. Please enlighten me. I did not understand why you wrote *you will be surpliced to know Mister Milton and I are bothered*, followed by something or other about *nuns* and a mention of *hens not laying*."

"Upon my soul," Mister Milton said.

Her mother's laughter rang out through the hall.

"Kate," Gertrude commenced, "I wrote, *'You will be surprised to know Mister Milton and I are betrothed. I hope you will continue to provide for us.'*"

Flabbergasted, Kate stared at her mother.

"Daughter, will you not congratulate us?"

"But...." Kate choked back her words. It would be the height of rudeness to say she thought the happy couple were too old to marry. She closed her eyes to block out their exchange of tender glances, an exchange that reminded her of the affectionate manner with which Sir Newton and Mrs Radcliffe always regarded each other.

Kate opened her eyes again. Two pairs of anxious ones scrutinised her.

"Lady Sinclair, I fear you think me bold to aspire to marry Mrs Corby." Mister Milton tugged his neck cloth as though it strangled him. "After all, when everything is said and done, I never anticipated the honour of becoming father-by-law to a countess." He paused to clear his throat. "Yet, when I first heard my Gertrude—I beg your pardon, my lady, for mentioning your mother with such familiarity. When I first heard Mrs Corby sing with the voice of an angel, I desired nothing more than to be blessed by her hand in marriage."

For a few moments, only the logs crackling in the grate broke the silence. Kate forced herself to speak. "By birth you are my mother's equal. What objection can there be to your marriage? Besides, I am not my mother's keeper." She beckoned to the butler. "Fetch champagne, the best wine for a toast." With a smile, she addressed them. "I congratulate you and hope you will be happy. As for your allowance, Mother, I shall stop it, instead I will dower you," she broke off and laughed before continuing. "It is ridiculous for a daughter to say she will dower her mother. Nevertheless I shall settle land *and* money upon you."

The butler showed Kate one of several small bottles.

She nodded her approval. "You may serve us."

She proposed a toast. "Long life and happiness to both of you."

The three of them drained their glasses.

"Thank you for your good wishes, Lady Sinclair," Mister Milton replied. "I shall send an announcement of our betrothal to *The Gazette*."

Faced with the couple's obvious joy, Kate thought of Captain Howard. She wondered if it was *ever* wise to love a younger man. No, it was not. She did not desire the captain either as a lover or a husband, so, in all probability, one day, she must endure the sight of him married to another woman. Of course it would be only right and proper because, even if a miracle changed her mind about remarriage, it would be selfish to wed him. She was too old for him, was she not?

At night, Kate tossed and turned, her mind filled with thoughts of Captain Howard. Before she left town, he seemed to be avoiding her. If she saw him in the distance, he had touched his hat but did not approach her. At Mrs Denninson's rout, he had chatted to many people but did not speak so much as a word to her and had appeared to be unaware of her presence.

Oh well, he would not be the first gentleman to cease his attentions when he received no encouragement. Yet she liked him, very much indeed, and had favoured him more than any other gentleman; and had he not promised she would enjoy his second kiss more than his first?

Sleepless, Kate got out of bed and struck the flint to light a candle. A glass of apricot cordial would soothe her. Back in bed she clutched the barley sugar stem of the small glass and regarded it suspiciously. Drinking in solitude. Had the captain driven her to it? Where was Captain Howard? What was he doing? Was he already making advances to another lady?

Chapter Twenty-Two

Edward rode Dark Lady down The Strand and then along Fleet Street, which was thronged with traders, coaches, drays, sedans, and pedestrians.

A woman wearing a stained apron held up her basket. "Buy my fresh mackerel, one for a penny, six for four pence."

The mare tossed her head. The stink of fish overwhelmed Edward. His nose twitched.

A man shoved his flat tray filled with pies toward him. "Hot baked Wardens. Hot."

They looked delicious but Edward was in no mood for food. He shook his head as he guided Dark Lady into the City through Ludgate to London Bridge, which was crowded with houses and shops. After Edward crossed it, he made his way through narrow streets full of mean houses surrounding the busy Pool of London until he reached The Merry Monarch.

He sighed, hardly daring to hope that, after many false claimants to the reward for information leading to Amanda's whereabouts, the latest informant would provide him with genuine facts.

Dark Lady's hooves clattered over the cobbles into a small stable yard. Edward dismounted in haste. After he handed the reins to a shabby groom, he strode into the modest hostelry, where he hoped to be given information about Amanda.

The landlord bustled into the small lobby of the dilapidated premises. A broad smile wreathed his tanned face and deepened his wrinkles. "Good to see you again, Captain." He wiped the palms of his hands on his leather apron.

"Good to see you, Smithers. I missed you after you left the navy."

"You got my message?" the erstwhile bosun asked.

"I was out when it arrived. Is the girl still here?"

"Aye, aye, Captain. My wife's giving her a tasty bite of bread and cheese."

"That is kind of Mrs Smithers. Please let the girl finish eating before you bring her to me."

Smithers ushered him into a tiny private parlour. "Aye, aye, sir, but let me make you comfortable first. May I draw you a pint of my home-brewed ale, or are you now so high and mighty that you'll only drink my best brandy?"

Edward grinned. "Nay, Smithers, I've not grown too top lofty to refuse the ale."

"Right you are, Captain, I'll draw a tankard for you before I send the lass to you."

* * *

The habits of the sea difficult to shake, Edward paced up and down the room as though he were on the quarterdeck. He picked up one of a pair of blue and white pottery dogs from the mantle. Tawdry ornaments. He replaced it.

While he sat, sipping his ale, he glanced around the dark, wainscoted room, bare of all other than two hard-backed chairs, a settle, and a small table.

After what seemed an age, a young girl, with wisps of mouse-brown hair straggling onto her forehead from

283

beneath her mobcap, sidled into the parlour. Her mud brown eyes stared at him as she bobbed a curtsey.

"Don't be afraid." Edward held out the pamphlet. He pointed to Amanda's portrait. "Do you know this young lady?"

The girl nodded. She seemed chirpy as a sparrow.

"Tell me her name and whereabouts."

The 'sparrow' appeared to consider her position before she removed her hand from her mouth. "If I tell you, you'll give me the money?"

Edward bit back a frustrated expletive. Always the money. Another red herring? "The reward? Yes, you shall have it if you help me to find her."

She scowled. "'Ow do I know you won't cheat me?"

Torn between amusement and irritation at the tiny girl's effrontery, he nearly laughed. "Tell me and you will find out."

"She's Mistress Amanda, and she's at Mister Kebble's house."

Amanda. This time the name was correct. "Kebble, the famous actor?"

Smithers entered the parlour and handed another tankard of ale to Edward while the girl answered the question.

"Yes, Mister, the actor. Only Mister Kebble's no more, so it be'nt 'is house."

"I don't understand, girl. What do you mean?"

"I'll explain, Mister."

"Not, Mister," Smithers interrupted, "you're working windward, he's a captain in Her Majesty's navy."

The girl hung her head.

284

"Thank you, Smithers, that will be all," Edward said.

Although he no longer commanded the man, Smithers saluted before he left the parlour.

"What is your name?" Edward asked the girl.

"Becky, sir. Oh I beg your pardon, Captain."

"Tell me why Mistress Amanda is at Mister Kebble's house."

"It isn't Mister Kebble's house. It's Mister Lucius's house now. Leastways I think it is."

"Mister Kebble sold it to Mister Lucius?"

Becky shook her head. She burst into a storm of weeping. "Mister Kebble's turned 'is toes up," she explained between sobs. She dashed forward, work-reddened hand outstretched. For a moment, he thought she would grasp hold of him. "You must come, Captain. I only 'ope the watchman 'asn't taken Mistress Amanda away."

"Why should he take her away?"

"Cause Mister Kebble's nephew, ~~Mister Lucius~~Mister Lucius, accused her of stealing some money but I don't believe she's a thief."

He glanced at his sharp-faced informant. "Take me to her," he ordered and left a coin on the table for his ale.

Followed by Becky, Edward hurried out into the stable yard where he lifted her up onto Dark Lady.

She squeaked while clinging to the mare's mane.

He settled himself on the saddle. "No need to be frightened."

With the help of Becky's directions, Edward guided Dark Lady through the busy streets and back across London Bridge to the late actor's tall, narrow house near Drury Lane. He dismounted, helped Becky to alight, tied Dark Lady to a hitching post, and promised to pay a stout lad a penny if he kept an eye on the mare.

A woman approached him, her vizard proclaiming her a prostitute, one of the many women plying their sorry trade who kept their eyes open for customers in this neighbourhood notorious for vice. He shook his head as he turned his back to her.

Edward ignored two other gaudily dressed females who sauntered toward him, their faces concealed by vizards. He hastened up the short flight of steps leading to the late Mister Kebble's house.

The gleaming brass lion's head knocker stopped him short. The hair on the back of his neck rose. He remembered that Kate told him Dr Moore's mention of a golden lion's head in his prophecy. Coincidence? No, more than coincidence. Edward banged the knocker against the darkened wood, while Becky scuttled into an alleyway, presumably to the servants' entrance at the back of the house.

Handkerchief in hand, a middle-aged lady clad in black opened the door.

"I am sorry to disturb you in your grief, but I have come to speak with Mistress Amanda on an urgent matter," Edward explained.

The woman sniffed, applied the handkerchief first to her moist eyes, and then to the tip of her nose. "With Mistress Amanda?"

"Yes, she is here is she not?"

"Yes, sir," she replied after some hesitation, "but I don't know if Mister Lucius will allow you to speak to her."

Edward held out the pamphlet.

The woman shook her head. "I'm only the housekeeper, Mrs Jennings, sir. I can't read."

"You can tell me if the picture is of Mistress Amanda."

She scrutinised the print of his sketch. "I think so, sir, but why do you want to find a girl accused of being an ungrateful thief?"

"Thief?" Edward feigned surprise while thinking that even if misfortune drove Lady Amanda to crime, she would still receive a warm welcome from her mother.

Mrs Jennings nodded her head. "Yes, sir, the girl's a thief—or so Mister Lucius will tell you. Mind you, I wouldn't have believed it of her, but Mister Lucius is sure she's guilty." She shook her head. "He even ordered Becky, the servant girl, to fetch the watchman. I expected to see him when I opened the door in answer to your knock."

Becky could be dismissed for not summoning the watchman. Brave of her to respond to the advertisement instead of obeying Lucius's order. "Mrs Jennings, even if you will not allow me to speak to Mistress Amanda, may I speak to your master?"

The housekeeper opened the door wider to admit him.

After stepping into a small, wood-panelled hall, Edward regarded the portrait of Mister Kebble in his prime when he had played the part of Hamlet.

"A lady of my acquaintance," Edward began with Mrs Corby in mind, "is devoted to the theatre. She has often remarked on the greatness of your late master's performances."

"Thank you, sir. Mister Kebble was more than a famous actor. He was a kind man. He even took Mistress Amanda in and trained her for the stage."

Edward remembered Kate telling him about Doctor Moore's predictions. He had forecast that Amanda might grace the London stage. A cold chill ran down his spine.

"Come, sir." Mrs Jennings led the way up the stairs to a comfortable parlour expensively furnished in red and gold.

"Has the watchman come?" asked the grubby man sprawled on a chaise lounge.

Edward whistled low as he always did when thoughtful. He did not like the look of the dishevelled fellow.

Mrs Jennings bobbed a curtsey. "No, sir, this gentleman is come in search of Mistress Amanda."

The man, presumably Lucius, passed his hand across his forehead. He blinked several times. "Who are you, sir, and what the deuce is your interest in the haughty chit?"

"Captain Howard at your service, sir. As for my business, it is a private matter."

"Lucius Kebble at your service, sir." He winked. "With regard to your business with the little beauty, I'll wager you'll have no more luck with her than I did."

Mrs Jennings gasped. Edward narrowed his eyes as Lucius tried to stand. The near empty decanter told its own story. The sooner he removed Amanda from the house, the better things would be.

"Take me to Mistress Amanda," he commanded Mrs Jennings in the tone he used on the quarterdeck.

She glanced at the heir, who fumbled with the decanter.

Lucius leered. "No harm in letting him view the pretty morsel while we await the watchman." He wagged a finger at Edward. "If she agrees to be nice to me, I might drop the charge."

Upon hearing those lewd remarks, Mrs Jennings cheeks flamed. "The charge seems to have been trumped up." Mrs Jennings opened the door and nearly bumped into Becky. "You've taken your time, my girl. Where's the watchman?" she asked.

Edward answered for Becky. "Instead of fetching him, Becky had the presence of mind to reply to my advertisement. She laid the necessary information which directed me to this house."

"Oh, was there ever such a miserable day sent to try me?" Mrs Jennings shut the door. She glared at Becky. "Him in there will be furious with you for not summoning the watchman." She snorted. "What were you doing girl, creeping around the house when your place is in the kitchen?"

Becky burst into tears.

"Any more noise and I'll clout you."

"You will not," Edward ordered. As usual he sympathised with the downtrodden.

The housekeeper did not spare him a glance. "Becky, fetch the watchman."

The 'bedraggled sparrow' thrust out her lower lip. "I won't."

Mrs Jennings raised her fists.

Becky put her hands over her ears, to prevent the housekeeper boxing them.

"Enough, Mrs Jennings," Edward commenced in an ice-cold tone, "take me to Mistress Amanda."

The housekeeper glared at Becky for an instant before she led him along a corridor, through the kitchen, and down the stairs to a cold cellar.

Where was Lady Amanda? He glanced around. In one section were shelves loaded with pickles and preserves. In another part he saw shelves laden with bottles of wine. Edward eyed miscellaneous barrels and trestles, a broken chair, and some lengths of rope which lay on the flagstones.

"Where is she?" Edward snapped.

"Mercy, she was tied up tight as could be." Mrs Jennings gasped. She pointed at the rope. "She's escaped. Mister Lucius will be beside himself."

"If Mistress Amanda was bound with rope, how could she have escaped?" Edward asked.

"Becky," the housekeeper shouted.

"Don't blame me," Becky mumbled. She sidled out of Mrs Jenning's reach.

"Why did I not lock the door?" Mrs Jennings asked without any sign of further regret over Amanda's escape. "Well, I'll not work for the likes of Mister Lucius. I've a bit of money put by, so I'll pack my bags and be off to stay with my sister until I find another position." Mrs Jennings turned to leave.

"A moment, if you please."

"Sir?"

"How old is Mistress Amanda?"

"She never did say, but I think she's twelve or thereabouts."

The right age, Edward thought. "Is she related to your late master?"

Mrs Jennings shook her head. "I don't think so, sir, but it's no use questioning me, I know little about her other than—"she broke off.

"What?" he asked.

"I did hear mention of the London Workhouse."

"There is a reward," Edward said, now certain Kate's daughter had *sought* shelter with Mister Kebble.

Becky tugged his sleeve.

"A reward?" Mrs Jennings said. "Upon my word, you sly creature, Becky, that's why you went to fetch this gentleman instead of the watchman."

Hands on her hips, Becky stepped forward. "No, it's not. I went because I like Mistress Amanda. I don't want 'er to go to gaol."

The girl stood staring at him in the dim light from a small, barred window set high up in the stone wall. Edward sighed, reluctant to leave Becky to face Lucius's wrath. Besides, he wanted to cross-question her about Amanda's possible whereabouts and, without doubt, Kate would also want to speak with her.

For a moment, he considered searching the nearby streets for Amanda but rejected the idea. After her escape, the girl had most probably disappeared into the crowded lanes and alleys with great speed. He looked at Becky. If she had untied Amanda, perhaps Becky knew where Amanda was going.

"My money, Captain," Becky squeaked.

"I shall give you the reward if your information leads me to Amanda. Now, pack your duds and accompany me. I will find you employment."

Becky sighed, despite the irrepressible amusement that appeared in her eyes. "After Mrs Jennings and I leave 'ere, what will nasty Mister Lucius do when 'e finds out Mistress Amanda's gone?"

"You will not be here to find out. Now, hurry along to fetch your things while I make certain the urchin is still looking after my horse."

In the narrow street divided by a noxious kennel overflowing with filthy water and rubbish, Dark Lady whinnied a greeting to Edward. He gave the ragamuffin his due and stood, deep in thought, by the hitching post. After some time, Becky, accompanied by another girl, came out of the passage which led from the back of the house. "'Ere she is, Captain, she was 'iding in the shed at the end of the garden wondering where to go."

"Becky says you are looking for me." Becky's companion spoke in a beautifully modulated tone. "Is it true? If so, why did you want to find me?"

A pair of blue eyes the same shade as Kate's questioned him.

"My dear child," Edward said, his voice thick with emotion.

Chapter Twenty-Three

Edward knocked on the front door of his godmother's house. Perkins, her butler, opened it. He looked down his long nose at Lady Amanda, who stood beside Edward, and at Becky, who peered from behind Edward, a small bundle clasped in her grubby hand.

"Step forward, Becky, there is no reason to be nervous." Edward looked at the butler. "Please summon the housekeeper to care for these girls."

Perkins slowly opened the door so they could enter. "Has my mistress been told of the young persons' arrival, Captain?"

Edward scrutinised Perkins from the tip of his shoes to the top of his wig. "There is a stain on your waistcoat, your buttons are not polished to an acceptable standard, and your neckband needs to be straightened."

Perkins shuffled his feet.

"In future, remember it is not for you to question me," he said in a voice cold enough to freeze barnacles.

Slight colour rose in the butler's cheeks. "I shall fetch the housekeeper, Captain." Without another word, Perkins disappeared through a door which led to steps that gave access to the basement.

Edward gazed down at Lady Amanda and drew Becky forward. "Your immediate needs will be seen to and you must bathe."

"Bathe?" Becky grumbled.

"Yes," Edward insisted. "And I daresay you are both in need of sustenance."

"What's that?" asked Becky.

"Food," Lady Amanda explained.

"No need to wait in the hall." Edward thrust open the door to an anteroom decorated in ice blue, its cold hue softened by the judicious use of richly coloured oriental rugs.

Lady Amanda eyed her surroundings.

No doubt about her identity lingered in Edward's mind. She bore an uncanny resemblance not only to Kate but also to Charles.

Edward shut the door. "Amanda, the lady I believe to be your mother has been searching for you. I brought you here to be looked after until I can tell her I have found you."

"Gawd," Becky stared at Lady Amanda with something approaching awe. "There we were as good as friends in the old gentleman's house, and me thinking you were an orphan."

Lady Amanda sank onto a chair. "Who do you think my mother is?"

"A great lady, but it is not for me to tell you who she is. You must wait in patience for confirmation you are her daughter and, if she wishes, for her ladyship to make herself known to you," Edward explained, confident he did not offer her false hope, and sure Kate would want to meet her daughter as soon as possible. He held out his hand. "Get up, child. Hold your head high as befits what I believe to be your true place in society."

Lady Amanda remained seated. "Why have you brought me here?" She rolled her eyes as though she was about to panic.

Edward sat on a box-like couch. He gestured to Becky to sit down, but she remained on her feet, her bundle clutched in her hands.

"Mistress Amanda," Edward began, for it would be premature to address her by her title, "where did you live before you resided with Mister Kebble?"

"At the London Workhouse."

Lady Amanda looked up at the blue ceiling, a background for painted angels with folded wings and gold halos.

"Before that?" he asked and held his breath while waiting for her reply.

"With Mister and Mrs Simpkins, who took me in when I was a baby and treated me like their daughter."

The reply almost confirmed her identity.

"What was Mrs Simpkins' Christian name?"

"Tabitha."

Incontrovertible proof.

Lady Amanda's stomach growled. She blushed. "I beg your pardon."

"Think nothing of it. You shall eat soon."

"Thank you, Becky is always hungry."

This child, rejected by her father, had inherited Kate's pride? Why did mother and daughter tug at his heartstrings? He sank beyond salvation in a sea of love for the mother and spontaneous affection for the daughter because she was so much like Kate. For the rest of his days on earth he wanted to protect them, to love them and make them happy. Edward tapped his chin with his forefinger. He dragged himself from a vision of Utopia, for that meant marriage, and he doubted Kate would accept his proposal, even though he did not covet her fortune and would ensure she remained in control of it. He dragged his mind away from Kate. "Mistress Amanda, why did you run away from the workhouse?"

Lady Amanda's cheeks turned coral pink. She glanced at Becky.

"Well, you see, Captain Sir," Becky began, "there was this old gent on what-do-you-call-it?"

"The committee." More colour flooded into Lady Amanda's cheeks.

"Oh yes, the committee," Becky said. "'E was always putting 'is hands where they shouldn't be, so Amanda ran away because she knew 'e was after her—if you take my meaning."

Edward clenched his fists. "Yes, I do, but, Mistress Amanda, why did you not tell the nurse in charge of your dormitory about the lecher?"

Her ladyship stared at a priceless oil painting of a tender-faced Mary, with Elizabeth, the infant Jesus, and young John the Baptist.

"She didn't tell because she wouldn't 'ave been believed," Becky chirped.

"I see. Mistress Amanda, why did you seek refuge with Mister Kebble?"

"He was a friend of my foster mother and father. When I was a little girl, Mister Kebble used to say that one day my face could make a fortune on the stage. So when I ran away, I'd already decided to become an actress. After I convinced Mister Kebble I was serious, he agreed to train me." She blinked her tears away. "I'll miss him. He could not have treated me better if I'd been his daughter. When I made my debut on the stage, no father could have been prouder of me. Yet he didn't let me go on stage again. He said I should wait until I'm older." Her eyes filled with tears. "What will happen to me now?"

"There is no need for tears. Your mother will provide for you," Edward said.

The housekeeper arrived. She bobbed a curtsey. "Perkins tells me these young people are to be taken care of."

"See to it that they have a bath and a good meal," Edward ordered. "I shall speak to your mistress, who will give you further instructions."

The housekeeper shepherded the girls out of the ante room. Edward followed them with the intention of going upstairs to join his godmother. Before he put his foot on the first step, a lackey answered a knock on the front door.

"Is Mrs Radcliffe at home? We must speak to her immediately."

Edward recognised the voice. Confound it! His business with his godmother must wait. He turned around. "Lord Kershaw." He inclined his head. "Mistress Martyn, I am sure my godmother will be relieved to see you." He glanced at the lackey. "Where is Mrs Radcliffe?"

"In the yellow closet."

Edward waved his hand at the servant. "Stay here. I will announce this lady and gentleman." He inclined his head to the couple. "My lord, Mistress Martyn, please follow me."

In the gallery on the first floor, Edward indicated a couch opposite a white granite fireplace, on the mantelpiece of which stood a pair of blue and white Delft vases. "Be good enough to wait here for a few moments."

He rapped on the door of his godmother's private closet.

"Come," Frances called.

Edward slipped into the room in which an ornately carved walnut strongbox stood on a gilt stand with legs that curved inward. Like everything else in Frances's house, the small room was furnished with elegance and comfort.

He bowed to his godmother and Sir Newton, who sat close together on a sofa upholstered with daffodil-yellow damask.

Frances looked up. Her smile welcomed him. "Edward," she murmured.

He kissed her but did not sit. "Urgent business calls me to the country. While I am away, I am entrusting a young lady and a servant girl to your care."

Of course, he could take them to Missendene Manor in a hired coach but it would cause unnecessary delay. He would ride there. With several changes of horses on the way, he could reach Kate in less than thirty-six hours instead of the seventy-two or more it would take to go by coach.

Frances fluttered her fan backward and forward. "Girls! You want me to take care of two girls. Who are they? Why do you ask such a thing of me?"

"Becky is a scrap of a servant girl who needs employment. As for Mistress Amanda, please trust me. At the moment, I cannot explain why I brought her here. Yet, when you see her, you might guess the truth."

Her curiosity aroused, his godmother's eyes glittered. "A mystery, how exciting. Who can your protégée be?" Her laughter tinkled. She looked up at him. "We ladies live such dull lives."

He laughed. "I would not have thought so."

"'Tis true, we are forbidden so many things gentlemen enjoy, such as clubs and coffeehouses."

"You are right." He kissed her cheek. "Until my return, please keep Amanda in seclusion. I depend on your discretion."

Newton flicked open his jade snuff box. "Deep, m'boy, very deep. Saw the way your eyes lit up when I mentioned seeing the Earl of Sinclair dressed as a girl. Suppose it was not him but the young lady you have brought here."

Foppish Sir Newton might be, but he was not a fool. "You are too knowing, sir." In dangerous waters, he changed the subject. "Mistress Martyn is here to see you, Godmother."

"Jane, here," Frances cried. "Thank God. I have been distracted with thoughts of what might have befallen her."

"I must warn you. She married Lord Kershaw clandestinely. I hope she has come to you for advice."

"An illicit marriage? How shocking! What could she have been thinking?"

Sir Newton inspected his tortoiseshell snuffbox. "Who would have thought that milk and water chit would be so wicked?"

Edward returned to the landing. "Lord Kershaw, I have told Mrs Radcliffe about your false marriage and am confident she will help you. May you have long and happy lives." Edward opened the door to admit them to the yellow closet. He intended to leave for Missendene without delay.

"Mrs Radcliffe." Jane burst into tears.

Frances waved her fan at Edward. "Don't leave." She hurried across the salon and hugged Jane. "Naughty child, why did you marry in haste? Where did you marry? Captain Howard tells me your marriage is clandestine. I am shocked. As for your poor parents, do you know they are frantic with worry? They feared someone murdered you."

The young woman returned Edward's godmother's embrace. "I am sorry, Mrs Radcliffe. I married in haste because I love Lord Kershaw, and I feared my mother would force me to marry Fenton, an odious man who is repulsive. Nothing would induce me to share the same fate as the Countess of Sinclair. I would prefer death to an arranged marriage to a much older man who is a libertine," Mistress Martyn concluded and then burst into tears.

Lord Kershaw put an arm around her shoulders. "Don't cry. As Captain Howard suggested, maybe Mrs Radcliffe will help us to marry in the country. If she does, we can return to London and present ourselves to your parents as man and wife."

Mistress Martyn's shoulders heaved. Kershaw patted her back. He whispered in her ear. Like an obedient child, she wiped her eyes with her wisp of a handkerchief.

Mrs Radcliffe shook her head at the couple.

Newton held Mrs Radcliffe's hand. "My sweet lady, don't upset yourself. You are not responsible for this rash pair." He looked at Kershaw and Mistress Martyn. "Sit yourselves down."

"Yes," Mrs Radcliffe said, "please sit." She glared at Lord Kershaw. "If you harmed a hair of her head you will have me to reckon with."

"Of course I have not harmed a hair of my angel's head, madam," Kershaw protested. He eyed Edward and then subsided onto a comfortable wing chair. "Never—" he sighed, "—did I imagine ladies, God bless them, cry at the least provocation." He coughed. "Yet you must not be thinking I mind. After all, a gentleman's duty is to console and protect his wife."

How soon could he be on his way? Edward wondered. Could he reach Kate in less than thirty-six hours?

"Captain, have you nothing to say?" Lord Kershaw asked. "Do you not think ladies cry at the least provocation?"

Edward thought of the many vicissitudes Kate faced with courage. "Not all of them."

Kershaw kissed "his angel's" hand. "Will you not favour me with a smile, my love?"

"Where did you marry?" Sir Newton asked.

"At The Fleet, after I ensured the parson was still in Holy Orders," Kershaw replied.

"More than likely you were duped." Sir Newton snorted and eyed Mistress Martyn with disfavour. "No, no, don't cry, my constitution cannot bear females who sob their hearts out in a most unladylike fashion." He raised his eyeglass to scrutinise Mistress Martyn. "I daresay you filled your head with nonsense from too many novels about love and marriage before you eloped."

"Shush, Sir Newton." Frances tapped his arm with her furled fan. She looked at the unfortunate bride.

"There is only one thing to be done. I shall summon your parents. Under the circumstances, I assume they will not withhold their consent to your marriage."

Tears rolled down Mistress Martyn's cheeks. "No, I beg you not to. Father will be heart-broken and Mother will be furious."

"You should have considered the consequences before you left in secret to get married," Sir Newton said. "No, no, please don't wail. Stands to reason you preferred Kershaw to Fenton."

For the first time since she entered the room, Mistress Martyn smiled. "I thank you for your understanding of my predicament, sir."

"My dear child," Frances began, "I have no doubt your parents will be delighted to discover you safe and well. They fear you were abducted by some rogue and forced to marry in the presence of witnesses in Fleet Chapel for your prospective fortune. They were also afraid you were subjected to unmentionable brutality. No, no, please spare poor Newton's sensibilities by not crying again. If you insist, I will not send for your parents."

Mistress Martyn wiped her tears away. "Mrs Radcliffe, do you truly believe my parents will be happy to see me?"

"Yes, I do, although they may be angry at first."

Enough was enough. "Good day to you." Edward bowed and left the salon.

Frances followed him onto the landing. "To think I wanted you to marry that silly creature."

"Let us be glad I had too much sense to be carried away by your match-making."

She eyed him. "Well, you cannot blame me. You are very dear to me, so I want the best for you. Don't look so grim. You see a penitent before you. I confess I was wrong."

He folded his arms. "About what?"

"The Countess of Sinclair." Frances sighed. "It seems she has not stolen your heart. You have given it to her."

Edward raised her be-ringed hand to his lips. "And?"

"My dear Sir Newton told me you love her, but I did not believe him. I thought you suffered from no more than youth's green sickness. Now I understand you are a man who knows his own mind. You have my blessings, if you wish to marry her."

He released her hand. "Thank you."

She stamped her daintily shod foot. "Is that all you have to say?"

"What else *should* I say?"

"Wretch," she said playfully, "are you going to marry her?"

"I doubt she will have me. However, I can fulfil one of her heart's desires and hope she will always think of me with kindness, if not affection."

"Bah, should she not wed you, she would be a cold-hearted monster."

Edward laughed at his godmother's unexpected turnabout and then went to pack some essential items.

Chapter Twenty-Four

The clock struck midnight. Kate surveyed herself in the mirror. Her thick plait lay over one shoulder and tumbled down her nightgown to her waist. The satin ribbons of her white-work nightcap—tied into a bow under her chin—fluttered with each swift rise and fall of her breast.

Jessie yawned. "I've run a warming pan through your sheets and turned back the covers, my lady."

"You are exhausted, Jessie, go and sleep."

"I'm not too tired to see you into your bed, my lady."

"No need," Kate said and sat by the fireplace.

"It is a little cold, my lady. Should I light the fire?"

"No thank you."

Jessie curtsied and withdrew.

Candlelight shone on the rosy pink walls of Kate's closet and flickered over her collection of miniatures: small but priceless paintings, such as one of an unknown lady by Nicolas Hilliard.

Fatigued, but not yet ready to retire, Kate went to the window and drew apart the cream damask curtains. She peered through a gap in the thin, pink muslin drapes, which protected her from the sight of anyone without.

Restless, she observed the tranquil north approach. In a midnight blue sky, the moon hung like the ghost of a becalmed ship. Where were her children? Was

Charles in town or at Sinclair Place? What of Amanda? Why had Captain Howard ignored her in London? No longer could she deny she loved him. Although she would not wed again, she would carry the gallant young man in her heart for the rest of her life. Yet was she as afraid of him as she was of other men? Curiosity and breathless excitement welled up in her.

She stared out into the moonlight. Had something moved? A horseman emerged from the darkness. The clock struck the half hour. Who could it be? A thief? For fear of highwaymen, no honest person would ride alone at night.

The figure reached the north door and dismounted. A knock thundered through the manor. Hardly a thief? Some stranger who had lost his way?

* * *

Covered with dust, Edward strode into Missendene. He handed his cloak to the sleepy lackey on duty.

The man gawped. "Captain Howard."

"I am come with urgent tidings for your mistress. Take me to her."

"I can't. She's retired for the night."

"Do as I ask. There is not a moment to waste."

The lackey hesitated.

Edward knew the layout of the manor. He thrust his hat, gloves, and riding crop into the man's arms. "Tell someone to attend to my horse." He turned to another lackey. "Go and tell her ladyship I have arrived with important news."

"Very good, sir."

305

Eager to speak to Kate, as soon as she was informed of his arrival, he hurried up the stairs with the intention of waiting on the second floor landing.

Mrs Corby, a becoming nightcap on her head and a candlestick in hand, came out of her bedchamber. Clad in a purple banyan, Mister Milton emerged from another room cramming a turban onto his shaven head.

A third door opened. Kate crossed the threshold of her closet, her hip-length plait freed from its coronet falling over one shoulder to her waist and swaying seductively with each step.

Edward caught his breath at the sight of her in the sumptuous nightgown that parted below the knees revealing a delicate muslin night rail.

"Captain Howard, what are you doing here at this hour of the night?" Kate asked.

He bowed to the three of them. "Milady, please accept my sincere apology for my rude intrusion. My only excuse is that I have news for your ears alone." He stepped forward and held the door of her closet wide open. "Come."

Kate's cheeks coloured up as she glanced at her mother and Mister Milton.

The reverend gentleman retired to his room, but Gertrude lingered. "Improper." She stared hard at Edward. "This is not fitting."

"Mother, I am sure the captain has good cause to seek me out at this hour of the night."

"Yes, I do." Edward bowed again. "Please excuse us, Mrs Corby. I apologise for disturbing your sleep. Do return to bed. I hope you will pass a tranquil night."

Gertrude clutched her lavender-coloured nightgown around her, looked at him indignantly, and then returned to her bedchamber.

Edward cupped Kate's elbow with his hand, guided her into her closet, and shut the door.

Kate sank onto a chaise longue, one slim-fingered hand pressed to her throat.

"Forgive me for not washing the dust away before I came into your presence but I have ridden day and night to reach you."

"Is something amiss with Charles?"

He shook his head. "No. Prepare yourself for good news. I have found Lady Amanda."

"You have found my daughter!" Kate swooned, sliding from chaise longue onto the floor.

"Kate!" Edward knelt. He cradled her head in his arms, his nostrils filled with her delicious fragrance.

Smelling salts. Edward grabbed a cushion and slipped it under her head. The door opposite him might lead to her bedchamber. He hurried through it. Yes, he was right. He hunted on her dressing table.

Edward opened a tiny silver bottle and sniffed its contents. His eyes watered. Salts, strong enough to wake the dead.

He hastened back to Kate—who made feeble movements with her hands—and knelt again and raised her into his arms. "I am sorry for breaking the news so abruptly. Never did I think you would faint."

She opened her eyes. "Neither did I. It is the first time I have done so."

"Sniff this, it will revive you."

He held the bottle beneath her nose. When Kate spluttered he helped her to sit. Firelight gilded her face.

Her eyes glowed like precious jewels with fiery depths. "You really have found Amanda?"

"Yes. God be praised, she is safe and well."

Kate stood.

To steady her, Edward put his arm around her waist.

"Where is she?"

He pressed her head to his chest and then stroked the tender nape of her neck. "Amanda and Becky, the little maidservant who helped me find her, are at my godmother's house."

"Oh, how good Mrs Radcliffe is. But have you told her the truth?" With each breath Kate took, her breasts rose and fell more rapidly than usual, the movement tantalising him.

"Lady Amanda bears so close a resemblance to you and Charles that I am sure Godmother will guess who she is. Don't worry. She is too discreet to tattle."

Kate looked up at him, her face transformed by joy. "Why did you not bring Amanda to me?"

"I wanted to tell you without delay. I made the journey from London in less than half the usual time. Had I brought Lady Amanda by coach, I would have been delayed. Also, I deem it wise to ask Milton to formally identify her and attest to it in a document signed by witnesses."

She squeezed her eyes shut. "Then you are not certain the young lady is my girl?"

"Yes, I am, but to establish her in society you need proof. Mister Milton can attest she is your daughter. Her foster father's heir can take an oath that he placed her in the London Workhouse."

"How good you are to me, Captain Howard. What have I done to deserve such kindness?"

"Even now, do you not believe I am your devoted servant?"

"Indeed you are. I can never thank you enough for finding Amanda."

"I am glad to be of service to you."

"Is there naught I can do for you?"

"Yes, give me a heart hitherto untouched by any other man."

She shuddered and withdrew from the circle of his arms. "You are foolish. I know not how to love. Besides, my husband disgusted me. I have no wish to give myself to another man, although I realise some wives are not only compliant but pleased to share a bed with their husbands."

"Shush. I am not a fool. I am a man hardened in battle who has borne responsibility for his crew." Captain Howard took her hands in his. "Long since, I guessed your husband treated you shamefully." The captain kissed each of her fingers before he spoke again. "Sweet heart of mine, trust me and all shall be well." He turned her hand over and pressed a kiss onto its palm.

* * *

Delight bubbled through Kate's veins. Although she would not admit it to Edward—as she now thought of him—he had melted her ice-bound heart. How could she resist the temptation to put her hands on either side of his face, draw him toward her, and kiss his mouth? Kate's body quivered. Her stomach contracted. Her toes curled. Nevertheless she kept her hands at her side. In her case, she was certain the marriage bed would lead to disillusionment, even though her gallant captain was cut from a very different fabric from that of her dead husband.

Confusion and bewilderment sparked by the emotion rushing through her caused Kate's cheeks to burn. Reunited with Amanda, and with the captain at her side, she could achieve anything. But what was she considering? Some months ago, when they attended the theatre, had she not indicated her frozen heart by dressing like an Ice Queen? Yet, it had not discouraged Edward. She sighed. Although she loved him, it would be unfair to marry him. He deserved a young bride, not one burdened by a miserable past with many responsibilities. Besides, the captain had not mentioned marriage. Perhaps he wanted no more than a liaison to which she would never agree. Her breath hissed between her teeth. What was she thinking? She would never trust her well-being to any man.

"Forgive me." Edward drew her into his arms again and cradled her close to his broad chest. "At this moment, I daresay the last thing you wish to consider is love. For now, all you care about is meeting Lady Amanda. You are right to call me foolish. I am a fool for speaking of my devotion to you while you are preoccupied with thoughts of your daughter." He kissed the top of her head and released her. "You must seek your bed. Have you recovered after fainting? Did you hurt yourself when you fell? Shall I summon Jessie?"

She wanted him to hold her forever, but she would not take advantage of him. "I have recovered and am unharmed. In answer to your third question, don't summon Jessie, she needs her rest."

Now that he no longer supported her, she swayed. His strong arm went around her again.

"With your permission I shall see you safely to your bed."

Kate shook her head. "That is not necessary."

Her mistrust hurt. Edward bowed. "I shall trouble you no further and seek accommodation in the nearest inn."

Kate opened the door to the landing and then rang a hand bell. "You will do no such thing. The bedchamber you occupied on your last visit shall be prepared for you."

"Thank you, milady. Tomorrow I shall leave. You may send Mister Milton to London to identify Lady Amanda." He made a formal bow of the correct depth. "Goodnight, milady, I will retire to my room."

"I have offended you," she said, filled with regret, her gaze intent on his face in the dim light.

He returned her gaze for a long moment, inclined his head and then left the closet.

Chapter Twenty-Five

In the coach on the way to Missendene Manor, Frances looked at Lady Amanda. "'Tis like a fairy story," she cooed to the young girl for the umpteenth time.

Edward exchanged an amused glance with Mister Milton. Since the clergyman had identified Lady Amanda, his godmother had not only likened the lost heiress's change of circumstances to a fairy story, but also to a play.

With remarkable speed, Godmother had provided Lady Amanda with a new wardrobe; and she had also ensured Becky was suitably attired. Moreover, Godmother allowed the girl to travel in the fargon loaded with baggage.

"Are you not excited, child?" Frances asked Lady Amanda when the coach turned off the rutted road onto the approach to Missendene Manor.

Her ladyship nodded and looked from Frances to Mister Milton to Edward, as though she sought reassurance.

"How different your life will be now you are acknowledged as Countess of Sinclair's daughter," Frances said.

Lady Amanda sighed. "I wish my father lived, I would have liked to meet him."

Edward exchanged a startled glance with Mister Milton.

The wheels crunched over thick gravel. When the coach halted, everyone descended and stood facing the arched entrance to the manor. The front door opened. Flanked by two lackeys, Kate stood on the threshold dressed in a gown and petticoat the colour of bluebells.

Lady Amanda lagged behind her companions, and before Edward could say something to reassure the young lady, his godmother spoke. "No need to be bashful, your mother is expecting us."

Frances half-turned, seized Lady Amanda's hand, and drew her forward.

Kate hurried toward them as fast as her full skirts and high-heeled shoes allowed. Frances released Lady Amanda's hand. Kate's arms circled her daughter. Tears spilled out of Kate's eyes. "This is where you belong. Safe at last with your mother."

Her eyes tear-filled, Kate's daughter withdrew from the embrace and stared at Kate. "I don't understand why you gave me to the Simpkins."

Edward cleared his throat. How could she reveal the ugly truth to the child?

Kate dabbed the tears with her handkerchief. "Come indoors, we shall speak later." She smiled at Mrs Radcliffe. "Welcome to Missendene Manor." Kate nodded at Milton. "Welcome back, sir, my mother will be pleased to see you. She feared a mishap on the journey. Captain Howard, you are welcome."

"I shall not inconvenience you for a moment longer than necessary. After the fargon arrives with the groom leading Dark Lady, I shall return to London." He made a stiff bow, still angered by Kate's suspicion that he would take advantage of her when he offered to see her safe in bed after she fainted.

To understand her fear of being bedded was one thing, to be suspected of seeking to take sexual advantage of Kate at her most vulnerable, was another. It proved how little she knew him.

Lady Amanda ran to him. "Please don't go, sir. You have been very kind to me. What will I do without you?"

Above her head, he looked into Kate's eyes.

"I second my daughter's plea," Kate said softly.

By his faith, how he loved her. Yet he now believed she would never reciprocate. It was agony to be near her, realising she would never be his.

"You are most kind, madam, but urgent business calls me back to town."

"What business?" his godmother asked. "With your uncle, Admiral Rooke's help, you have been cleared of all charges. But as he told you, it will be some time before you are given a new command."

"Congratulations, Captain, on a successful outcome to the charges brought against you," Kate said, her hands trembling.

"Thank you, milady," he replied, wondering if she feared he would be severely injured or lose his life at sea.

Kate clasped her daughter's hand. "No need for all of us to linger here. Come indoors."

With Amanda beside her, Kate led them into the manor house, and then up the stairs to a withdrawing room with several mullioned windows, polished oak floors, and chairs upholstered in velvet, the colour of old gold.

Gertrude rose from an armchair. "My dear child," she puffed, one hand pressed to her bosom. "I always wanted a granddaughter, but was not told of your birth."

"You did not want me." Lady Amanda removed her hand from Kate's and clutched Edward's.

"To the contrary," Edward said, "you were snatched from your mother at birth, and since that dreadful day she has never ceased to pine for you."

"Is the captain telling the truth?" Amanda asked Kate.

"Yes, Daughter." She beckoned to her butler. "Serve my guests with wine."

Charles entered the withdrawing room. He bowed so low the beaver hat in his hand brushed the floor. "Sinclair at your service, sister."

The children stared at each other. "I have seen you in my dreams," Lady Amanda said.

"And I, you." The quiver of Charles's upper lip betrayed his emotion. "Have they not told you we are twins?"

Amanda sank onto a chair. Charles perched on the arm and enfolded her hand in his.

Kate approached Edward. "My brother-by-law underwent a change of heart and allowed my son to visit me. Charles and Amanda will be thirteen next week. In three years, under the terms of his father's will, Charles will have more say over his life, and in five years, he will come into his inheritance. I assume Mister Sinclair fears Charles will have naught to do with him then, and he is frightened that he will be almost penniless when deprived of the income from my son's estates which he now enjoys."

"Then all is well that ends well," Edward said.

Kate pressed her hand to her throat. "I can never thank you enough for all you have done for me and mine."

His senses swam when he breathed in the scent of her spicy perfume mingled with sweetness. "Have I not told you I require no thanks?"

"Nevertheless, you have it. Will you not stay here instead of hurrying back to London?"

Did she want him to put up here? Really want him to do so?

Her eyes pleaded with him. "If not for my sake, for Amanda's. She seems fond of you."

''As you please, milady.''

* * *

Kate tossed and turned all night. With both children safe under her roof, she should have sunk into peaceful repose. Yet tonight it was impossible. After she had dined with her family and guests, she had withdrawn to her closet and then sent for the twins.

Her son had strode in and smiled at her before Amanda stood in the doorway hesitant to enter.

"Come and sit down, sweetheart," Kate had said. Amanda sat in the chair farthest from her. "Tell me why you ran away from the London Workhouse," Kate coaxed. "Did someone mistreat you? If so I shall ensure the person is punished."

Becky, Amanda's faithful shadow, came forward and shut the door behind her. "Amanda, I beg pardon—I'm not used to 'er title—Lady Amanda won't tell you. As I've already told the captain, that nasty committee member, Sir Clive, was always putting 'is 'ands up the prettiest girls' skirts, but before 'e could corner Amanda, she ran away."

"What? Oh my poor child, I shall lodge a complaint and ensure Sir Clive is never again received in polite society."

Amanda's cheeks flamed. "But then everyone will know what he tried to do to me. They'll whisper and stare and say horrid things."

Kate pressed her hand to her heart. "Very well, I shall not report him but you may be sure I will find a way to ruin him and have him removed from the Board. He shall be prevented from making free with innocent little girls."

"Were I older, I would challenge Sir Clive to a duel to the death," Charles said.

"Why was I taken from you?" Amanda asked.

"Leave the room, Becky," Kate ordered.

The girl raised her eyebrows at Amanda, who nodded.

"Father falsely believed a woman who gave birth to twins had slept with two men," Charles said after Becky left. "To be revenged on Mother, he kept me and sent you away."

"Amanda, I have been searching for you since the day your father died," Kate explained. "Before then he kept me immured in a manor in the dreary wastes of Northumberland. Until he died, I thought of you every day. Afterwards, I continued to think of you while I searched." Kate swallowed her sobs. She hoped her daughter would never find out that her father gave orders to murder her.

Amanda bunched her apron in her hands. "Truly?" she asked, as though she did not believe her. "I mean, how did you search for me?"

"I employed agents. Should you doubt my word, I have correspondence to prove it."

"Why didn't Mister Milton tell you where I was?"

It was not going to be as easy to forge a bond with Amanda as it was with Charles. "Amanda, your father made not only the midwife in attendance at your birth, but also Mister Milton, swear a sacred oath that they would never speak of the matter. After your father died, his conscience goaded Mister Milton into breaking his vow by telling me the Simpkins' reared you. Were they good to you?" Kate asked, her voice trembling when she spoke the last words.

Amanda nodded. "Yes, no one could have had kinder parents. Of course they were not really my parents, but that's how I think of them. Mother used to complain Father spoiled me but she pampered me. If Mother insisted Father should cane me for some wrongdoing, he would take me into another room." She giggled. "Instead of whacking me, he whacked the floor to mimic the sound of a beating and make Mother think he struck me. He could never bear to hurt me. If anyone such as Sir Clive held ill-intentions to me during his lifetime, I think he would have committed murder for my sake."

Thank God her daughter's childhood had been happy until she went to the workhouse. "You must miss them very much."

Amanda twisted a fold of her satinet petticoat. "Yes, I do, and I always will."

318

"Of course you will." Kate hesitated before she spoke again. "I know I can never replace them in your affections, but I hope you can learn to love me and your brother." Kate went to Amanda. "Sit next to me on the sofa."

Charles stood. He smiled encouragingly at Amanda who resisted the gentle pressure of Kate's hand.

"Come, child," Kate said, "it will be easier to share confidences when we are sitting close to each other."

Amanda acquiesced. Settled on the sofa, Kate slipped an arm around Amanda. "What of Mister Kebble?"

"What of him?" Amanda asked.

"Was he good to you?"

"Yes, he looked on me as a granddaughter, but he was a strict teacher." She tensed. "But his grandson, Mister Lucius is a pig. A fat sot of a pig and I hate him."

Kate frowned. "Why do you detest him?"

"He wanted to bed me. When I escaped his sweaty hands, he accused me of theft and then ordered Becky to call the Watch." The hard expression in Amanda's eyes softened. "Thanks to her, the captain rescued me."

Charles smiled at his twin. "I am really glad he found you."

Amanda yawned. Her eyes drooped.

"Bed for you," Kate said, "for both of you."

Amanda left the closet, but Charles lingered for a moment before he bowed and kissed her cheek. "You are superb, Mother."

"And you are a son to delight any mother's heart. Good night, Charles."

Her dreams of reunion with her children had come true, so why could she not sleep? Perhaps it was because of Captain Howard's formal manner toward her.

Kate drew the bed curtains apart. She fumbled candle. Beyond the circle of light cast by the fire, long shadows crept across the room, giving it an unfamiliar appearance. She glanced at the clock on a table by her bed. Dawn already, she would seek peace in her private retreat, the pavilion by the lake.

* * *

On the morning after Kate and Lady Amanda's reunion, Edward pushed back the bedcovers. A frustrated groan escaped him. He was certain physical consummation of his love for Kate would free her from fear, delight her, and set her heart afire. Yet he doubted he would ever have the opportunity to make her his own and prove she had no cause for trepidation.

How he wished that tonight he could wait for everyone to retire before he made his way discreetly to Kate's bedchamber.

He rose, thrust his feet into his slippers and drew on his crimson and gold nightgown. He shivered, only partially with cold, while he poked the embers of the dying fire and added more logs. One luxury he had observed Kate enjoyed, were fires, regardless of the season.

How long should he stay at Missendene? Lady Amanda looked at him whenever she spoke and hovered near him as though she took comfort in him. Charles sought his company and asked if he could ride

320

with him this morning. Should he stay at the manor for the children's sake? As for Kate, did he imagine her eyes softened whenever she looked at him? If it were true, what was its significance?

He drew apart the sea green curtains, folded back the wooden shutters, and looked out of the window along the sweep of the drive bordered by symmetrical gardens and orchards.

The pale sun hung low in the east and the last dusky fingers of night clung to the horizon. Edward hoped this new day would not place another barrier between him and Kate. Yesterday, he believed she would never reciprocate his love, but was he mistaken? Should he put his injured pride aside and carry out his earlier plan to beguile Kate with all the love, patience, and tenderness at his command? Not for the entire world did he want to risk dismaying her with unbridled passion. If he pursued her, he must control his insistent desire and give her the fulfilment he was certain she never experienced in bed with her old satyr of a husband.

Why not visit Kate's bedchamber tonight and, if she consented, claim her for his own? A wave of heat flooded him. His stomach tightened. In violent response to a vision of Kate's slim body in his arms, he shook with painful hunger only she could satisfy.

Edward answered his question. He could not visit Kate tonight for fear she would assume he expected her favour in return for finding Amanda.

A dip in the icy lake would cool him in more ways than one. He grabbed a towel.

Beyond the cluster of immaculate stables and other outbuildings at the rear of the manor, the serene lake reflected dawn's radiant colours and a white pavilion on the shore.

Out of sight of any other building, Edward stripped off his nightgown and night rail. He plunged into the clear water and swam to the farther shore.

* * *

Kate opened the door of the pavilion. After the initial shock of seeing Captain Howard naked, Kate admired his well-proportioned body. In silence, she watched Edward cleave through the water, turn and swim back.

He emerged from the lake. Droplets, which glistened by the light of the pale sun, clung to every part of his muscular body. Never before had she judged any man beautiful. Paintings and sculptures of either naked or partially clad males, depicting classical Roman or Greek myths, always struck her as unreal. Yet with his broad chest, narrow waist, and well-formed arms and legs, Captain Howard's body surpassed those representations of male perfection, despite a scar from his navel to his groin. A swift breath escaped her. Greek sculptors of old marked their work with a small flaw in order not to arouse the jealousy of their heathen Gods. Well, no pagan deity would envy that disfigurement which did not repulse her.

Handsome as Apollo come to life, the captain stood on the lakeshore. His physique was so different from her late husband's that he could have belonged to another species.

* * *

Edward stooped to pick up his towel. He straightened and saw Kate framed by the arched doorway of the pavilion. Embarrassed, he tried to ignore his arousal, knotted the towel around his waist, and strode toward her.

Kate's cheeks flamed. Not since he saw one of his friends' scantily clad young sisters, whose chamber he mistook for his own, had he seen a lady as discomposed as Kate.

Edward tried to ignore his pulsating flesh, pushed his hair back from his forehead, and bowed. "My lady, I did not expect to see you here at this hour."

The countess sighed. "I could not sleep."

The time of truth presented itself in an unexpected manner. "Neither could I, for thoughts of you lying sated in my arms."

Her cheeks scarlet, his lady retreated into the pavilion.

Edward followed. He shut the door. "At last, we are alone. Since we parted after I told you I had found Amanda, you cannot imagine how much I have longed for this moment."

Kate studied the floor. "We should not be here with you near naked and me in my night attire."

In spite of her mild reproof, she did not sound annoyed.

How should he respond, he wondered, while forcing himself to observe the interior of the pavilion, the white painted shutters at the windows, a bookcase, low tables, several cane chairs and a couch piled with cushions, a folded quilt, and several colourful shawls?

Never before did she appear more desirable than now, clad in her turquoise blue nightgown lined with pale fur, her braided hair snaking over her right shoulder, and her face innocent of powder and patch. "My love, my dear, dear love." He breathed deep. The traces of her perfume, attar of roses blended with sandalwood, filled his nostrils. "My heart's desire," he murmured. "Heart of my heart, please don't be afraid of me," he breathed. "I promise I will never hurt you."

The twin sapphires of Kate's eyes gazed unwaveringly into his.

* * *

Despite her apprehension and lack of clothes, Kate yearned for the captain to kiss her again. No more than a kiss, she assured herself. Now, although she often declared her aversion to even the smallest intimacy, for the first time she wanted a man to overcome it, and she wanted Edward to be the one to do so. Indeed, she could imagine no other man capable of laying her fears to rest.

Head tilted, Kate continued to gaze into his eyes. Unlike men of Mister Stafford's nature, Edward did not seize hold of her. His body aloof from hers, he lowered his head. She closed her eyes waiting for his kiss. To her delight, his lips did not ravage her mouth. Instead, they teased, titillated, and promised greater rapture.

Breathless and delighted, Kate drew her head back, raised her hand, and traced the outline of his mouth with the tip of her finger.

"Say my name," he beseeched.

"Captain Howard," she whispered, enthralled by his full, firm lips.

"Edward, call me Edward," he urged.

Kate hesitated. Formal mode of address protected a lady from the risk of disrespect engendered by the use of Christian names. Her sense of humour surfaced. When they first met, on a mad whim, she invited him to call her Kate, although she would have been outraged if he had done so. She suppressed a chuckle. Ridiculous to think of disrespect when, clad in her night attire, she faced a near naked gentleman.

"Oh, Kate, you know not how much I adore you."

Her tumultuous heartbeat resounded in her ears. Her cheeks burned. She trembled. "Edward," she murmured, her eyes half-closed.

* * *

Never before had he been rewarded with such sweet surrender. He expelled his breath with a sigh of deep satisfaction. Fully aroused, Edward wondered if he would be able to contain his desire long enough to satisfy Kate. If the door had not clattered open, he would have gathered Kate in his arms.

325

Chapter Twenty-Six

"What the deuce, Countess?" a boy's voice asked.

Edward turned. The Earl of Sinclair's eyes blazed at him. Although Edward liked the young earl and hoped to become his father-by-law, he deplored his unexpected arrival in the pavilion at such a crucial time in his relationship with Kate.

"My boy." Kate reached out her hands to Charles.

"Uncle Sinclair is right," the earl spat, his child's face contorted like a gargoyle's. "You are a whore, my lady."

Edward crossed the pavilion with long strides. "To address your Lady Mother thus, my Lord, proves you are no better than an undisciplined puppy, if not worse. Her ladyship is *not* a whore." He frowned, humiliated by the necessity of offering an explanation to a thirteen year old boy. "Unbeknown to me, when I took an early morning dip in the lake, milady was in the pavilion."

"I am not a small child to be easily gulled," Charles snapped.

To reassure Kate, Edward smiled at her. "My lord, I hope you will offer us your apologies and your congratulations."

The sob that caught in Charles's throat betrayed his age. "Congratulate you on the occasion of my discovery of you undressed and Lady Sinclair clad in her night clothes?"

"Yes," Edward insisted, aware of Kate's obvious bewilderment. "Congratulate us. You are the first to know the countess has consented to marry me. Milady, pray tell his lordship you have agreed to be my bride."

Head bent, Kate sank onto the couch. Edward eyed her anxiously, knowing she felt trapped. Yet to deny his claim, would destroy whatever little faith her son still had in her. "Charles, will you not felicitate us?"

"I shall, despite my shock when I came upon you in such damnable circumstances." His lips a thin line, Charles bowed with excessive formality. "I trust you will be as happy in your marriage, my lady, as I am to be free of my uncle for the time being."

"Neatly put." Edward cursed the unintentionally hearty note that had crept into his voice, for he would never deliberately patronise his future stepson.

Edward crossed the small space separating him from Kate. Her hands in his, he drew her upright, and then kissed her cheek before going to retrieve his attire from the lakeshore.

Charles had given him the opportunity to overcome Kate's reluctance to remarry. Fate had played into his hands. When fair means did not triumph, perhaps foul means justified the result. Besides, in love and war, the rules of fair play did not always apply.

Convinced Kate would marry him, he dressed without undue haste and whistled a merry sea shanty on his way back to his bedchamber.

* * *

Kate patted the couch. "My dear son, please stop scowling and sit next to me."

327

Charles stared downward and shifted his weight from one foot to the other before standing still.

"It grieves me that you must return to your uncle within the week. I wish you could remain in my care until you come of age. However, if you so wish, when you are eighteen, you may boot him out of your life."

Charles's eyes glinted like granite. "My lady, you may rest assured that when the time comes, I shall be delighted to kick my uncle out with the hope he has not exhausted my revenues, in spite of my trustees best efforts on my behalf."

"Put all thought of it out of your mind. I am more than wealthy enough to provide amply for you and your sister."

"Thank you, but I hope it will not be necessary." Charles studied her face. "Besides, when you marry Captain Howard, will your fortune not pass into his hands?"

"We have not discussed it, but he might be content for the marriage settlements to be in my favour."

Her son removed his hat and twirled it around and around. "He is much younger than you. Why should he marry you if not for wealth and property?"

How adult Charles was for his age. "My boy, when you are older you will understand."

"Has he bedded you? Are you with child? Is that why you agreed to marry him?"

Kate's breath hissed. "'Pon my word, you are both impertinent and uncommon sharp for a boy of your years."

Charles drew himself up to his full height. "Life in my uncle and aunt's custody has honed my wits. Apart from Mister Milton, no one had my best interests at heart."

Despite the maturity of his words, childish colour stained her son's fair cheeks.

During the remainder of Charles's precious boyhood, Kate wanted to earn his love and respect. She also wanted him to experience security and happiness in the few years separating the last of his childhood from adulthood. "Sit you down, Charles."

He obeyed and then seemed to be looking fixedly at his silver shoe buckles.

"Look at me." When she spoke with authority no one disobeyed her. Although Charles pouted childishly, he did not defy her. She cupped his chin with her right hand to force him to return her steady look. "Although I am acquainted with many gentlemen who admire me, I have never bestowed kisses on them. Moreover, I have always tried not to be alone with any one of them."

Kate increased the pressure of her hand to enforce her words.

"So say you, but when I discovered you alone with Captain Howard, he was near naked," Charles protested with a cold expression in his blue eyes.

She must marry Edward or forfeit any hope of her boy's good opinion of her.

"Bah, it signified naught. This pavilion is my retreat. Foolish child for thinking ill of me. I come here for solitude not to seek male company. Chance brought Captain Howard here. Neither of us are liars. The captain has already explained that unbeknown to him I was here while he swam in the lake."

"Please release me, my lady."

"Very well." She put her hand on her lap before she spoke again. "You must become better acquainted with us and decide whether or not you believe us."

Tears slid down Charles's rounded cheeks. "I know not what to believe. I shall consult Mister Milton. He will tell me what is true and what is false, but I want to believe you, Mother, I do, I do." A small sob escaped him before he dried his tears with the back of his hand.

She would marry the captain to gain her son's trust, but first she had much to discuss with Edward in private. A tremor ran through her. Perhaps marriage to a gentleman she loved would not be as…as painful as she feared. Her husband-to-be had never given any indication he would use her as roughly, as her late husband did.

Kate drew Charles's fair head to her bosom. "There, there." She patted his back. "You are no more than a boy attempting to play a man's role. As for Mister Milton, say whatever you will to him. Perhaps he has not told you he is the new incumbent of Missendene parish."

Charles sniffed. "It is good of you to give him the living."

"Oh, he is an old acquaintance whom I am pleased to help. Besides, I can never repay his kindness to you. I am sure you are as glad as I am that he is to be married and hope he will be very happy."

She basked in Charles's admiration. It really was out of the question to risk her son's trust with a denial of her forced betrothal. Yet, despite Edward Howard's unscrupulous seizure of an opportunity to marry her, at the thought of being held by him in sickness and health from the day of their marriage, a delightful glow spread through her.

"Mister Milton is to wed?" Charles withdrew from her embrace. "Who is he to marry?"

Kate laughed. "Your grandmother, who yearned to meet you from the day you were born." She stood. "The hour grows late. I must return to the house." She opened the door. "Look, there is Jessie with a cloak to hide my nightgown." Kate waved a finger at him. "By the way, how did you know where to find me, Charles?"

"Jessie said you might be here." His lower lip quivered like a small child's before he looked up at her. "Mother?"

Her heart sang. Again he had called her Mother. "Yes?"

Charles stood and regarded her anxiously. "After you marry Captain Howard, you will not allow him to beat me, will you?"

She enfolded him in her arms. "Never," she said with the ferocity of a vixen protecting her cub. "If anyone lays so much as a cruel finger on you, he will rue the day. As for the captain, he approves not of corporal punishment. Although the threat of a court martial has been removed, he is still on half pay as a result of his intervention between a brutal commander and a sailor."

"What of my sister? Would you allow the captain to chastise her with a rod?"

"I promise he is too kind of heart to apply the rod to a female. Now, come and breakfast with me in my apartment. I will invite Amanda to join us and tell her I shall marry Captain Howard."

* * *

In the evening, Cook excelled herself, and after Kate and her guests had supped, Charles, who sat at the opposite end of the table to her, stood. He raised his glass and looked from one to another, including Captain Howard, who sat on her left.

What was her son about? Kate wondered, while admiring his thick hair which fell to his shoulders in natural waves and curls.

"My lord, ladies and gentlemen." Charles smiled at his sister. "I propose a toast to my lady mother and Captain Howard who, this day, plighted their troth."

Silence greeted his announcement before his grandmother pushed herself to her feet. "Betrothed to an insignificant captain on half pay when you could have married a duke or a marquess?" she shrieked.

Mister Milton stood. "My dear," he said to Gertrude after he had cleared his throat, "you forget there are those who will censure you for marrying an insignificant man of the cloth." He coughed. "Let us be upstanding and drink to the future bride and groom."

"As you please," his betrothed said grudgingly.

Marriage, Kate's mind screamed, although earlier on, she had been optimistic. *I swore never to marry again, but now I am committed to Captain Howard.* She looked at her son, who inclined his head to her. His composure and his immaculate dark blue coat and breeches, gave him the appearance of a fourteen or fifteen year old. Everyone stood. "To both of you," they chorused as they raised their glasses, drank, and then surrounded them to shake the captain's hand and offer Kate congratulatory kisses.

Mrs Radcliffe's voice rose above a buzz of congratulations and conversation. "My dearest boy," she began, before she kissed Edward on the cheek, "I don't deny I had grave misgivings."

Edward feared his godmother was about to commit a *faux pas* and voice her earlier disapproval of Kate. However, to his relief, she came to an abrupt halt.

"My dearest boy," she repeated, "from the depths of my heart, I wish you and your bride-to-be every happiness."

Sir Newton patted Mrs Radcliffe's back and smiled at her. "Hear, hear," he said.

Kate smiled her thanks at the elderly couple, and Amanda pressed a kiss on her cheek.

* * *

Kate snuggled down in her tester bed while Jessie added logs to the fire before snuffing out the candles.

Jessie yawned. "Do you require aught else, my lady?"

"No, away to your bed," Kate replied.

Alone, Kate stretched, yawned, and looked at the flames, which coloured the walls and played with flickering shadows.

Someone tapped on the door between her bedchamber and her private closet. Whoever it was opened it before she had time to respond.

"Who is there?" Kate demanded.

"Charles. I hope you don't object to my being bold enough to visit you so late at night, Countess."

Why had he come? To berate her again or to discuss a problem?

Although she did not want her son to address her as Countess, delight at his presence bubbled up in her. "My dear child, I am your mother. You may approach me whenever you please," she said, puzzled by his visit to her bedchamber at so late an hour.

Charles shut the door and stood with his back to the frame, darkness shrouding his face. Silence lay between them like a soft blanket until she broke it. "We have many lost years for which to make amends. Come closer to me and explain why you are here at this hour of the night."

While he approached her with quick footsteps, Kate sat. First, she piled the bolster and pillows against the bed head. Next, she patted the edges of the warm quilt. "Sit here."

Charles hesitated beside the bed.

"No need for embarrassment," Kate coaxed.

His face averted, he sat on the edge of the bed as far away from her as possible.

"Do you have something particular to say to me?"

He nodded.

How she longed to tenderly pat his rounded cheeks. She refrained. Charles might reject such an affectionate gesture.

"I have come to apologise," he mumbled. "No gentleman should call his mother a whore."

"True, but I prefer honesty to deceit. Do you believe I am one?"

He flung himself at her in a paroxysm of weeping. "No," he replied when his sobs subsided. "I don't think ill of you, and I hate those who blackened your name to me."

Kate held him in her arms for a while before she unbuttoned his coat and waistcoat. "Take these off before you remove your shoes. This night you shall sleep in my bed secure in my love."

Charles hesitated for a long moment before he flung off his velvet coat and embroidered satin waistcoat. He removed his shoes while Kate rearranged the pillows and raised a corner of the quilt. Her heart sang with joy. "Get into bed, child."

Exhausted by emotion, her son soon fell asleep while Kate propped herself on her elbow and delighted in every detail of his precious face. Now, in the quiet of the sleeping manor, all that remained to complete her happiness was to ensure Amanda's contentment.

A discreet knock startled Kate. To prevent Charles being disturbed, she slipped out of bed and opened the door. Illuminated by a candle, garbed in a magnificent scarlet nightgown embroidered with fantastical sea creatures and fronds of seaweed, Captain Howard stood facing her.

"Why are you here?" she asked in her most haughty tone.

Edward smiled. His teeth gleamed white. "I have come to kiss you again."

"In my bedchamber, at this hour of the night!"

"Or elsewhere if you prefer." A laugh caught in his throat.

"'Pon my word you are too bold, please leave."

"Do you really judge me impudent? After all, we are betrothed." A flame leapt in the hearth, its light revealing his eyes burning like coals.

Kate stepped back.

With the speed of a rope snaking down from the mizenmast, Edward scooped her into his arms. He kissed her mouth without allowing her a moment to mention Charles's presence. She flailed his chest with her hands while he carried her toward the bed. His kiss seared her lips. Her hands stilled. Desire, more intense than any he previously invoked, churned deep within her.

Edward tripped but locked her tighter in his arms. Yet, while he steadied himself, Kate slipped free and looked down at the stumbling block, Charles's shoe.

"My apologies for nearly falling with you." Edward reached out, presumably to snatch her into his arms again with or without her consent.

"Shush, I am not alone."

"What the devil do you mean? Who is your bedfellow? One of your handsome lackeys?" he snarled and marched out of the room.

Incredulous she stared after him. How dare he accuse her of licentiousness? Kate drew a deep breath. She understood. Edward suffered jealousy equalling her own when she saw him with Mistress Martyn through the window and assumed he had deceived her.

Oh my love, my dear love, she grieved. *How could I have been so foolish?* She must go to Edward and speak to him without delay. Kate groaned. What should she say? She pulled on her nightgown, opened the bedchamber door, and tiptoed out of the room.

She traversed the dark, deserted corridor before ascending the winding stairs to Edward's bedchamber. Tremulous, she tried to slow her breath in order to quieten her heart. She tapped on the door. No answer.

She raised the latch and then pushed the door to open it. Locked from within. Her breath and heart tumultuous, she knocked.

"Who is there?" Edward demanded from the other side of the door.

"The Countess of Sinclair."

"Do I know you?" he asked in a stern voice.

"Don't be foolish." She put the candle down beside a Chinese vase standing on a carved wooden chest.

"Foolish? I asked who knocked on my door at this hour of the night."

Baffled and taken aback, she caught her breath for a moment. "Captain Howard, please don't engage in a ridiculous game."

"I suggest you return to bed, Countess."

Her annoyance increased. She pounded the door.

"Who is there?" came the captain's harsh voice.

What did he want of her? "Lady Sinclair."

"Milady, should you not be abed?"

Intolerable, his voice now sounded amused.

Pride stung, dictating she should leave. Yet she remained. Tears gathered in her eyes. Why did he not open the door?

A draught extinguished the candle. In total darkness, Kate slumped. She tried to catch her breath. What had the captain reduced her to, no more than a pitiful creature who longed for a kind word from him? With an effort, she straightened her back. "This is ridiculous, please let me in. I must talk to you."

"Who is there?"

Infuriating man! "Kate," she snapped, goaded almost beyond endurance.

The door opened. Candlelight streamed out into the darkness.

"I came to tell you Charles is sleeping in my bed."

Strong arms enfolded her. They banished the last dregs of her confusion. "Kate, my Kate, just Kate, beautiful Kate. When we are alone, I cannot see the countess. I only have eyes for Kate, the lady I adore."

After her captain drew her into his bedchamber, he pushed the door closed with his foot. Secure in his arms, she pressed close to him. His mouth covered hers. He guided her to the bed. Her ivory-coloured nightgown pooled on the floor next to his discarded night rail. The candles burned low. He released her tresses from their plait. "You cannot imagine how often I dreamt of this," he murmured as he ran his hand through her hair.

She raised her face to receive his kiss, her hands on his warm back.

Edward clasped her upper arms. He held her at a little distance from him. "Why are you here, Kate?"

Befuddled by the question, at a moment when she hungered for him, she could not speak.

He repeated his question.

"To tell you I want no misunderstandings, and…and to say I love you."

"Ah," Edward breathed in a low tone. He gazed at her, his eyes soft by firelight. "Heart of my heart."

Despite her mild protest, he kissed her. This time his lips skimmed and teased until she trembled with desire, still fearful, but well-guarded and fortified by his ardent love.

* * *

Before dawn, Kate got out of bed without waking Edward. She put on her linen night rail and nightgown. For a moment she paused to admire her captain. She twined a curl of his dark hair around her finger. She must return to her bedchamber.

No one stirred in the dark corridors. When she entered her room, she slid into bed careful not to wake Charles. A smile curved her lips. Only the essence of romantic poetry could put into words the miracle of her betrothed's tender lovemaking and her total surrender to its delights.

She blushed at the memory of kisses sweeter than nectar, of hands so gentle that they soothed her fears, and of a restrained, muscular body that evoked a rhythm leading to mutual bliss hitherto unimaginable.

Gloriously aware of her entire body, recently adored, caressed, and kissed by her husband-to-be, Kate smiled and closed her eyes. She slept without the memories and fears which had plagued her since the day she had married her late husband.

* * *

Kate opened her eyes to a room full of sunlight, bright as the sweet memory of Edward's passion.

"Well, well, my lady, 'tis not like you to sleep well past noon," Jessie commented. "Are you feverish?"

Kate giggled. To her own ears she sounded like a foolish girl burning with love. "I am well."

Her tirewoman's nose twitched. "After I brought your morning chocolate and found you sleeping, Lord Sinclair returned to his bedchamber. He's out riding

339

with Captain Howard." Jessie curtseyed. "Come to think of it, my lady, I've not yet wished you joy, but I do," Jessie said, looking at her knowingly.

Did Jessie suspect she and Edward passed the night in joyous abandonment? So what if she did? At heart, Jessie was a romantic.

Kate quivered like aspen keys in the breeze. Her breasts ached for more caresses and kisses.

Jessie poured some chocolate. She handed her the dish of thin cut bread and butter.

"Thank you, I am ravenous. I could eat a whole loaf."

"Well, there's a welcome change, my lady. For months you've done no more than fuss over your victuals, and you have scarcely eaten enough to keep you in beauty."

Jessie spoke true. Until this morning, her appetite had deserted her. Were her cheeks hollow? Thank God for face creams and powders, rouge, and patches to enhance her appearance. What to wear today? Edward must have eyes only for her.

A tap on the door. Jessie opened it, laughed, and then turned to Kate. "My lady, Lord Sinclair and Captain Howard beg the favour of an informal levee."

"Ask them to wait in my closet and close the door."

"Very good, my lady."

Kate got out of bed. She pulled on her nightgown. "My hair, my face." She hurried into her dressing room.

When she was neat and tidy, Kate returned to bed. "Jessie," she commenced, "admit the earl and Captain Howard." With a rush of love for them, Kate relaxed.

Upon entering the bedchamber, Edward captured her attention with a raised eyebrow. He approached the bed. Bent over, he whispered in her ear. "Join me in the orangery as soon as you can."

Like an eager puppy, Charles took a couple of steps after Edward.

Kate, all impatience to snatch a private word with her love, put a firm hand on Charles's shoulder. "We must not neglect your sister. Why not pass the morning with her until we dine? You and Amanda need to become acquainted with each other."

"As you please, my lady," her son replied.

If George and his wife had done little else for her boy, they had ensured his manners were exquisite, but she wanted to see him tousled after enjoying country pursuits. How she hoped the Sinclairs would permit him to attend her wedding.

The captain of her heart smiled.

"You may go, Jessie."

"Thank you," Edward said. "You have spared us the necessity of seeking privacy in the orangery." He lowered himself onto a chair by the fireplace. "My heart, after we wed I want you to enjoy all of your current privileges. Therefore, I wish you to remain in charge of all your financial affairs and in full control of all your properties."

"That is very generous of you. Are you sure?"

He nodded. "I have only one request."

She looked away from him. Money, everything always came down to that. "What is it?" she asked, forcing herself to speak in an even tone.

"In the unlikely but unhappy event of your death, I want to be named Amanda's guardian in your last will and testament."

"Thank you, Edward." Her heart beat fast. "It is not Amanda's death I fear, it is yours. I love you so dearly that I could not bear it if you died at sea."

"Heart of my heart, don't grow pale and tremble. I have given much thought to this. You cannot trade at the Royal Exchange, but if you instruct me, I can on your behalf, so I shall resign from the navy."

"Are you sure that is what you want?"

"Yes, I think that instead of having shares in merchant ships, you might want to own a fleet of them. I would find it interesting to oversee their construction and sail on them, perhaps with you by my side. And when the marriage settlements are drawn up, all your property shall remain yours to do with as you see fit. I never want to be accused of marrying you for your money."

"I did not expect such generous unselfishness," she said, amazed by his words.

He smiled at her. "All this is for the future. For now we must decide where we shall live after our marriage. Could you bear to live in a more modest style? I would not be at ease in any of your late husband's houses."

"Yes, if you don't expect me to give up Missendene. I bought it with the profits from my business interests with the intention of bequeathing it to Amanda if I found her."

"Could you tolerate living in my house in Chelsea? If it is too small, we can enlarge it. And there are many good schools in and around the village, one of which Amanda could attend daily."

"Yes, oh yes, Edward, I do believe that for your sake I could tolerate anything."

He laughed. "What a child you are at heart. I don't want you to tolerate anything which does not make you happy." His dimpled chin jutted forward. "I am a sea captain, so I hope you will obey one command."

"What?" she asked, startled and a little apprehensive.

"No more levees. I warn you, milady, I shall be a jealous husband." Edward stood and marched to the bedside. "In future, I alone will advise you where to put your patches," he whispered in her ear.

"Captain," she protested, "that is an outrageous suggestion."

"A charming one," he said, his eyes alight with laughter while she giggled like a carefree girl.

She stared up at him. "I cannot imagine why you love me."

"I have asked myself that question. My only answer is you are Kate. My Kate. In fact, I think I have loved you since the moment we met, although I was too much of a fool to realise it." He took a deep breath. "My heart, I promise you that if we are blessed with children, I shall never separate you from them."

More children, why had she not thought of that? Kate's eyes brimmed with tears. Her cup of joy overflowed. She had moored in a safe harbour. "Edward," she murmured and held out her arms to him.

Epilogue

Rain lashed down, rattling against the windows. In the grounds of Missendene Manor, treetops whirled. Ill omens?

"A message from Captain Howard." Rose handed it to Kate.

"Sit still, my lady." Jessie put the last pin in Kate's coronet of plaits.

"What does he want?" Amanda asked.

Kate waved them all away while she broke the seal. How she loved her bridegroom. She could never repay him for everything. Kate could scarce breathe for happiness. She handed the note to Amanda. "Captain Howard's brother has negotiated with your uncle on my behalf. In return for a financial settlement, he will allow Charles to live with us."

Amanda clapped her hands.

Money, thought Kate. Did everything in the world have a price, including her son?

Her hand steady, she applied powder, and then tinted her cheeks and eyebrows. The mirror reflected her inner radiance.

Kate stood, pleased with her ruby red wedding gown and sumptuous cloth-of-gold petticoat.

Charles would give her away. Amanda would hold her train.

"Here, Mother." Amanda handed her a tussiemussie of fragrant red and white roses.

Kate remembered the day when Edward gave her out of season roses. She recalled tucking a red one into the neckline of her gown. Afterward he had compared the red blossom and her white skin to an inner battle, an allusion to the War of the Roses. He had been right. She had been at war. Now, thanks to him, she was at peace.

Jessie looped the end of her ivory fan over her wrist. "You are beautiful, my lady."

Amanda pointed to the window. "Look, it has stopped raining."

Yes it had. Outside, the clouds parted. Sunlight flooded the bedchamber.

* * *

Glorious colour spilled through the stained glass windows. A good omen? Kate hoped so. She crossed her fingers while she trod down the aisle of Missendene Manor's private chapel.

Although aware of family and friends, her eyes focussed on Edward's beloved figure before the altar. She adored him. Nothing she did for him from this day forth could ever prove how much she loved him. Within the cocoon of her silks, Kate shivered with desire when she reached the altar. Her bridegroom, handsome beyond belief, looked his best in a dark blue coat, which blazed with gold epaulettes and buttons.

Later Kate could not remember the words of the service conducted by Mister Milton, but she did remember Edward's warm embrace, followed by her children's congratulations and hugs.

* * *

Edward turned from the altar with Kate at his side.

His bride smiled up at him. "Dr Moore's prophecy came true. I did not need to seek my daughter. You brought her to me."

Edward rested one hand on Charles's shoulder and beckoned to Amanda with his other hand. "Come to us, Daughter. At long last we have found you, so our proverbial cup runs over with joy." He smiled to encourage her. Already Charles called him Father, but Amanda did not. When she stepped toward him with an uncertain smile, he wanted to put an arm around the ill-done-by child and hold her close to his heart. However, he sensed it would take time for him and Kate to gain her complete trust. Yet of one thing he was sure, for so long as they lived, they would not only love Kate's children but also do their utmost to guide and protect them.

"Till death do us part, heart of my heart," he murmured into his bride's ear.

Rosemary Morris books published by Books We Love

Historical 18th Century
The Captain and the Countess
Far Above Rubies

Regency
Sundays Child
Mondays Child

About the Author

Rosemary Morris was born in 1940 in Sidcup Kent. As a child, when she was not making up stories, her head was 'always in a book.'

While working in a travel agency, Rosemary met her Indian husband. He encouraged her to continue her education at Westminster College.

In 1961 Rosemary and her husband, now a barrister, moved to his birthplace, Kenya, where she lived from 1961 until 1982. After an attempted coup d'état, she and four of her children lived in an ashram in France.

Back in England, Rosemary wrote historical fiction. She is now a member of the Romantic Novelists' Association, Historical Novel Society and Cassio Writers.

Apart from writing, Rosemary enjoys classical Indian literature, reading, visiting places of historical interest, vegetarian cooking, growing organic fruit, herbs and vegetables and creative crafts.

Time spent with her five children and their families, most of whom live near her, is precious.

* * * *

Did you enjoy The Captain and the Countess? If so, please help us spread the word
•Recommend the book to your family and friends
•Post a review
•Tweet and Facebook about it

Lightning Source UK Ltd.
Milton Keynes UK
UKOW02f0838270616

277155UK00001B/2/P